DRIVE ME WILD SERIES #2

by
AMY BOOKER

eBook ISBN: 979-8-9859875-7-7

Print ISBN: 979-8-9865651-2-5

Published by Renaissan Publishing Limited, Cuyahoga Falls, Ohio

www.amybookerauthor.com

For Jeanette

Foreword

Author's Note

If you've read my previous books, you'll know that the chapter names are all song titles. Music has been an integral part of my life, and it always sets the mood. Whether it's the overall energy of the song, the lyrics, or even just the title, that tone carries through into my written words on the page. The playlist and a link can be found at the back of each book, or you can find them on my website: www. amybookerauthor.com.

Chapter 1

Hide & Seek

Chelsie

I'm really getting sick of funerals. Between my dad's death less than a year ago and now Wayne Bailey, the head mechanic at Mischief Motors, my one black dress is at least giving me my money's worth. I didn't know Wayne very well. I don't think anyone did. He kept to himself except to yell and swear at the paparazzi that follows my half-sister Normandy and her billionaire husband, Brandon. He was always chasing someone away from the gate to the depot property like it was his front lawn.

Normandy and I are co-owners of Mischief

Motors, and now that she's discovered she's pregnant with their first baby, a lot of the day-to-day operations are slowly being transferred to me. I'm in charge of the fleet inventory of classic and exotic cars we rent out to our elite clients, which keeps me busy, and now my responsibilities are expanding slowly. I suppose now that means I'll be in charge of replacing Wayne, too. Though I don't have the first clue on where to start with that task.

"You must be Chelsie." An older woman touches my arm warmly. I noticed her in the front row during the funeral service, nearly wilting in the Vegas sun with silent tears flowing freely down her pale cheeks. She must be Wayne's wife. I didn't make it in time to be a part of the procession, so I can only guess. Her bright white short hair, and sparkling blue eyes, contrast with the melancholy expression on her face. "Thank you so much for coming. Wayne talked about you all the time."

I am extremely surprised by this. I didn't think Wayne even registered who I was. And he was at Mischief from the beginning, so he kind of saw me grow up. I guess we never know who's paying attention. "Oh wow, that's so sweet to hear. Hopefully, it was good things." I give her a smile in an attempt to cheer her up. An ache in my throat forms as I wish I could somehow alleviate her apparent emotional pain. "I'm so sorry for your loss. I know Mischief isn't going to be the same without him."

"I know your dad used to say they built those garages around Wayne since he was almost always there." She sighs, placing a hand over her heart. "He just loved working there. He loved his cars more than anything. Even more than me sometimes, I think."

"Oh, I'm sure that's not true." Though I am anything but. With the amount of time Wayne spent at the garage, I'm frankly surprised he had a wife. And she seems so sweet; I can't believe he'd want to be away from her as much as he was.

"I'm not unrealistic about my spot on the list of Wayne's interests," she chuckles, her cheeks coloring. The sudden smile makes her years younger in an instant. It's amazing how a smile can do that. "We accepted each other as we are, or were, I guess. I need to get used to saying things in the past tense now." Her smile disappears as quickly as it came, and my heart lurches.

"How long were you two married?" I ask, curious now as to why I didn't know about her after all these years.

"Can you believe it was sixty-five years this year?" She shakes her head as though she can't believe it herself. Gripping a sparkling blue pendant around her neck, she goes on. "He got this sapphire for me to mark the occasion. He was so proud he looked up what was a proper stone to buy for sixty-five years, but I would have been happy with just a card."

The necklace is absolutely gorgeous. Wayne had good taste and a spectacular jeweler from the looks of it.

"Well, it is beautiful and matches your eyes. He definitely did good." The color returns to her cheeks a little with the compliment. "I can't picture myself being with someone sixty-five days, let alone years. It must have been true love for you both."

She touches my arm again, her warm fingers giving it a slight squeeze. "It was. But there's love out there for everyone. You'll find yours." She gives me a wink and a sly smile as if she knows something about my love life I don't. A small chill rushes through me as the wind picks up around us. "When you find some time in the next week or so, could you call me? I understood from Wayne that you're in charge of the cars at Mischief, and well, he had a bunch of classic cars he collected over the years, and I don't have any idea what to do with them now."

"You're looking to sell them?"

"I don't know if they're worth anything, but I trust you to tell me what they could go for. Even if you don't buy them, you could help me sell them to other people. If you can. I know you're very busy."

"Of course. I'd be happy to help you with that." And now I'm dying to find out what kind of treasures Wayne kept for himself and what shape they're in. It would be kind of funny if they're all rusted-out clunkers. But it would also be amazing if they were in prime condition. "I'll give you a call. I'm sure we have your number at the office somewhere."

Patting my arm again, she says goodbye, and another chill spirals down my spine. April in Las Vegas is relatively warm if you're in the sun, like today, so there's no reason for all these chills. While the wind here always has a bite to it, it could be I'm coming down with something. I hope not. I don't have time to be sick.

"Isn't Mrs. Bailey the sweetest thing?" Normandy comes up from behind to stand with me and watch Mrs. Bailey speak with another group of mourners.

"She is. I can't believe I never knew she existed."

"Yeah, if I hadn't gone through all the HR and tax stuff, I wouldn't have known about her either. He sure was an expert at keeping secrets. We were notified of Wayne's death by a family friend."

Her words hang between us, neither acknowledging how many secrets have been uncovered lately. When our father died, we learned the hard way that he kept a connection to the Vegas underworld a secret, and she was kidnapped and shot by one of the local crime families. She was fortunate to be released with only a wounded arm, but it shows how dangerous family secrets can be. I doubt quiet Wayne had anything so nefarious going on in his life, but you never really know anyone, so I can't assume anything.

"She wants me to check out Wayne's cars and help her sell them. I guess he's got quite the collection."

"Interesting. Let me know how it goes or if there are any we could use at Mischief." She nods at me as a smile tugs a corner of her mouth upward. Pregnancy suits her; she's glowing and only a few months along. "That's all your department, so do your thing. First, though, I think we'll need to find a replacement for Wayne as soon as possible. We can't have a gap in that position for any length of time. Broken down cars are bad for business."

"I figured as much. Do you want me to handle that too?"

She grimaces at first, but I can see her switching into planning mode. "Would you want to?"

I shrug. "I may as well, while I'm taking things on. I'm sure finding a decent mechanic can't be that hard."

That statement will come back to haunt me in so many ways.

Chapter 2

Arsonist's Lullaby

Noah

"Yeah, well, you know what, Gus? You can go fuck yourself. And this job." I throw the oily rag I'm holding onto the ground between us. "I quit."

"You can't quit in the middle of a job." He raises his hands in disbelief and points to the car on the lift behind me. How can he be so dense?

"This shouldn't even be a job, and you know it," I hiss through gritted teeth, trying to keep my voice from carrying into the waiting room where the customers are. It would not go over well if they knew how this asshole operated. And while I'm not going to be a part of it anymore, I have been up to this point, so I'm just as guilty. "If you hadn't poked a hole into that muffler with your pen while showing that lady what was "wrong" with her entire exhaust system, she could have gotten at least another six months out of it. She only came in for a fucking oil change."

His neck reddens as he glances around at the other mechanics who have stopped to observe our showdown. They're also fully aware of how Gus does things, so they're as complicit as I have been. I'm just the first one to call him out on it.

"Fine. Five years and all I've taught you is down the drain. Get the hell out of my shop. You've got 24 hours to take your tools off my property, or I'm confiscating them." He shoots venomous glares at everyone who's stopped to stare. "And you, dipshits, get back to work."

All he's taught me. Right. The only thing he's taught me is how to swindle unsuspecting customers into repairs they don't need at prices they can't afford. *Asshole.* And, great, now I need to figure out how to move all my tools out of here and where to store them. They will not fit into the apartment I'm temporarily sharing with my brother, Theo.

Shit. My brother is not going to be pleased about this. He's aware I haven't been happy with this job for years, but he's still going to freak out at me just up and quitting without having another job lined up.

Lord knows he's hated his job, too but refuses to do anything about it. Mr. Responsible Casino Boss won't understand that sometimes you have to follow your gut and get out of toxic relationships, especially those with employers.

When I get home, I call just about everybody I know and their brothers to find someone with a truck and a garage I can store a huge rolling tool cabinet. It takes me a couple hours, but I'm able to lock down both for tomorrow afternoon. Finding people willing to move anything, especially in the heat of Las Vegas, is like looking for an honest casino. They are few and far between.

Then I start searching online for job openings for auto mechanics. Those are almost as hard to come by from the looks of it. I haven't searched for a new job in over five years, and the slim pickings are discouraging. Maybe I did fuck up by quitting like I did, or at least I should have found something else before leaving. Well, it's too late now. I've made this mess; now I've got to clean it up.

"You're home early." Theo enters the apartment and tosses his keys into a bowl by the door, sliding a curious glance at me while shrugging out of his suit coat and kicking his shoes off. We have very different work uniforms. "Everything okay with you?"

"Not really." I go back scrolling an employment site on my phone, not finding anything on this one either. "I quit my job today."

Silence. Theo freezes at the entrance to the kitchen, I assume to process what I've said. But he's not responded to it.

"Gus fucked over another old lady who didn't deserve it, and I just couldn't do it anymore." I shut off my phone and toss it on the leather couch cushion next to me. Staring at my phone isn't going to make jobs magically appear on the screen. I need to unclench my jaw, but my frustration is getting to me. "So, I told Gus to go fuck himself, and I'll pick up my tools tomorrow."

"And, you have something else lined up, right?" A deep frown creases his brow, and I can sense the bitter, warning tone in his voice. He's not going to like my answer. He's always been the practical one, overthinking and rationalizing everything, planning everything in advance. On the other hand, I tend to wear my heart on my sleeve and act on impulse. He's a people person, and I am more of a puzzle person. I'd much rather figure out why an engine is frozen on my own than talk to somebody about it.

"When is your house going to be ready again?" I knew he'd jump on my case about this. He's staying with me while he waits for the house he recently bought to vacate, but that's not happening quickly enough for me now. "And, no, I don't. But I started looking as soon as I got home. I'll find something. I'm not worried," I lie. I am, in fact, *extremely* worried. If the quick search I did on my phone is any sign, there aren't a lot of places hiring auto mechanics with my advanced skill level. As a matter of fact, there are exactly none.

"Actually..." He rubs his chin thoughtfully as he rocks on his heels.

"What, actually?" That's an oddly swift change in his mood that I didn't see coming.

"I may have a lead on a job for you." He loosens his tie and leans in the doorway, his tall frame filling the space. "You know Brandon Carmichael, that billionaire guy who married that chick from the car place, right?"

That's a lot of hoops for my brain to jump through, but I get there. "Yeah, Mischief Motors. What about him?"

"He's in the process of buying Bliss Casino since the Mamana family had it taken away from them by the government for all of their illegal shit."

"Good for him," I say flatly. I don't understand what this has to do with me at all. Sometimes my brother can be very unhelpful.

"No, idiot. That's not what I'm trying to tell you. I was going to say he had to rearrange meetings with the state regulators today because he had to attend the funeral of the head mechanic at Mischief Motors. So, they might have an opening."

"Oh, really?" Now that sounds interesting, indeed. They are known for keeping a varied inventory of classic and exotic cars. I would love to get my hands on truly challenging projects like those kinds of vehicles would be. I can picture fabricating the needed parts myself in my head. I snap out of it after realizing the entire situation. "Wait, their mechanic just died, so I should just walk in and offer my services? *'Hey, I heard your guy died, so here I am.'* That's kind of fucked up, man."

He shrugs at me. "Or you can wait until they post for the job and compete against a million other mechanics in the area looking for work. I say, shove your foot in the door while it's open. It couldn't hurt."

That last part is dubious. It could hurt if I showed up at their garage with them still grieving for their previous mechanic and me wanting to jump into his spot. It's presumptuous. But Theo does have a point. If I wait too long, it could be filled as soon as they post the job. I don't want to risk missing out if I have the inside information I can use.

"I'll think about it." It's not like I have much else to do now that I'm unemployed.

Chapter 3

When You Were Young

Chelsie

"So, what qualifications are we looking for?" I ask Normandy. We're putting together the job listing for Wayne's replacement, but we're both stumped on what he did. Because he did *everything*. "We can't just put 'mechanic' because he did so much more than that."

She swivels in her chair, rubbing her pregnant belly absently. "I thought you knew cars, so I assumed you'd know what it takes to keep them going." She smirks, and I can't tell if she's being sarcastic.

"Sure, I know *about* the cars, like their pedigrees,

and the story behind how Dad found and bought them. I know all their names but *not* how to fix them." I sigh, shutting my laptop, and propping my feet on her desk as I usually do when we talk. "Can't one of the other mechanics take over?"

Normandy shakes her head at me. "No. All of them are apprentices. Wayne was teaching them, too, for credit at the local community college. None of them are certified in anything. There's no way any of them could fill his spot."

"Great. So, we need to find a teacher too? Norm, this is going to be impossible." I run my hands down my cheeks and take a deep breath. "We're going to need a dang miracle. Some amazingly talented and certified teaching mechanic needs to walk in from off the street and offer himself up to be employed by us. Oh, and for a reasonable salary too."

"Crazier things have happened." A slight grin steals across her face, and she gives me a knowing look.

I scoff. "Just because you landed a billionaire at Dad's funeral doesn't mean we're all lucky in all things. I don't think this is going to be that easy. Wayne was one-of-a-kind."

There's a knock on the open office door behind me, and a smooth male voice floats in. "Sorry to interrupt, but I understand you may have an opening for a head mechanic?"

Normandy and I stare at each other briefly, our

eyes big. I do my best to keep my mouth from dropping open in disbelief and rub at my arms for the hair that is now standing on end.

She recovers first, standing and offering a hand to shake to the man. "We are, indeed. I'm Normandy Carmichael, one of the owners here. And you are...?"

I slide my high heels off the desk and turn to see who this potential walk-in miracle might be. When my eyes land on him, my stomach lurches. *Noah Thompson. You have got to be fucking kidding me.*

"I'm Noah...."

"The job's been filled. Sorry." I blurt out, practically jumping from my seat and almost dropping my laptop as it slides down my thighs before I catch it. I keep my face down and turned away from him, not wanting him to recognize me. I'll be mortified if he remembers me.

"Nonsense," Normandy says, purposely ignoring me and giving Noah a broad smile. Does she not notice I'm in distress over here? "We just started looking."

"Oh, cool." His voice is still as sexy as it was in high school, if not more so now. *Damn him.* "Actually, my brother Theo runs the poker room at Bliss Casino, which I believe is now yours too. That's how I heard about a possible opening here." He sounds nervous. *Good.*

"Ah, that's fantastic. Well, you heard correctly, we are now looking to fill a spot recently...vacated."

"Sorry about the circumstances." He almost sounds like he has sympathy. I know this is, in fact, a lie. He doesn't have a sympathetic bone in his body. He wouldn't know compassion if it rose up and bit him on the ass.

I dare to glance up at him, tall, dark shaggy hair, a perfect amount of scruff on the jawline, deep brown eyes under a perfectly shaped brow. He's almost too pretty for words. *Still too pretty.* It's been what, seven years since high school? And he's only improved with age, which hardly seems possible. He was perfect to begin with. Back then, I could have sworn he hung the moon and the stars; he was so swoon-worthy. I crushed on him for years. He just didn't know I existed. Well, he did for a split-second when I worked up the courage to ask him out in the hallway one day after class during our senior year. My best friend, Mackenzie, talked me into it, and he cruelly rejected me in front of his friends and then laughed about it. As if the thought of going out with me was the most disgusting and hilarious thing anyone had ever heard of. I was mortified.

I've never forgotten that day, and I don't think I ever will. His friends didn't forget about it, that's for sure. I couldn't walk the halls without somebody pointing and laughing at me. As if I would have the nerve to think I could be with someone like Noah. Mac told me to ignore everyone, but that's extremely hard to do when you're a teenager. Every little flaw is magnified a million times, and every little dig by Noah's friends tore me down and apart. His friends didn't need to worry about my nerve. It was made clear I wasn't worthy. I wasn't going to make that mistake again. Hot Topic had nothing to do with it. It was me that was the problem. Back then anyways. Since then, I've hardened my shell. More like lacquered, or even better, petrified.

"Chels?" Normandy's harsh tone pulls me out of my flashback.

"What's that?" I shake my head a little to clear the dark fog of the past.

"I was telling Noah you would show him around and tell him about the job."

I arch an eyebrow at her. Does she not remember the conversation we were just having before this guy showed up? Neither of us has a clue what the job entails.

"Okay...." Glancing back at Noah, I find him smiling at me expectantly. *Sure, now that you need a job, you'll be decent to me. Asshole.* "First, do you have a resume? References? What happened at your last job? Why do you need this one? Did you quit? Or were you fired?"

Noah pales at my barrage of questions, taking a small step back. *Good. Be afraid of me, jerk.*

"Chelsie, geez!" Normandy titters nervously, walking around the desk and putting an arm around me, squeezing way too tight. "Sorry about my sister.

She's been upset since Wayne passed away, isn't that right, Chelsie?" She pulls me into her side harshly again. I still don't find this amusing.

"I completely understand," Noah says, his head bobbing, licking his lips as he finally meets my gaze.

Recognize me yet, buddy?

I smirk at him and cross my arms, waiting for it to dawn on him who I am as he sees me, but nothing happens. *Does he really not know who I am?* I was that forgettable to him. Of course, I was. But now, I have his attention, and if he wants the job, he has to be nice to me. The thought makes my stomach churn. That's right, he's only being nice to me because he has to.

When our eyes meet, some crazy current flows between us, and the hair on my arms is back at attention. All these years, and he still makes me weak-kneed, but now it looks like I might be affecting him, too. That can't be right, though. It was made clear to me long ago that I'm not Noah Thompson's type.

My shoulders drop with a sigh, and I resign to having to deal with him on this now, whether I want to or not. If nothing else, it's *my* job to find Wayne's replacement.

"Fine." I slide out of Normandy's grip and brush past Noah to the open office door. I take a deep breath as I pass him, and it's a mistake. His cologne is light and fresh and makes my head spin a little.

"Follow me, and I'll show you around." I don't glance back to check if he's moving as directed as I head toward one of the back garages.

If he can act like his rejection never happened because I'm sure it was so trivial to him that he doesn't remember it, so can I. *I think.* Though, to be honest, just the thought of him hurts my heart with fresh pain echoing still from that day. I've spent the last seven years trying to forget Noah Thompson, and the asshole walks into my business looking for a job. *I was looking for a miracle, not a curse.*

Chapter 4

Young Folks

Noah

Chelsie is confusing as hell. First, telling me the job was filled, and then the charged look that just happened between us, and now she's practically running away from me. That was a roller coaster I did not see coming when I came in here. I'm glad I did come, though, because it sounds like I might have a solid shot at the job. *If* I can win Chelsie over.

I catch up to her as she pushes through an exit door, and I need to power walk to keep up with her as she barrels into yet another door to another garage. I have to say, I don't mind lagging a bit; the view from behind is stellar. The curves on her are beyond enticing, and the shape of her legs in those tight jeans with those high heels...*Yikes.*

Once inside the next garage, she turns to face me, a hand on her hip and disdain in her eyes. "This is where Wayne did all of his repairs." She waves to the line of car lifts and wall of tools and cabinets. Mechanics in their Mischief Motors uniforms are working on a few cars in different phases of repair. They all look young. Well, younger than me.

"What certifications do you have?" Her eyes are narrowed as if in challenge again. *Does she doubt that I'm qualified for this position?*

"It might be easier for you to tell me what certifications you're looking for." I give her a small smile, trying to stay modest but confident. It's a fine line. "I have a lot." *Shit, that was too cocky.*

She swallows hard, abruptly uncomfortable, and avoids my eyes. "Can you teach?"

"Excuse me?" I was not expecting that question at all. I guess we're skipping the certifications.

"Teach. You know what that word means, right? To show someone else how to do something?" She crosses her arms again. She does that a lot, and it's incredibly distracting since it draws my eyes to the exact area of her body I should not be paying attention to. "Can you teach these apprentices for their college credits?" She points to the mechanics spread around the garage. I didn't realize this was a teaching gig. While I've never officially done it, I always seem to be mentoring somebody.

"Yeah. I could do that." I'm hoping my cocky has turned to confidence.

She eyes me warily yet again. I don't know what I did to piss this woman off, but I must have done something. She's been nothing but rude to me this entire time.

"So, what *did* happen at your last job?" She tilts her head, curious, her long chestnut hair swaying with the movement. Something about her is so intriguing. I want to know what is going on behind those angry eyes.

This is going to suck, but I need to be honest here. "Well, my last boss, who I worked for over five years, was unscrupulous, to put it mildly. He basically conned an old woman into a repair she didn't need, and it wasn't the first time. So, I told him to go fuck himself." *Shit. Swearing in a job interview is probably not a great move.* "I mean, I told him off."

Her eyes dance brightly, and a smile takes over her entire being. She's radiant when she smiles. *Hot damn.* "Oh my god, did you really? That's amazing." Her laughter is deep and heartwarming, like she means it. Did I just break through?

"Yeah. I couldn't work for someone like him anymore. I'd come home and want to shower in bleach to clean my soul."

Her laugh fades, and she eyes me again, but this

23

time it's not warily; it's with something else entirely. If I didn't know better, I'd think she was having inappropriate thoughts about me. I guess turnabout is fair play in the naughty thought department.

"I can put together a resume if you need one. And I can give you references to check for my qualifications if you want." I flash a quick smile. "Although, my last boss wasn't too happy about how I left, so who knows what he's going to say about me. My coworkers will stand up for me, though, I'm sure."

She nods, and it seems more to herself than in response to what I said. She silently walks past me and out the door, so I follow, unsure what we're doing now or where we're going. She takes a right and heads into another garage. This one is large and full of cars. A *lot* of cars. Classics, exotics, limos, SUVs, you name it. I get goosebumps taking it all in. This is an automotive lover's dream garage.

"Whoa." It's not very articulate, but it's the best I can do at the moment. "This is impressive."

She still doesn't say anything but watches my reaction intently. I'm sure my eyes have lit up like Christmas trees as I examine the different makes and models. I have never seen such an incredible collection and am rendered speechless. I'm supernaturally drawn to the line of cars, tracing my hand gently along chrome curves, bending to view better angles of the fantastic designs, and peeking into windows to admire lush interiors. After a few minutes, I glance up and find Chelsie staring at me, an impish smile making her mouth twitch. Her dark brown eyes are unreadable, though. I get the feeling I will have a tough time figuring her out.

"Your father had an impeccable taste in cars," I say, walking back toward her slowly. I am undeniably attracted to her. Something about her trips a switch in me; the more I get to know her, the more interesting and intriguing she becomes. I want to learn more. I want to know everything about her. But I need a job, too. So, I have to force myself to play it cool.

"He did." Her voice is tearful and cracked. And, looking up at me, her eyes grow sad. I shouldn't have brought up her late father. That was kind of insensitive of me.

"I'm sorry, I shouldn't have brought it up...."

"No, no. It's fine." She glances around the garage. "It's not like he's not *everywhere* in this place anyway." Letting out a deep sigh and straightening her shoulders like she's about to face a firing squad, she continues, "Right, so when can you start?"

I think she just offered me the job. Can that be right? "Seriously?"

"Seriously." Though she obviously isn't pleased about it. That's not confusing at all.

"I can start tomorrow."

"Whoa, easy there, Tex. How about Monday?"

She chuckles, her cheeks flushing slightly. She's damned mesmerizing when she blushes. "I'd like those references you mentioned first. I'm not completely irresponsible." She shrugs with a smirk. "Just a little irresponsible. I'm going with my gut hiring you. Don't make me regret it."

"Noted. And, I won't." I can't believe I got the job. Just like that. Not that Chelsie or her sister are pushovers, but it seems too easy. I've never been hired on pure intuition before, and it's a bizarre sensation to be taken at my word on something so important. It almost makes me want to do the job even better because of it in a strange way. That makes zero sense to my logical brain, but it is what it is.

Theo is going to be miserable to live with for the next few weeks while he gloats about giving me the idea to come here in the first place. I can deal with that. What I don't know if I can deal with is working with Chelsie Blake. There's something about her I can't put my finger on, though I'd like to put my hands all over her and those curves. And thoughts like that are precisely why this will be pure hell. *How am I supposed to work around a woman who drives me to distraction?*

Chapter 5

I Like the Way You Die

Chelsie

Once Noah gives me his references and leaves, I head into the office I've been using and shut the door, leaning against it and trying to gather my bearings. I cannot believe he just walked in, and I just offered him a job. I am going to be working with Noah Thompson. Daily. In close proximity. What the hell am I thinking?

He didn't recognize or remember me, though I'm not surprised. I was pretty forgettable back then. But it still hurts to think about how he made fun of me when I asked him out. Part of me wanted to believe he only did that to appear cool in front of his friends, as everyone tries to do in high school. I always thought I saw something in his eyes that looked like shame, but I figured it was what I wanted to see. I didn't want to believe he could be so cruel just for the sake of it.

I didn't notice a wedding ring on his finger, but then I've heard a lot of mechanics don't wear rings because they're hazardous or something, so it might not mean anything. Not like he'd be interested in me anyway, or me in him either. If he didn't want me then I'm not instantly worthwhile now. Or maybe I should forgive a simple high school rejection. Maybe I could forgive him if it were simple and not as devastating to me as it was. *Maybe*.

A knock on the door at my back startles me, making me jump. I turn quickly and open the door, surprising Normandy.

"Whoa, were you waiting by the door or something?" she asks.

"I was just about to open it when you knocked. What's up?"

"Are you okay? You look like you've seen a ghost." Her brow furrows with concern.

Am I that upset? I need to work on that if I'm going to be working with Noah. The last thing I want is for him to know what's going on in my head about him.

"I'm fine. Did you just come here to ask me that?" My patience is running very thin now, though

I'm trying to keep myself in check. Normandy didn't know about Noah and me when she pulled me into this.

"No, I wanted to find out how things went with Noah." She walks past me and sits at my desk, her high blonde ponytail swinging as she moves. *Come on in.* "Did you give him the job?"

I turn and roll my eyes so she can't see. "Yes. He's starting on Monday. Though I still have his references to check first." I sit across from her and drop my face into my hands. "I can't believe he just walked in here like that."

"Why were you saying the job was filled when he first showed up?"

I peek between my fingers at her, debating internally how much I want to tell her. One, it's embarrassing as hell. The guy I had the biggest crush on in high school, who broke my fragile teenage heart, shows up at my work out of the blue. And, two, seeing him again brings all those feelings and more to the surface that I've pushed down for years. That was in the past. We've both grown up a lot since then, I would hope. I don't want to open that can of worms.

"I don't know," I shrug, playing aloof. "Why do I say most things? I'm a mystery."

She stares at me intensely, examining me for any sign of being disingenuous. But she's a great poker player for a reason; she can read people.

"You're lying." A smile starts to grow as if she's coming to some sort of realization. "You know him, don't you?" She sits up, pulling on that thread of an idea. "Did you used to date? Work together? It didn't seem like he knew you, though."

"He doesn't remember me."

"I knew it!" She claps her hands and rubs her palms together like the evil sister she unexpectedly is. "Remember you from where? How do you know him?"

I sigh and lay my head down on the desk. "High school."

"You went to high school together? Was he that cute back then too?"

I groan. This is not happening. Normandy does *not* really want me to rehash and relive the nightmare that was high school. Especially not the incident with Noah.

"C'mon, Chels, I want details."

"Norm, to be honest, I don't want to talk about it." I lift my head and stare her straight in the eyes, trying to express how much I don't want to talk about this. Not right now, and not with her.

She takes in my gaze and demeanor, and her smile morphs into worry, but she nods. "Then we won't talk about it." She switches gears. "What are you doing for dinner tonight? Why don't you come over to our house to eat? Brandon's in New York tonight, and I could use the company."

Normandy was kidnapped not long ago by an organized crime family that were rivals of our father, who were demanding a ransom from her billionaire husband, and she still has difficulty being alone sometimes. The thought pulls on my heartstrings, but I have my own demons to face tonight, and I want to do it on my own. If I'm going to be able to face Noah Thompson daily, I need to kick the brittle skeletons of emotions out of my closet before Monday.

"Thanks for the offer, but I'm just going to head home tonight. I'll take a rain check for the next time Brandon's out of town?"

She nods again and stands to leave. "Alright, but if you change your mind, you know where to find me."

I watch as she leaves my office, and I can't believe this is my life now. It's surreal at times like this. I've lost a father but gained my half-sister in my life regularly and gained this job working alongside her that I never imagined. And now Noah's back in the picture and rocking the boat. *He's just going to be an employee. Settle down.*

Just an employee, my ass.

I spend that night talking with my best friend Mackenzie about the whole situation over a bottle of wine, and she is of the belief that it's a positive thing he didn't remember me.

"I mean, imagine you run into someone you were a total asshole to years ago while applying for a job. How awkward would that be?" She twirls a long magenta lock of hair around her finger as she speaks. "That would be so difficult to explain, right?"

I glare at her. "That's what is happening to *me*. Someone who was an asshole to *me* comes to *me* for a job. What was I supposed to say? *'No, you were a dick to me in high school. No way I'm hiring you.'* I couldn't do that."

"I know. I still can't believe Noah Fucking Thompson now works for you." She mutters into her glass, "You still should have let me kick his ass for you back then. I'm still game for that."

Smirking at her, I stand to grab a refill. "He certainly would have remembered that much, at least." I can't help but laugh, picturing it. She would have had too much fun getting back at him for me.

Mac and I have been best friends since the seventh grade, and we're always overprotective of each other. After the Noah thing in high school, she brought me out of my shell and helped me overcome it. Her motto is *'the best revenge is letting go,'* which eventually worked for me. Not only did I move on from Noah Thompson, but I found my own confidence. Though now it feels like that is being tested.

"So, what's going on with you and Cooper? Neither of you has mentioned the other in a while. I take it things have cooled off?" There's a conspiratorial tone in her voice that I'm not crazy about. Mac is forever trying to play matchmaker with me.

Cooper is the guitarist for the rock band that Mackenzie manages, Murderous Crows, and a total player. We've hooked up a few times but never considered anything more than that. And that's how I like it, though: no strings, no complications, no broken hearts. It works for us.

"Nothing's going on. I just haven't seen him in a while." I shrug, flipping through my albums to find something new to play. "I've been too busy with work lately."

She tsks at me, "All work and no play makes Chelsie a very dull girl."

Grinning at her, I shoot back, "And what about you, Ms. Matchmaker? Where are all of your hot dates? I'm feeling a whole pot and black kettle vibe happening here."

"Touché." She pouts a little, crossing her arms over her chest. "I'm barely home enough to date either. The pickings are slim when we're on the road, and there's no way I'm dating a musician. I know how they are while touring, and no, thank you."

"You could have your pick of anyone." And she could. Mackenzie is stupidly attractive. She's always had guys fawning all over her, but nobody ever catches her interest. It doesn't help that she's a workaholic. "Don't give me that crap."

"While I don't believe that, I'm starting to think my soulmate might be pizza or this wine. This is a fantastic wine." She giggles, and it's contagious.

"Well, I think my soulmate will be the eleven cats I end up with one day. That counts, right?" We both start laughing harder, the wine kicking in now.

All this talk about soulmates, and my brain instantly switches to Noah. *Not good.* I will need to work much harder to get him out of my system this time. Especially since we'll be in such close proximity almost every day. I'm going to need to build up some emotional fortitude if I'm going to survive this. *Well, if I'm going to survive him.*

Chapter 6

Come Closer

Noah

Monday morning comes around, and since I haven't heard anything to the contrary, I show up at Mischief Motors, ready to start work. Chelsie said she would check my references, so I assume she did that, and everything went well. Though, I'm dying to hear what Gus had to say. He's an asshole and a con man, but I don't think he's spiteful or vindictive. I did give him five good years, which is more than anyone else has. And he should know he was lucky he got that much from me.

When I enter the front garage, it's empty, and it

looks like all the offices are dark. Music is playing softly overhead, though, so somebody must be around. I'm not sure of the business hours either. Maybe they're open 24/7. I walk through the garage and push open the back door to check the other garages for signs of life. As I step out, I run into someone entering the garage, and after a quick blur and a bump, my chest is burning with a hot liquid that smells an awful lot like coffee. It is so hot I'm afraid it could seriously burn me, so I pull my t-shirt over my head, wad it up and use the dry sections to wipe down my front.

"Oh my God, I am so sorry. Shit." It's Chelsie. She ignores her broken mug spread in pieces around us on the ground and grabs my shirt to take over, drying me off. I do not argue or put up a fight. Her hands on me is a great fucking way to start the week and a new job. "I didn't expect you...fuck, never mind. I'm sorry." Glancing up, she reads into my smirk and dirty thoughts and stops what she's doing. *If you touch me like that, you'd better expect a reaction.*

"That's hot," I say, leaving it open-ended as to my meaning.

Her cheeks catch fire, and she shoves my shirt into my chest.

"Yeah, well, I said I was sorry." She avoids looking at me and squats down to pick up the shards of her coffee mug. This puts her in a compromising position in front of me, but I think I've had enough fun at her expense. I don't want to push my luck with her.

Crouching down to help, I try to lighten the mood. "So, employee orientation here is a little different...." I laugh, but she doesn't join. Instead, she gets even more flustered and accidentally slashes the palm of her hand with a piece of broken ceramic.

"Shit, shit, shit. Fuck this day," she hisses, standing and shaking her hand in pain. I grab it and examine the cut. Her hand is soft against my callouses, so delicate and smooth.

"I don't think you'll need stitches. Luckily, it's not that deep."

Her cheeks flare again, and she yanks her hand away. "What, are you an EMT too?" She's doing everything she can to not gawk at my bare upper body. It would be comical if it didn't make me feel so bad. I'm not about to put that dirty shirt back on, though, no matter how uncomfortable we both might be.

"No, but I've seen enough mechanics with gashes and cuts to tell when more than a Band-aid is needed."

"Well, I need to clean this mess before somebody else gets hurt." She bends down again and starts collecting mug pieces.

"Go clean your wound, and I'll take care of this." I take the pieces from her and start picking up more.

She stares at me for a second but then heads into the garage I just left. Figuring out Chelsie Blake is going to be complicated.

As I'm finishing up, she comes out and hands me a bag with a Mischief Motors shirt, and she's still not looking at me. "Here, wear this. I guessed at the size."

I pull the shirt out of the bag and put it on, buttoning it as we both stand awkwardly. The shirt fits fine, and when she finally glances at me, I notice a mixture of embarrassment on her face but also anger. I hope I haven't done something to piss her off. Maybe I should have put the dirty shirt on.

"Thanks for the shirt."

Nodding, she ignores the comment. "Right. Follow me. You have paperwork to fill out." She turns on a high heel that only brings her to my shoulder and swings the door to the garage open wide before marching through. I hesitate for only a second to watch her go, then follow her to her office.

"How's your hand?" I ask, sitting across the desk from her.

She waves me off. "It'll be fine. Don't worry about it." Opening a folder, she quickly flips through the papers inside, slams it shut, and hands it over to me. "Here, fill these out. It's tax and insurance forms." She follows up with a pen thrust at me. I jerk back to avoid being stabbed in the chest with a ballpoint pen and take it from her, noticing she's careful not to let our fingers touch in the process. I wonder if I'm getting to her like she's getting to me.

I fill out the requisite paperwork while Chelsie takes off somewhere else. When I finish, and she's still not back, I stand and start looking at all the framed photographs on her office wall. Pictures of her and her father taken over the years in front of various classic cars. Ranging from young to not long ago, it's quite a visual history of their relationship. Her teenage years are particularly interesting since she looks nothing like that anymore. She's almost unrecognizable, but those pictures tickle something in my brain. I can't pinpoint what, exactly, but it's an odd déjà vu type of sensation that makes zero sense.

"Are you done?" Chelsie asks from behind me, startling me out of my inner thoughts about her. Her tone is sharp, and she doesn't sound happy. I don't think I've seen or heard her happy except for when I told her about Gus last week.

"Did you call any of the references I gave you?" Thinking of Gus makes me wonder if she talked to him after all.

"I called all of them. Why?" The corner of her mouth raises, and she meets my eyes for the first time today. An intense fire rages inside her; I just know it. "Are you worried about what they said about you?"

"I doubt I would have to fill out all those forms if they said negative things," I smirk right back at her.

Two can play at this game. I like flirting games, and playing with her could be fun.

She raises an eyebrow, questioning my logic. "Are you so sure? I could have had you fill those out just to torture you." Licking her lips, she crosses her arms over her chest, again drawing my eyes there. *She needs to stop fucking doing that.*

Not only am I distracted by her breasts, but now I'm thinking about her torturing me. She is already doing that, but the possibility of intentional torture of a sexual nature makes my mouth go dry, and my palms start to sweat. *Fucking hell.*

"Fair enough. I guess I'm glad Gus didn't throw me under the bus."

She chuckles a little at this. "He wasn't too happy saying decent things about you, but he did. But I can understand why you quit there. He seems like a real peach."

I shrug noncommittally. If Gus said decent things about me, I'd feel like a total asshole if I started bad-mouthing him, even if he deserves it. I keep my karma in check and keep my mouth shut.

"Okay then..." She turns and heads out the door, and I assume I'm supposed to follow her, so I do. *I think I'd follow Chelsie Blake just about anywhere.*

Chapter 7

Bright Eyes

Chelsie

I lead Noah to where he'll be working, show him the various systems and duties he'll be handling, and leave him with his apprentices. Initially, he looks a bit like a fish out of water as I observe from open garage bay doors, but he quickly acclimates and is running the show in no time.

"How goes the new recruit?" Normandy sidles up next to me, taking in the scene I've been quietly watching from the sidelines, hopefully unnoticed.

"I got him to take his shirt off this morning...." I tease.

Her head whips around to stare at me. "You what? Chelsie, we can't...."

"Relax. It was an accident. We ran into each other in a doorway. I spilled hot coffee on him."

Her shoulders sag in obvious relief, but I'm curious what she thought I meant. "Oh. Okay, good."

I arch an eyebrow at her. "Good? I doubt burning a new employee is good. I also broke my favorite coffee mug and cut my hand while cleaning up." I hold my palm up to show her the bandage. "It's been a great start."

"I meant good, in that the reason he took his shirt off wasn't something...else." She eyes me sideways. "You know there's no dating of employees, right? That could be a legal nightmare."

Now it's my turn to glance at her and scoff, "Not. A. Problem." Shifting away from her, I head back to my office, but she catches up and walks with me.

"What are you up to today? Besides burning people and injuring yourself, that is?" She's almost got a weird excitement around her today, and since she learned she was pregnant, she's not been in the best of moods. Morning sickness still hits her at all hours of the day, making her miserable to be around most of the time.

"The usual Monday crap." The sensation that I'm not going to like what comes next washes over me. "Why?"

"I just got off the phone with Mrs. Bailey. Remember her? Wayne's widow?"

"Yeah..." I'm not seeing where she's going with this.

"Well, she wants you to call her to set up a time to appraise the cars, and she wants you to do it soon. I don't know why but she seems to be in a hurry to get rid of those cars."

That's strange. She didn't seem to be in that big of a rush last week when I first talked to her about it at Wayne's funeral.

"Okay. I can give her a call." I study Normandy, wondering how to broach the next topic. "So, what's my budget for purchasing vehicles?" Not too long ago, I was asked to sell off some of the inventory, and now she seems anxious for me to buy more cars. It's not a clear message. But then, she did marry a billionaire, so maybe he's funding some of the business now, though Normandy hasn't told me anything of the sort. Since we're co-owners, I would think she'd tell me something like that.

"Well, see what she's got first, and then we'll work out the details if you think any of them would be worth buying." She shrugs and splits off to go into her own office.

I stare after her, wondering what is up with her chipper mood. Normandy is not someone I would describe as jovial by any means, so her weird attitude today is disconcerting.

After I arrange to meet Mrs. Bailey at her house later this afternoon, I leave my office to find Normandy to tell her the plan. I find her talking to Noah in the lot between the garages, and a pang of jealousy sparks in my chest at the two of them together. It's irrational. Normandy is madly in love with her husband and vice versa, so even the thought of her being unfaithful to him is completely insane. She would never. And to be honest, I don't think Noah would do anything with a married woman either, but I can't help my feelings when they pop up unbidden like that.

I shove it down and approach them, anxious to tell Normandy about my plans.

"Hey, Chelsie," Noah says smoothly, tipping his chin at me.

I kind of nod at him but focus on Normandy. I'm not here to talk to him. "I just got off the phone with Mrs. Bailey. I'm going to head over there in a few to check out Wayne's cars. Do you want to come with me? I wouldn't mind the company. It's a bit of a drive into the desert."

"No, but you should take Noah with you."

My gaze snaps up to him. *No. Don't suggest that.* I do not want to be in a car for any period of time with him.

"Well, no, I...." I can't get words out. I can't get stupid words out because I'm freaking out like a silly kid. Whenever I'm around him, I devolve into my brittle high school self, and I hate it.

"Take me where?" His eyes seem to light up at the idea. Damn it. *No. No. No.*

Normandy glances at me but answers him, "She's going to look at your predecessor's car collection. His widow wants to be rid of it."

"Really, you don't need to...." I can't seem to finish a thought around these two.

"I'd love to go with you." He smiles, and my chest tightens at the sight. "It might be helpful for me to check them out mechanically, you know, before you buy anything. You don't want to end up buying a lemon."

I glare at him and throw a hand on my hip for good measure. "I highly doubt Wayne would have invested in lemons."

He reddens, but I can't read the reaction. It could be embarrassment or anger. "I didn't mean he would. But you don't know how long the cars have been sitting. Lots of things can go bad on a car if it sits idle."

His words don't help me decipher his mood. But regardless of what he's feeling, I do not want him to come along for this.

"Really, Norm. I'm capable of handling this."

She shakes her head at me. "I think Noah is right. A mechanic's eye would be useful." She pats my arm and turns to head toward her car. "You two figure out the details. Call me later, and we'll talk budget if we need to, okay? Goodbye, Noah."

And with that, she gets into the car waiting for her and leaves. She doesn't get to drive herself anywhere anymore and always has security around. It took a while to get used to that for both of us.

Noah and I stare after the car, and when it's out of sight, it turns awkward between us. Of course, it does. This is never going to be comfortable or easy.

I turn to face him, studying him closely for the first time. He's aged well. I still see young, high school Noah in some of his features. His eyes are the same delicious chocolate brown they've always been, but they now have seen some life experiences and matured. All of him has, and he's still damn attractive. He's always been tall, but he used to be lanky and lithe. Now he's filled out, more muscular and stronger.

"When do we leave?" His voice breaks me out of my ogling, and I have to pretend I wasn't just staring at him with admiration.

"A half hour. Meet me out front." I ignore if he says or does anything as I go back inside. I need a cool drink. And a cold shower. *Stat.*

Chapter 8

Honey Whiskey

Noah

So, mixed messages are a thing. And they're what I'm getting from Chelsie Blake. She acts as though she hates my guts for some reason I still don't understand, and then I catch her looking at me like I'm some sort of snack. I don't mind the snack part since she looks just as tasty, but her vibe contradicts that. Maybe I'll gain some insight on this field trip we're taking to look at the car collection.

I'm leaning against my car at the scheduled meeting time, waiting for Chelsie to come out. My breathing stops when she emerges from the garage, and my heart bounces around in my rib cage while I

47

take her in. I've thought she was enthralling since I met her last week, but just now, when she doesn't know anyone is looking at her, she's more than pretty. She's literally breathtaking, as my lungs have just proven.

What the hell is wrong with me? I can't be thinking these kinds of things. She's my fucking boss, for fuck's sake. And it's my first damned day of work. If I keep this up, it's a surefire way to get myself canned. Something I'm not in a position to do at the moment. But damn, if this is how I'm reacting to her on the first day of work, the foreseeable future will be a sexual tension-filled nightmare. I spent most of the day thinking about her with her hands on my chest, distracted or looking for her out of the corner of my eye. It's hard to get work done around here.

When she glances over and catches me staring at her, she blushes, and I think I do too, but I do my best to cover it up. I don't know if I succeed, but luckily, she's looking away, so she couldn't notice my reaction. I have got to pull my shit together when I'm around her, or else I will find myself in trouble very quickly.

"Are you driving? Or do you want me to?" I ask as she approaches me.

Putting a hand up to shield her eyes from the lowering sun, she replies, "I'll drive."

I don't argue, but I was hoping I'd get to drive. Being a static passenger is going to be difficult. At least if I were driving, I'd have something to do with my hands and something to concentrate on. Now I'm going to be stuck in a car with a beautiful woman who I can't keep my mind off of for who knows how long, and I'll need to somehow keep it professional.

We start heading past the airport towards Henderson, the sun setting behind us. She keeps the radio volume high enough to make conversation difficult, so I fix my gaze out the passenger side window and tap my thighs along with the music for something to do. I didn't think it would be this awkward between us, but she's not making it easy.

Fifteen minutes in, she turns down the music. "So, tell me about yourself, Noah." She keeps her eyes on the road, so I think she's being polite. I'm sure she doesn't give two shits about me personally and is just making small talk. I'll take it, though. It's better than nothing. Maybe the problem is that she's got a boyfriend. Of course, she's got a boyfriend, if not more than one. I should have assumed that.

"What do you want to know?" I'm not being coy. I don't do well with that type of demand. Do they want to know my sign? Or my favorite color? The options are endless, and I'm not one to tell my life story to a stranger, no matter how gorgeous they are. Maybe *especially* not if they're gorgeous.

"I don't know." She shrugs, confirming it's just the small talk she's after. "Tell me about your family, I guess."

Okay, that's a direction, at least. "Well, it's just me and my older brother Theo. He's staying with me temporarily until the house he just bought is ready to move in."

"How much older is he?"

"Just a couple of years, but he's super smart and flew through school, so we didn't really get to go to school together."

Her hands grab the steering wheel tightly. So much that her knuckles whiten with the pressure. After a few seconds, she releases her stranglehold on the leather and eases up.

We drive in silence again for a while before she asks, "Where did you go to school?" The white knuckles are back, and I can sense her muscles tense up next to me. Why is she being so intense? I do not understand the vibe right now.

"Coronado." I glance at her for a reaction, but she's not giving anything away. She's got no emotion now. Her jaw is set, and her eyes are narrowed as if she's focusing hard on the road ahead. "Where did you go?" I realize I should have asked her about her family, too. I took all the questions and didn't ask anything about her.

She presses her lips in a quick scowl, then evades my question. "We're here." The car turns into a long driveway on what almost feels like a farm or a ranch. We're on the far eastern edge of Henderson now, and the houses here sit on much more land. The setting sun casts a warm amber glow on the white wood plank exterior of the home. It's only this kind of older architecture outside the city limits where you see houses not made of stucco and all looking alike. It makes homes like this unique.

I can spy the oversized garage behind the house, and I'm getting excited to check out what's in there.

When Chelsie pulls up to the house and shuts off the engine, she narrows her eyes at me sternly. "Be nice. This poor old woman just lost her husband of sixty-five years, and we're not going to swindle her in any way, shape, or form, got it?"

I'm taken aback by the venom thrown at me from out of nowhere. I stare back at her in disbelief. Does she think I came out here to take advantage of this woman? "Did I not tell you the story about why I quit my last job?"

The intense staring contest between us continues for a minute, neither of us breaking away. I swear I could reach over and pull her into a kiss, and I think she would let me from the way she's looking at me, but I know I can't. Fuck, do I want to. It's excruciating how much I want to. Memories of her touching my chest flash through me like heat lightning, making it worse.

She blinks, coming back to herself from somewhere else. I think I was with her wherever that was and am dragged back with her.

"Fine. Let's go." She shoots me another dirty look

and pushes open her car door to step out. I take my time and watch her as she goes before following her to the house where Mrs. Bailey waits for us outside the front door. Chelsie's smile is so warm and authentic; I instantly want her to smile at me that way. I suddenly want that desperately more than anything.

What the fuck is wrong with me? This is not going to fly. I've got to pull it together, or I may need to quit this job. One fucking day. It's only been one fucking day. And it isn't even over yet.

Chapter 9

Double Down

Chelsie

Mrs. Bailey is so happy to see us; I can't help but smile back at her. It reminds me she's all alone now, without Wayne. They never had children, and it didn't seem like there were a lot of friends at the funeral last week. That's got to be a hard adjustment for her after so many years together with her husband.

She opens the door wide for us. "I see you brought your boyfriend with you. How sweet."

That stops me short, and I sputter, "Oh, no. This is *not* my boyfriend. This is..."

"I'm Noah," he interrupts, holding out a hand to

Mrs. Bailey, a winning smile curving his lips. "I have the honor of stepping into your late husband's shoes at Mischief Motors, and I must say, they are enormous shoes to fill." *What a charmer.*

She takes his hand sweetly into her own, smiling back at him with admiration. "Oh, that's so sweet of you to say. Wayne sure did love his job and those cars. I often wondered if he loved them more than me." She chuckles softly as she pats his hand.

"Oh, I don't believe that for a second. Actually..." He reaches into the back pocket of his jeans and pulls out something to hand to her. She takes a sharp breath as she takes it, one hand covering her mouth and now tears in her eyes. "I found this on Wayne's desk. It had a place of pride among everything, so he was sure to see it all day, every day."

I peek over Mrs. Bailey's shoulder and see a yellow-edged photo of a much younger her and Wayne. A wedding photo. It's a gorgeous picture, and the love between them is evident. Instead of looking at the photographer, they're looking into each other's eyes. It's beautiful. And to think, after sixty-five years together, he still cherished this photo. It's incredibly romantic.

Damn it. She's getting misty-eyed, which makes me do the same. That was sweet of Noah to bring for her.

Holding the photo to her chest lovingly and wiping at her watery eyes, she finds her voice.

"Thank you for this, Noah. You have no idea how much this means to an old woman like me."

He lowers his head and shoves his hands into his pockets, his cheeks warming at her gratitude. I don't know what he thought the picture would do, but he didn't expect the two of us women to start crying over it.

I brush at my own tears with the back of my hand. "So, where do you want to start, Mrs. Bailey? I noticed the big garage out back."

"Well, we can start by you calling me by my first name, which is Jeanette. 'Mrs. Bailey' makes me feel like an old lady." She laughs, leading us into the living room. Placing the photo on top of an upright piano, she asks, "Would you two like something to drink? Some iced tea, maybe? Or Coffee?"

"Nothing for me, thank you." I want to get this over with, so I can get away from Noah. Being around him has me on edge, and I don't like the feeling. I'm nervous for no reason, and I hate it. I hate that he has any effect on me still.

"I would love some iced tea, thanks." Noah takes a seat on the sofa, making himself at home. I stare at him in disbelief. This isn't a social call. We have a job to do here. As much as I love Mrs. Bailey, if I were alone, it would be a different story; I'd stay all evening to chat with her. But I don't want to "hang out" with Noah.

She catches me glaring at him and frowns, her

brows furrowing in confusion, though I don't know why she would be confused about that. I flash a smile and sit in the chair furthest from Noah, resigned to the fact we're now going to be here a while. I sigh inwardly and lock my fingers on my lap to keep them from fidgeting. I don't want to be impolite, so I need to go with the flow here.

Over the next two hours, we listen to stories of Wayne's escapades at Mischief Motors, including some hilarious anecdotes of things gone wrong, but all was fine, and a lesson learned. I also discovered she would go on trips with Wayne when he went to buy his own cars for his collection, just like I did with my dad. It was his weekend passion, and she enjoyed sharing it with him. I can understand her willingness to go along to share that time together.

After Noah's third glass of iced tea and at a lull in the conversation, I stand and stretch. "We should start looking at the cars before it gets too late." He nods his agreement and stands with me.

"Oh, no. It's too late in the day now." Mrs. Bailey glances out the window at the now dark sky. "There aren't any lights in that old garage, so you'll need to come back during the day to inspect the cars. I'm sorry our visit got a little carried away there. I should have considered that but chatting with the two of you was so lovely."

I glance over at Noah, and he's looking at me,

doubt that matches mine on his face. But we can't argue with her, so we have to go along.

"Okay, I can come back tomorrow afternoon." My schedule is flexible, so I can be here whenever she wants. "Not a problem."

"I can't come during work hours with the apprentices...." Noah's voice fades, but his point is made.

"Well, the two of you must come together." Mrs. Bailey is convinced of this for some reason.

"No, really, I can just...." I try to say.

"Nonsense." She pats my shoulder and pushes me toward the door, Noah following behind with a smirk. "The two of you work out when you can come together next, and just let me know. I'm almost always here."

"But..." She's not letting me sneak a word in.

"But nothing. You two have a fine rest of your evening, whatever you're doing." She gives Noah a wink. *What the hell?* "I look forward to seeing you both again soon."

She gives us a small wave as we step out and then shuts the door behind us. We both stand there in shock, looking at the closed door.

Noah turns to me. "What just happened?"

I shake my head at him. Unsure how to answer. "I don't know. But apparently, we'll be back." I turn on my heel and head back to my car, muttering to myself in a chiding imitation of Noah. "*I would love some iced tea, thanks...tell me more about your weekend trips...I can't come during work hours...blah blah blah.* Give me a break."

He's behind me laughing as he follows to the car, and damn it, it makes me laugh a little, but I try to hide it as best as I can. I don't think I succeed, though.

Once we're on the road back to the depot, he turns down the music. "So, do you want to grab a drink or something? It's still kind of early."

I glare at him. "Didn't you have enough to drink at Mrs. Bailey's?"

"You mean my new friend Jeanette's?" The grin taking him over is so contagious I can't help but reciprocate it. When he smiles like that, there are zero problems in the world, and everything will be fine. I need to remind myself it's a lie. It's all a lie.

"You think giving her that wedding photo won her over, don't you?" My tone is back to sarcastic, but I can't help it.

"What?" He's incredulous, his eyes flashing. "I didn't give it to her to win her over. I gave it to her because it was the right thing to do." He stares at me, and I can sense the weight of it on my skin. He's studying me, and it's all I can do not to stare back at him. "Is that what you think of me? What is your problem with me, anyway? You didn't want me in this job in the first place, but I have no clue why that is. You don't even know me."

Really? I don't know him? Oh, I know him too well. That's the problem. He's the one that doesn't know me. Doesn't remember me. Doesn't remember humiliating me. He never wanted to get to know me. *Screw him.*

"No. I do not want to get a drink with you," I say sternly, avoiding everything else he just said. I am not about to delve into my reasoning for anything with him. "Fraternizing with employees is against company policy. Even if I wanted to. Which I don't." There. That should nip that in the bud. I can't believe he asked me out. He must be riding the high of winning over Mrs. Bailey and think he can do the same thing with me. *Sorry, buddy.*

"Ouch. Okay, then." He almost sounds hurt. And I *almost* care.

Chapter 10

New Girl

Noah

I don't know what the hell I did to piss her off, but whatever it was must have been devastating because Chelsie is not letting it go. I just wish I knew what the fuck it was. I haven't even known her long enough to offend her. After being completely shot down by her for asking to grab a drink, we ride back to the depot in silence. Message received. Loud and clear.

Once at the depot, she drops me off at the door and takes off. Doesn't say goodbye. Doesn't say a word. *Fine*. She doesn't have to like me. She just has to sign my paychecks. I'm okay with that. But I'm not really. That's a lie. Besides finding her extremely attractive, something inside me twists at her dislike of me. I want her to like me. Actually, I want more than that, but I'll take liking me as a start.

I get she didn't want to hang out at Mrs. Bailey's, but I thought it would be rude to look at the cars and leave. The woman just lost her husband and is still adjusting to living all alone. It didn't hurt anything to take a few minutes to talk to her. After a while, Chelsie was just as involved in the conversation as I was, so she can't hold that against me. And how was I supposed to know the garage didn't have lights? I've never heard of such a thing, but the house is relatively old, so I didn't question it.

So, we need to go back another day to check out the cars. Big deal. It's not the end of the world like Chelsie is making it out to be. On my way home, I replay every interaction I've had with Chelsie, and for the life of me, I can't think why she has such a problem with me. Is it a 'type' thing? She doesn't think mechanics are good enough for her? That wouldn't be a first. I've come up against that before, and it was total bullshit. I don't peg Chelsie as being the judgmental type. Not about that, anyway. I guess I need to leave it alone and leave her be. It's going to be difficult, considering I can't stop thinking about her, but I'm not an idiot either. I know my limits, and I think I've just hit it with her.

Chelsie and I avoid each other as much as possible the rest of the week, and neither of us brings up a return trip to Mrs. Bailey's. If we don't do something by the middle of next week, I'll try to start the ball rolling. For now, I'll let Chelsie move at her own pace on it. I don't need to insert myself into the middle of her business dealings. I was merely along for the ride in the first place.

It's still a crazy work environment, though, as I often find myself thinking about Chelsie from out of nowhere. I'll be in the middle of a repair job with one of the apprentices, and I'll suddenly stop and zone out. I need to get my shit together since she obviously wants nothing to do with me. Well, sometimes, it's obvious. Other times, I have no fucking clue what is happening in her head.

On Saturday, my best friend River talks me into going out for drinks and seeing a local band he swears is "on the verge of something big." He works with the singer sometimes on construction projects. They're called Murderous Crows, and they opened for Indigo King when they were in town last year and were pretty good, so I don't mind seeing them again. Unfortunately, the show is at a local dive bar, Raven's, where my ex-girlfriend Melissa bar tends. It's been a long time since I've seen or talked to her, so I'm not sure what the reception will be. We're not unfriendly to each other, and things ended somewhat amicably last year, but I wouldn't go out of my way to seek her out. I hope she's not working tonight, so I can enjoy myself.

When we arrive at the bar, it's surprisingly empty. There appear to be regular bar patrons, but not many people are here to see the band. Melissa is working, so I grab a table and send River to the bar to buy our drinks. I'm not a chicken, but I want to have fun tonight, not get into any drama.

"So, this gig wasn't announced because it's a showcase for a record label or something. That's why there are so few people here." He sets our beers down and sits across from me. "Melissa said 'hi,' by the way." I'm sure his tone carries all of the unfriendliness that was implied.

I smirk at him and then check out the crowd, noticing a table full of guys in polo shirts and designer jeans. They must be the label reps since they stick out like sore thumbs.

"Isn't that Mackenzie something or other? I think we went to school with her, didn't we?" River asks.

I glance in the direction he's pointing and see a tall woman with long dark violet hair talking to a guy with way too many tattoos. He must be with the band. But River is right; I think we did go to school with her. "Roberts. Mackenzie Roberts. And yeah, we were in the same grade but didn't have any classes together, I don't think." I survey the crowd, seeing if I know anyone else or if anyone catches my interest. With Chelsie Blake constantly on my brain, a distraction away from her would be nice. A few more people have straggled in since we arrived, but not many.

The band comes on and plays, and they're outstanding. The singer seemed a bit out of it, but other than that, the music and the songs were great. When the band's set ends, I glance at the label people, and they seem to be impressed too. We could have just witnessed the birth of the next great rock band.

It's still early when the band ends, so River and I stay a little longer, enjoying ourselves and having a decent conversation. As longtime friends, we can sometimes end up butting heads or be at each other's throats about dumb shit, but we can have a decent time together most of the time. This night is one of those times.

"No, I'm going to finally tell him what I really think of him," a loud voice sounds from behind me, and my shoulder is pulled, turning me around roughly. It's Mackenzie Roberts, and she's got a finger pointed in my face. *What the fuck?* "I should have kicked your ass in high school for what you did to Chelsie, and I have half a mind to do it now to make up for the lost time."

"Mac. Stop it. Come on." I glance over and

surprisingly find Chelsie pulling on Mackenzie's arm, desperately trying to pull her away from me. "Please, Mac. Don't. You're making it worse."

What the hell is going on? Make what worse? And what is Mackenzie talking about?

"What the hell did I do?" I shrug my shoulders at Mackenzie, trying to prove my ignorance of the cause of her anger. I've had a few beers, and I'm not thinking clearly, but this is sobering me up fast.

A sharp fingernail is pushed into my chest as Mackenzie leans in, getting right in my face. She's kind of tall for a woman, I note to myself. "What did you do? Seriously?" She scoffs and glances at Chelsie, who now is frantic and has given up on pulling Mackenzie away but has buried her face in her hands. "You humiliated my best friend and broke her heart senior year. That's what you fucking did. Asshole."

"What?" I have no clue what the hell she's talking about.

"Don't play dumb. I was there and saw the whole thing. You knew what you were doing, showing off in front of your so-called friends by making fun of her. And when they went on making fun of her for the rest of senior year, you did nothing. Absolutely nothing. You were a total dick, and you're lucky Chelsie is a much better person than you, or you wouldn't have a job."

That's enough for Chelsie, and she turns and runs toward the restrooms at the back of the bar. I'm stunned. I do not remember any of this. It was at least seven years ago, but that sounds dramatic. I would remember something like that. At least, I think I would. Could I have done that? It does not sound like me at all.

"Mackenzie, I really don't remember anything like that happening. I swear."

She crosses her arms, her eyes narrowing. "It doesn't matter if you remember it or not because *we* do, and it definitely happened. Chelsie remembers it, and it's shaped how she's dealt with guys ever since." She shifts her weight uncomfortably, and I think she's going to take off after Chelsie now that the steam of her anger is dying.

"That was high school. It was years ago." I shrug, trying to think of what to say to make any of this better. It's hard since I don't remember my accused crime. Chelsie's shitty attitude toward me makes complete sense now, though. And I am surprised I got the job despite what I allegedly did or didn't do to her in high school. "I am not the same person I was back then. I don't think anyone is the same as in high school. Are you?"

"Of course not. My point is your flippant actions back then had real consequences that continue through today. You might want to own up to them."

She turns and heads back the same way Chelsie went.

"But..." I don't even finish. She's halfway across the bar now, anyway.

"What the hell did you do to her, dude?" River half laughs, half scoffs. "I don't remember anything like she talked about. But then again, I wasn't in your inner circle at that point either."

I rake my hands down my face, trying to remember any incidents like Mackenzie described. *Did I humiliate Chelsie? How?* Even in high school, I can't believe I would be that cruel.

"I don't know, man. I don't know."

"Hey Noah, how are you?" A quiet female voice behind me says.

I turn from my locker to find a girl staring at me, her hands pulled into her sleeves nervously so only her fingertips show. She's wearing an oversized hoodie that seems to be swallowing her whole. Her dark brown hair is pulled into a sleek ponytail, and her eyeliner is too heavy but interesting. I'm sure I've probably seen her before, but if so, I don't remember her. She's kind of pretty in a way, though.

"Hey," I say. Not sure what this is about. I can see Troy and Eric coming up the hall toward me, my new

friends from the varsity football team. They, of course, wouldn't be friends with me if I were still on junior varsity, but whatever. I've been moving up in the world since I made the team.

She stares at me for a while, working her bottom lip over with her teeth, before speaking again. She's nervous for some reason. Her bottom lip is interesting too. "I was wondering if you'd want to hang out sometime...with me?"

Did she just ask me out? I don't think I've ever had a girl ask me out before, and I'm kind of shocked.

"Yo, Thompson, what's hip, what's hot, what's new?" Troy comes up, offering a fist to bump, so I do, and then again with Eric. They both stand beside us, alternating their gazes expectantly between me and this girl, whose name I still don't even know.

After a minute of awkwardness, Eric says, "Look, man, if we're interrupting whatever is going on between you and Hot Topic over here, we can catch you on the flip side," he snickers and starts backing away. Troy starts to do the same. Shit. No. I'm just starting to fit in. I can't blow this now.

"What? Ew. No. I don't even know this girl." As I move to follow them, I slide a disdainful glare her way, but as I see her distraught expression and tears starting to form in her eyes, I can feel my soul turn to cinder and ash. Fuck. That was a complete dick move, but she'll get over it. She was pretty; she'll find someone else.

I wake up in a sweat and glance at the clock. It's the middle of the night, and though I feel like I just fell asleep, my mind is still cluttered by my dream.

My dream. I remember now. *Holy fuck. Now I know why Chelsie hates me. Mackenzie was right.*

Chapter 11

God Complex (Mojo)

Chelsie

The rest of the weekend both flies and drags by, and I spend most of it in bed, flipping channels on the TV, binge-watching dumb reality television and serial killer documentaries to keep my mind off the incident Saturday night with Noah. After making such a scene at the bar, I'm finally talking to Mackenzie again. She crossed a line, talking to Noah like that. And she called incessantly to apologize until I finally gave in and answered her. It still puts me in a horrible position. Noah was blissfully unaware of what happened in high school, and I wasn't about to tell him. Now I can never show my face again in public, especially not at work.

Monday morning comes, and I text Normandy that I'm too sick to go in. And again, on Tuesday. It's Wednesday morning, I sent the same message, and she's now banging at the door. I throw on a robe and head downstairs to let her in. *Remember, you're sick. Act sick.*

When I open the door, she stares at me from head to toe, a snarl of distaste on her face. "Get dressed." She pushes past me and drops her purse on the counter, making herself at home. To be fair, this did technically use to be her home. She signed over her half of our dad's house to me when she moved in with Brandon.

"What? Why?" I shut the door and turn to her. Even pregnant, she's gorgeous. She's had that California beach thing going for as long as I can remember, and the baby glow amplifies it. It's not fair.

"We're going to the doctors. I made an appointment for you with mine since I didn't know who yours is...." She announces this so casually like it's normal for someone to make appointments for others like this. It's not normal. At least, not for me.

"Norm, I don't need a doctor. I'll be fine. I just need rest...." I shuffle to the island and sit, propping my head in my hands. Even with all the sleeping I've done the last few days, I'm still exhausted.

"And a shower...." She scrunches her nose and backs away from me.

"Haha. Very funny." I make a snide face at her. "Despite my haggard appearance, I *am* clean. I just feel like shit." Not everyone can pull off her no-makeup glamour but come on.

Pressing the back of her hand to my forehead, she says, "You don't have a fever. What are your symptoms?"

Seeing the concern in her eyes makes me hesitate to answer. I don't want to lie to my sister, though every instinct in me also doesn't want to talk about why I'm hiding out here.

She must catch something in my expression that gives it away. "You're not sick, are you? What's going on?" Ever since our dad taught her how to play poker, she's been able to read people like they're freaking nursery rhymes. I've been unable to hide a single emotion around her my entire life. I don't know why I even bother trying.

I draw in a long breath and hold it before letting it out slowly. There's not going to be any getting around this with her. "No. Technically, I'm not sick. But I'm not exactly well either."

Sitting down next to me, she squeezes my arm with a warm hand, her expression softening. "Talk to me."

So, I do. I tell her everything, from what happened in high school to Saturday night at the bar.

My humiliation is now laid bare for her to witness, along with the rest of the world, because the universe apparently doesn't like letting things go.

"And that's why I'm here in my pj's, feeling sorry for myself and watching shitty TV." I rest my chin on my forearms, avoiding Normandy's intense gaze. She's studying me, and I'm not sure why. Does she not believe everything I just said? I can't take it anymore. "What? Why are you staring at me like that?"

"Noah has been asking about you like crazy. Every morning when I get in the office and when I leave in the evening, he asks if you're doing okay." She shakes her head slightly. "He even asked for your number so he could call you himself, and while I thought it was very sweet, I didn't think it was appropriate, so I said no. I guess I'm glad I didn't give it to him."

"Thanks for that." My voice is starting to turn raspy from talking so much.

Her eyes spark with curiosity. "Why did you hire him if you knew you'd be stuck working with him after what he did to you?"

Her question surprises me. "Do you not remember me trying to say the job was already filled? Geez, Norm. Selective memory much?"

She cringes as she remembers. "Yikes. Yeah, I guess I kind of steamrolled that whole conversation, didn't I? It just seemed too good to be true, him showing up out of the blue like that when we needed him."

"If it seems too good to be true, it probably is."

"Well, you can't hide away here forever. You'll need to come back to work eventually." She taps her chin thoughtfully. "Can we fire him? Do you want me to do it? Or do you want the privilege?" Her conspiratorial grin is wicked but not all that convincing.

"I don't want to fire him," I sigh. "I don't even hate him."

"Firing him could be a legal fiasco. I was kidding." She pauses and stares at me. "You don't still like him, do you?"

"I don't know, Norm." I groan. Not sure what I feel about anything anymore.

"Well, even if you did, tear that thought right out of your head. There's no dating employees, so the problem is solved for you. You're welcome."

"Gee, thanks."

"And what about Mac? Have you talked to her?"

"Yeah. She called me non-stop until I accepted her apology. I can't stay mad at her for very long."

"So, what are you going to do?"

"I don't know. Nothing. I'm not going to do anything." I rub my temples, fending off a headache. "There's nothing to do. I'll be back at work tomorrow."

"That's the spirit." She rubs my back as she

stands to leave. "Don't ever let a guy make you feel this way about yourself. You are gorgeous, smart, talented, and funny as all get out, and any guy would be lucky to worship at your feet."

"Damn, do you have to leave so soon? I could get used to this...."

"Nope, that was your one sisterly pep talk for the year. We need to ease into these things."

She leaves, and I think about everything Normandy said, particularly the part where there is no dating employees, so feeling this way is pointless. Even if Mackenzie did mortify me at the bar on Saturday night by bringing up my past feelings for Noah, it doesn't mean anything now. Now it is all a moot point. I can't date Noah, even if I wanted to. *So how the hell do I stop wanting to?*

Chapter 12

HY, How Are You?

Noah

By the time Chelsie returns to work on Thursday, I've had almost a week to think about what Mackenzie told me. And since remembering the incident she referred to, I've thought about nothing else. Even though it happened a long time ago, and I was a different person back then, Mackenzie was right; it doesn't negate my responsibility for my actions.

Normandy had said Chelsie was sick those days she didn't come to work, but I think I know better than that. The confrontation I had with Mackenzie on Saturday night forced her to stay away from work.

I get it. I could see how upset she was that night. And I don't blame her for reacting this way.

When she does return to work, I steer clear of her for most of the day, giving her whatever space she needs. I'd bet most of my savings I'm the last person she wants to be around right now. Even I'm having a hard time living with myself at the moment. I spent the past week doing some deep-dive soul searching, reflecting on high school and the whole clique dynamic that runs rampant. I had gotten so sucked into the vortex of 'popularity' that it blinded me to everything else, like what happened with Chelsie.

I learned the harsh lesson about popularity when I blew out my knee halfway through the football season and couldn't play anymore. All of a sudden, my so-called 'friends' were no longer my friends and barely spoke to me. I was damaged goods. And all the true friends I had before making the team, but abandoned along the way, couldn't trust me anymore, with good reason. I was an island. The land of misfit toys incarnated. The only person that still talked to me was River, but we've known each other all our lives.

Hearing what I did to Chelsie and how I humiliated her, in light of my self-reflection, is shameful but doesn't necessarily surprise me. I'd be shocked if she was the only person I did that to since, according to River, I was a dick to everyone during that time. I was an asshole back then, and she did not deserve to be treated like that.

It's strange how my brain just decided it was okay for me to forget things like that. It just said, *'Nope. This is too horrible. We don't like this part of you. Let's put this in a box and never discuss it again.'* How fucked up is my head that I can just shove incidents like that aside to make me feel better about myself? That shouldn't be how it works.

Part of me wants to talk to Chelsie about it. Apologize to her for being an ass back then and treating her so poorly. Try to explain myself, even though my reasons are meaningless. But another side of me wants to avoid the confrontation altogether. I don't want to see the hurt I caused in her eyes. I don't want to face the fact I've hurt people, regardless of how long ago it was.

"There you are." It's Chelsie, and she's found me where I've been taking inventory of our parts and supplies in a back room out of everyone's sight. It was the perfect hiding spot where I could still get work done. Until now, of course. "I've been looking for you all afternoon."

When I turn around, I don't see a broken woman as I expected since she has been out of work for so long. Instead, I see a strong woman with tired eyes, reticent to talk to me but determined.

I'm not sure how to react. I am not prepared for a

casual conversation or small talk. On the best of days, I suck at that.

"I've been here." I try to smile but doubt I pull it off.

"Well, I needed to find you because Mrs. Bailey wants us to come by today. If you're busy, I can tell her we'll try for another day...." She glances down, looking everywhere but at me.

"Today is fine," I say, trying to keep the excitement out of my voice. I'd been wondering if we would ever make a return trip, though now it seems tarnished somehow. I'm reminded she's known all along who I was. She even pretended not to know anything about me the last time we went to Mrs. Bailey's, asking me where I went to high school. Was she just fishing to check if I remembered her?

She nods, chewing on her bottom lip. "Okay. Cool. I'll meet you out front then." As she leaves, the memory of her biting her lip that day in school flashes behind my eyes, bringing the whole incident into my mind again. A heavy sadness cloaks me as I wind up the shop before leaving. I'm not sure what I'm sad about exactly. It doesn't have a focus. It's just an all-encompassing mood I can't seem to shake.

When I meet Chelsie outside, I don't say anything. I give her a polite nod, slide into the passenger's side of her car, and put on my seatbelt. There aren't words I could say to make up for what I did, so I'm not going to waste her time trying to think of any, let alone say anything. Words won't mean anything or make a difference at this point, so I remain silent.

We ride the whole way to Mrs. Bailey's in silence, the only noise in the car coming from the car stereo. I again spend the trip gazing out the window at the passing scenery, trying to ignore the intense energy that flows between us like a current whenever we're in the same space. The air in the car is charged with electricity, making me afraid to move for fear of sparking something. My hand itches to reach over and touch her thigh to be connected to her. I'm not even thinking sexually about her; I'm just soaking in her presence like a starving man at a buffet.

Mrs. Bailey is at the front door like last time when we arrive, so I wave a quick 'hello' but don't stop to chat. I go straight to the garage behind the house. If there aren't any lights, I want to use as much daylight as possible before it sets and goes away. Chelsie seems to have stopped to chat, so she can do the niceties this time without me. I need to separate myself from her for a little while. After that drive, my head is a bit fuzzy.

At the garage, I lean down to grab the handle to the main bay door, but as I try to lift it up, it doesn't budge. It's locked. I try a side door, and it too is locked. Looking back at the house, the two women are standing in the yard in front of Chelsie's car, talking away like we're here for another social call.

Making my way back to them, Mrs. Bailey holds out a set of keys to me, not pausing in the story she's telling Chelsie. She had to have known I needed these keys but made me walk all the way back to grab them? That sadness that surrounded me earlier is morphing into plain old grumpiness.

I take a deep breath, trying to calm the fuck down because my emotions today are all over the freaking place. I unlock the main garage door, and when I lift it up, I am greeted with the cleanest garage I have ever seen. I knew Wayne was meticulous by how he kept his shop at Mischief Motors, but this is a whole other level. The floor shines in what light does get in from the west-facing door like a fucking showroom. There are ten cars, five per row, an eclectic collection of older makes and models, and all in pristine condition. Holy shit, this will cost Chelsie an arm and a leg if she even wants one of them. All ten would be insane.

I start my inspections with the car nearest me, a 1967 Chevy Camaro with a cream paint job and black vinyl roof. The restoration is impeccable, and the upgrades impressive, but still in line with the style of the classic car. Wayne seems to respect the car's original form but also had the sense to upgrade without going over the top and turning them into bloated muscle cars on steroids.

"Noah!"

At the sound of my name, I glance up and find

Chelsie and Mrs. Bailey both staring at me expectantly. Apparently, they've been calling my name for some time now, but I've been lost in classic car land.

"Sorry, I got a little obsessed and tuned out." My neck heats with embarrassment, so I lift a hand to it, covering it best I can.

"Oh, I know *that* look." Mrs. Bailey is smiling at me with a faraway look, remembering something or someone else, and most likely, some other time.

Chapter 13

Nearly Forgot My Broken Heart

Chelsie

Once Noah snaps out of whatever dreamland he's traveled to, we go car by car while Mrs. Bailey observes from a lawn chair at the entrance to the garage, drinking an iced tea. He takes pictures and videos and rattles off notes for me to write down in a notebook about each car, so we can put it together later. Any attempt at an accurate valuation would be dicey since neither of us is qualified to do that. We'll need to bring in a professional for this.

I do my best to focus on the cars and not on him caressing and manhandling the curves and various features of the vehicles like they belong to a woman, but it's difficult. I'm sure a lot of it is in my head, and I'm projecting my dirty thoughts on what he's doing. The entire drive here was silent, which made my other senses sharper, and my physical awareness of his body right next to me was so heightened I could swear he felt it too. It was a wild and intense feeling but not entirely unpleasant. Again, I'm probably projecting.

Throughout our inspections, there are several moments where I need to pull Noah out of his admiration trance to get to work. As it is, we only make it through half of the cars before it gets too dark to see clearly.

"I guess you'll have to come back to do the rest." Mrs. Bailey doesn't sound too upset by this. I think she likes the company. She probably misses Wayne something fierce, and having us here fills that space for a little while.

"Mrs. Bailey, do you have anyone lined up to take care of the yard for you?" Noah peers sternly at the overgrown grass patches. Vegas grass is rare, and it's hard to have a natural lawn like other places. It's usually patchy and sparse and hardly survives for long during the summer. It can grow out of hand quickly in the middle of spring.

"It's Jeanette, honey. Don't forget." She wags a scolding finger at him but smiles. "And the neighbor's boy was going to handle it, but I haven't seen him in a while. I think it may have been just one of those niceties people say they're going to help with without really intending to do anything."

"Well, do you have the equipment here? I'm happy to come back and take care of it for you." Noah's tone sounds disappointed in all of humanity for offending Mrs. Bailey and eager to help if he can. My chest tightens around my melting heart. *Damn him. Being charming.*

She puts her hand on her chest in appreciation. "Well, I'd be so grateful if you could do that for me. There's a shed out back with Wayne's lawn equipment. I'd be happy to pay you for your trouble."

"Don't worry about it. I'll be by tomorrow after work if that's okay."

The hand on her chest flies to cover her mouth as she gets emotional. "Oh, that's so kind...."

Noah steps up and wraps his arms around her gently, letting her cry it out, and I've never seen a man so kind to a woman before. I can't stop the tears in my own eyes, and I need to choke down a sob from escaping. In the dying light of the day, watching Noah absorb an old woman's grief and loss with so much grace is something I'll never forget.

In that singular moment, my entire opinion of him starts to shift. He might not be the high school jerk that broke my heart anymore. He might now be the gentle soul that comforted a grieving widow when she needed it most. And I can't *un-feel* these feelings. They're seared into my heart now. I can almost feel the ice start to thaw a little bit. And to be honest, it scares me a little.

"We should be going." I can tell Noah is getting a bit uncomfortable, and I figure I can do some saving. "It's getting late."

"Oh, my goodness, you're right. You two have been here a long time, haven't you? I'm so sorry to keep you so late." Mrs. Bailey dabs at the corners of her eyes with a handkerchief. "I do enjoy watching the two of you work. You're so good together."

Noah and I glance at each other at her comment but turn away just as quickly. The suggestion of us being 'good together' is unnerving, especially with our history.

"Goodbye, Mrs. Bailey," I say, giving her a hug of my own. "I'll see you soon."

"Oh, won't you come with Noah tomorrow?" Her eyes are beseeching, practically begging me to come by. How can I say no to this woman?

I turn to Noah for his reaction, and he only shrugs, his face unreadable.

"I'll see what I can do," I say, not wanting to commit to anything if this whole thing blows up between Noah and me. Who knows what'll happen with us between now and tomorrow evening?

"Okay. You two have a fine night. Be safe." We

watch as she heads slowly into her house and waves from the door to the two of us.

Waving back, we go to my car, still silent, and I begin the drive back to the depot.

After several minutes of silence, I can't take any more. "If you don't want me to go with you tomorrow, just say so. I'll understand."

"You'll understand what?" He sounds angry, though I don't know why he would be. "Because I don't understand anything, Chelsie. Not a damned thing. All of a sudden, you're being nice to me? When did that happen? I must have missed a memo or something."

"Noah, I've never *not* been nice to you."

"You're barely civil to me. How can you even say that?"

He's not wrong, but he has to understand why. "What did you expect from me, Noah? To just forget everything that happened back in high school? To not carry that hurt with me somehow? And not feel it more when you pop back into my life?" I grab the steering wheel tightly, trying not to become overemotional, but I'm failing. "I'm not a robot without feelings. You hurt me, Noah. You fucking hurt me. And it wasn't just you. When word got out about what you did, everyone, and I mean *everyone*, looked at me like I was a joke. I was a *fucking joke*. Do you think anyone wanted to go out with me after that?

No, they didn't. And it followed me, too, until the end of senior year. Yes, it was long ago, and that's part of the problem. I have spent *so* many years hating you and what you did to me. *Hating you.* And seeing you brought it all back up again. I'm allowed to feel that."

Finally getting the chance to say these words out loud, and to him, is supposed to be cathartic. I didn't think I would ever have the opportunity to do this, and I should languish in the joy of telling him how I've felt all this time. And now that I have... I don't feel any better. I *thought* I would feel better. Instead, I can see him out of the corner of my eye, and he's shrinking into his seat as I talk. The force and passion of my words and emotions beat against him, and I feel like shit. I feel like total shit. This was not my intention at all.

"I'm sorry." I loosen my grip on the wheel and take a deep breath. "I didn't mean to blow up at you like that. And now I feel like shit. So, I guess we're kind of even."

"No. We're not." His voice is a quiet rasp and full of so much emotion I almost swerve. "We're not close to even. You could toss me out of this moving car, and we still wouldn't be close."

"Well, I won't be doing that, as tempting as it sounds." I qualify, "Not today, anyway."

I glance over and see I at least got a begrudging smirk out of him. That's progress.

"Chelsie, come on. It's not funny." He gazes out

the window again at the passing lights. "None of this is funny."

"No," I agree. "But it's not devastating anymore. I got through it. It's not the end of the world like we're making it. It can be fixable if we want it to. *Anything* is fixable if we want it to be."

He eyes me cautiously, not giving in quite yet. I can't believe I need to be the one convincing him of this, considering how friendly he used to be with me not long ago. In fact, just last week, he was *very* friendly when I spilled my coffee on him. And now my thoughts are drifting to his smooth bare chest under my fingers. And this is not going to do at all.

Chapter 14

Trouble

Noah

I can't believe Chelsie is the one trying to convince *me* that everything is going to be okay. From her reaction this past weekend, her missing work the last few days, and just blowing up at me, which, to be fair, is all deserved, to joking and wanting to make me believe it's all fixable is giving me emotional whiplash. I don't know what to think, let alone how to react.

"Anything is fixable, huh?" I ask, skeptical of this new positivity she's trying to convince me of. "So, you're missing work for days because of me. Isn't that big of a deal?" My stomach twists just thinking about the entire situation.

"I didn't say it wasn't a big deal. Obviously, it was a big deal to me." She grips the steering wheel a little tighter, her jaw clenching. "But it doesn't have to continue being a big deal. We're both adults now. We can control our emotions." Her throat bobs as she swallows hard, trying to do just that - control her emotions.

Suddenly, I can't tear my gaze away from her neck, wanting desperately to brush my lips along her skin just to find out if it's as smooth and delicious as it looks. She catches me staring at her and shifts uncomfortably. This is so many levels of wrong. She's my boss, for Christ's sake. I can't be having erotic thoughts about my boss.

"Dinner?" I blurt out the question, and even I'm surprised by it. I don't know where it came from. I wasn't even thinking about food, but since I've said it, I think I would like to have dinner with her. Maybe we can move past this awkwardness once and for all, now that she's gotten the anger out of her system for the most part. At least, I hope she has. There's no reason we can't be friends.

"Say what now?" The disbelief in her voice would be offensive if I didn't know where it came from. The same goes for the laughter that follows.

"Dinner. Supper. Food. A meal. You do know what it is, right?" I can't help but chuckle at the eye roll that answers my question. "Do you have dinner plans?" I internally cross my fingers that she doesn't. It feels as though we've moved on to a place where we can start this all over and forget the incident in high school ever happened.

"Noah...I don't know." Her entire body has stiffened, and I swear fear and panic are taking her over.

I put my hands up, "If you don't want to, we don't have to. I just thought, since we're being adults, we could have a meal with adult conversation."

She smirks at me and gives me a wicked side-eye. "And what exactly is an 'adult' conversation? We complain about the soaring cost of gas and our bad knees?" I must wince a little at the reference to a bad knee because she cringes, probably knowing it hit a little too close to home. "Sorry. I didn't mean...." She looks stricken that she's offended me or hurt my feelings.

"It's fine," I say, reaching over and touching her arm. I have to pull away since electricity sparks between us when my skin meets hers. I do my best to recover quickly. "You'll need to try harder than that to hurt my feelings."

"I'll keep that in mind." The sly grin she flashes at me makes me think we're on our way to at least friendship. I can live with that. For now. At least she didn't acknowledge the electrical storm brewing around us. I can't believe she didn't notice it, though.

"Let's grab some pizza at the Island. I think there's a hockey game tonight. Or, we can work on our adult conversation skills." I give her my own sly smile. This flirting thing could become addictive, especially since I think it's working.

Eyeing me cautiously, she flips the turn indicator, turning the car toward the Island casino. It's a dive, but the pizza is terrific, and the drinks are cheap.

"Fine. A quick dinner." The warning tone in her voice is half-hearted but charming.

The hockey game is on the big screen in the enclosed patio attached to the casino, and we take our pizza and beer to a table we're lucky to snag. Chelsie wouldn't let me pay and insisted on buying her own, making a comment about this not being a 'date.' So, if I needed any reminder of that, there it is. It's crowded with the game going on, but the noise fills any awkward silences we might have. The local team is winning, which seems to elevate the mood of everyone in the room, which is also helpful.

I'm surprised to discover that Chelsie is a hockey fan and is quite passionate about the penalties that the referees miss against our team. It's nice to know we have something in common, and it makes me wonder what other interests we might share. Once the first intermission starts, the patio quiets down, and we're left to talk to each other again.

"So, what else are you into besides hockey?" I ask, taking a sip of my beer. The way Chelsie pulled such a one-eighty in the car on the way here is still kind of messing with my head a little. I need to figure her out, and the only way to do that is by asking questions since she doesn't ever offer anything up about herself.

The odd look she gives me makes me think she's searching for ulterior motives for my question. "...Lots of things, I guess. Hockey, obviously. Football. Music." She shrugs with a small smile and averts her eyes. Damn, she's downright bashful all of a sudden, a side to her I don't think I've seen before. She's usually a hard ass. "I don't know, the usual stuff."

Her softer side is doing something to my insides that I have no business feeling. It's making me start having thoughts I've told myself aren't a great idea. Not with her. Not with Chelsie. And not only because she's my boss, but because I've already hurt her in a colossal way. It would be insane to even consider any relationship with her, but I can't stop myself. I can't stop thinking about her all fucking day, and I can't help but stare at her when I'm in her presence. Like I'm doing right now.

When she glances back at me, she catches me

staring at her, but I don't look away. I can't look away. I'm enthralled by everything about her. The long dark hair that she constantly runs her fingers through, her deep brown eyes that seem to notice everything about everyone, even things they don't want to be seen. There's a sadness behind those eyes she covers well for the most part, but I see it. I know that pain, not only because I feel my own, but because I know I caused at least some of hers.

She's studying me too. She hasn't looked away and appears lost in her thoughts as she examines me. It's almost as though we're seeing each other for the first time. As if maybe my high school idiocy didn't happen. Perhaps she's seeing the real me, not the asshole I used to be. I'd like her to know that I've changed. I've grown up and grown into a better person.

"Can I get you guys some refills on your drinks?" A server snaps us out of our intense staring contest.

"Yeah, that would be great, thanks." I could use another beer or three. Either to help me get over whatever feelings I've started to have for Chelsie or to give me the courage to find out what they are and pursue them. I know that's the worst idea in the world, but my heart is fucking dumb.

Chapter 15
Will It Tear Us Apart

Chelsie

What in the world is going on here? I'm supposed to hate Noah. As a matter of fact, I did hate Noah until a few minutes ago, didn't I? And now we're staring at each other? Gazing into each other's eyes? *Bitch, please.*

"What is your game, Noah?" I ask, crossing my arms and leaning back to check his reaction to my question. It surprised him. *Good.*

"What makes you think I have a game?" His confident smile tells me he's deflecting. He's having thoughts. Maybe the same thoughts I've been having about him all night. Hell, all *week.*

We've gotten along so well this evening, and nothing was awkward until I had to open my big fat mouth and say something stupid and accusatory. I couldn't just leave things alone to play out however they were going to play out. Nope. I have to ruin everything like always.

I glance up to the big screen TV taking up an entire wall and pretend to be interested in the game again, though, since intermission, I've been too focused on Noah to care. At least we're winning. That much I can pay attention to. Otherwise, it's a blur of gold and black and grey.

The server returns with our beers, and I eagerly take a long sip of mine to pull my nerves under control. It makes no sense, but whenever I'm around Noah, I'm hurtled into a time machine and thrown back to high school all over again. Only this time, I not only feel the butterflies of the initial crush I had on him but the crushing weight of the humiliation that followed everything trying to kill those butterflies. The poor things keep battering against my chest, probably trying to escape their cage. And in no time, I'm in metaphor land. Next thing, I'll be comparing him to a summer's day. *What the hell?* Maybe I should slow down with the beers. Or speed up. I can't decide at the moment.

"Are you okay?" His brow creases with concern. He has the prettiest eyes. I always thought so. "You seem a little out of it."

"I'm fine. I was just admiring your eyes. They're still pretty." I smile as a grin spreads on his face at my words. Whoa. What the total fuck am I doing? Did I just say that out loud? To his face?

Yeah. I seem to be jumping into the shallow end of the pool head first here. This is not cool. I take another long swig of my drink while I try to gather my thoughts. How many beers have I had now? I can't remember.

He blushes. *He fucking blushes.* I just made Noah Thompson blush. But again, he doesn't look away. He's obviously admiring me. I don't think I've ever seen a guy openly admire me like this, and I don't know what I'm supposed to do while he's doing it. Do I stare back? Smile? Wink? Ignore it and play it cool like it happens to me all the time? Instead of any of those cool things, I get the feeling I appear terrified because I feel that emotion pretty hardcore now too.

"*Your* eyes are the most interesting color I've ever seen," he murmurs, leaning forward to get a closer look, his face mere inches from mine. I can't help but alternate my gaze from his eyes to his lips as he gets closer. I swear he is about to kiss me, and I will most certainly let him. His voice is low and full of air. It's probably the air I can't seem to catch as I wait for him to make a move. "You have honey-colored streaks in them catching the light. It's so interesting."

Damn. I guess a kiss isn't forthcoming.

"Interesting? You've said that before. Is that good or bad? Or just...interesting?"

He chuckles and reaches up a hand to trace a finger along my cheekbone, his calluses rough, and he pushes the hair out of my eyes. "Interesting is always an incredible thing."

His eyes skim down to my lips, and he leans closer. I'm afraid to move. I *can't* move. I'm frozen to the spot. Noah Thompson is about to kiss me. In public. He's still smiling, and his warm breath tickles. I close my eyes, hungry for our lips to meet when the crowd around us unexpectedly goes crazy as a goal is scored. Noah and I jump back and away from each other and back to reality.

He seems a little stunned by the sudden turn of events, and I'm feeling the same way. Were we about to kiss? Or is that just something I was hoping for? I turn away and try to compose myself. If he was going to kiss me, he would have kissed me. He had to know the opportunity was presenting itself since I'm pretty sure I was more than obvious about it. I'm not exactly subtle about those kinds of things.

We turn our attention to the game, avoiding looking at each other and not speaking, but completely *aware* of the other person right next to us. When the second intermission hits, I have to ask what is going on. I'm too confused, and I don't like it.

I take another swig of my beer, this time draining it. *How many is that now?* Before I do anything else,

I need to figure out if I just got rejected. My mind is racing with possibilities and opportunities, and words aren't making sense. *Uh oh.*

"So, what was that doing?"

We both frown at my words, and he stares at me in confusion. "Huh?"

I try again, talking a little slower, but end up slurring everything together. "What was the thing doing before? Just then. With the eyes and the mouth. Thing. Your mouth."

He still stares at me, confused, but starts laughing again.

"Wow, someone has had a little too much to drink." He waves at someone across the room, so I turn and wave too, but I don't see anyone in particular paying attention to us. My vision is getting a little blurry.

"Well, I know who you're talking to, but I've had drinks-a-plenty tonight. Today. No, tonight was okay. I really think it was okay. Won't you? I should probably stop having this. You know?" Suddenly a wave of sadness washes over me, and I don't know why, but I don't want to be here anymore. I want to go home so I can cry. My watery eyes focus on Noah, and my voice is clear. "I need to go home."

"Yes, ma'am. That is the plan. I'm just waiting for our bill so I can pay before we go." He's still smiling at me, and that makes me sadder for some reason.

"Okay, you do you." I stand and start weaving my way toward the exit back into the casino to leave, but he wraps an arm around my waist and pulls me to him, my back against his chest. *Wow*. He is strong. And solid. *Damn*.

"Whoa, slow down there, Speedy." He pulls out his wallet and throws some bills on the table. I assume it's enough to cover our bill. I didn't want him to pay for everything. This isn't a date. Norm would kill me.

"Norm's going to call the police on us. I just know it." Why can't I shut up? I need to shut up. I need to get home, but there is no way I can drive right now. "Can you drive a taxi?"

I peek open my eyes and glare at the sunlight streaming through my window. God, it's way too bright. Is something wrong with my eyes? And wow, my head. Holy migraine, my head hurts. Even the slight movement is making me nauseous.

Last night's events hit me like a tidal wave, and the fact that I got drunk in front of Noah makes me even more sick to my stomach. I don't remember how the night ended. I roll onto my back and take stock. I'm in bed. It is my bed, thank God. And I have pajamas on, so at least I had the sense to do that when I got home. I need water, some ibuprofen, and to pee like a racehorse, not necessarily in that order.

I glance at my watch. *Shit. It's after nine o'clock. I'm an hour late for work.* I whip the covers off me and swing my legs over the side of the bed as I sit up; and I should have done that a little slower because a wave of nausea crashes into me, and I have to steady myself and swallow hard to keep it down. I notice then my feet have hit something solid. My feet don't usually touch the floor when I sit on the side of my bed because it's raised up pretty high. I look down and find my feet planted on Noah's bare back. *Noah is sleeping on the floor. What the hell?* I yank my feet up and off him quickly to not wake him. That would be awkward.

"Chels? Are you here?" Normandy's voice calls from downstairs as a door slams. *Shit. Shit. Shit. I need to change the locks.*

What the fuck am I going to do? Do I wake up Noah? What do I tell Normandy? She'll kill me if she thinks Noah and I have something going on. Did something happen between us last night? I don't have time to think about this, and my skull is about to crack open it hurts so bad.

I hear Normandy come up the stairs, and panic sets in. What the hell do I do with Noah? I leap off the bed and over him carefully, not stepping on him.

"I'll be right down," I call, and shut my bedroom door and lock it. Rushing over to Noah, I crouch down and shake him gently. "Hey, wake up," I whisper, trying to keep my voice low, so Normandy doesn't hear me.

He rolls onto his side and gives me a smile when he sees me. "Hey, you. How are you--"

I clamp a hand over his mouth, stopping him from saying anything more. His eyebrows shoot up in surprise, and I put a finger to my mouth, indicating for him to keep quiet. I mouth the name *Normandy* and hook a thumb over my shoulder toward the locked door, letting him know we're not alone in the house.

He nods that he understands but shrugs his shoulders in a *'What do I do?'* fashion while sitting up. His dark hair is spiking out all over the place, and it only dawns on me at that moment he's naked except for his boxer briefs. Good lord, the body on this man. I have to make a concerted effort not to gasp or drool. I turn away from his rock-hard abs I'm dying to touch to verify their firmness.

I need to shake myself out of the trance the sight of his body has put me in and pull myself back into the present. As my head continues to pound, this is incredibly difficult. I glance around, knowing Normandy will be at my door any second. *The bathroom.* I refuse to shove him into a closet. It's the only choice.

"Go, go, go," I whisper, pointing to the open door to the bathroom and simultaneously helping him up from the floor. I don't even have a second to consider why he was sleeping on the floor next to my bed or why that may have happened. I'm starting to think I don't want to know the answer to those questions.

Noah follows my desperate instructions and heads into the bathroom, and I can't stop myself from admiring everything about the view from behind as he goes.

"Chelsie? Why is the door locked?" Normandy is jiggling the doorknob. Wow, no such thing as boundaries with my half-sister. I did not miss this since we didn't grow up together. I guess I'm getting a crash course in sisterhood. *Lovely.*

I open the door and block the doorway. "Norm. What are you doing here? And what if I had... a guest?" I don't know how else to word that at short notice to my brain. She knows what I mean, though. "It's awfully rude of you to barge into my house uninvited."

She takes a step back, surprised by the venom in my words. I'm shocked too, but I agree with what I've just said as I listen. So, there's that.

"I'm sorry, Chelsie. I hadn't considered...." She tries to peek over my shoulder into the bedroom, presumably to see if I actually do have a guest.

"Yeah, well, you should think about that next time." I put a hand on my hip, exaggerating my disapproval of her actions. "Why are you here?" I'm still being a bitch, but I've got our head mechanic hiding in my bathroom, and I don't know why. I want to find out the reason as soon as possible because I'm dying to know what happened last night.

"You didn't show up at work, so I got worried." Her brow furrows, and she grows a little suspicious. "Noah didn't show up to work either, but his car is at the depot, which is strange. His apprentices haven't heard from him either."

Shit. This is not good. I need to think fast. "He had a doctor's appointment or something. He told me about it yesterday. He took a half day."

She arches an eyebrow at me, still suspicious, but I hold her gaze. I hope to God I'm a good liar. I haven't had to lie like this ever, I don't think. "And what about you?"

"I didn't know I had set hours." Which is true. We never talked about my schedule at the depot. I always showed up early and stayed late. "And I just overslept, is all. I'll be in shortly. Is that okay with you, mom?" The sarcasm drips off the words, and I cringe inside. Normandy doesn't deserve me acting like this toward her, but my head is about to explode; I have my high school crush half naked, hiding in my bathroom, and she did come into my house unannounced and uninvited. It's not a great combination to encourage me to keep my composure.

The hurt in her eyes at my outburst makes me feel worse, which I didn't think was possible. She nods and turns to head back downstairs without saying a word.

I'm torn between going after her and letting her go so I can find out what happened from Noah. In the end, I do nothing and just stand in my bedroom doorway, allowing my brain to catch up to everything that's happened and been said in the last three minutes. I'm moving in slow motion, but the headache accelerates more as I wake up.

The door to the kitchen closes, and I let out the breath I was holding the entire time Normandy was here. At least she didn't slam the door. Thank God for small mercies. And now I feel like complete and total shit for reacting that way to my sister. I will need to do some significant damage control once I get to work to make up for this.

Work. Shit. Now to deal with the nearly naked man in my bathroom so he can get to work too.

Chapter 16

Cupid's Arrow

Noah

I can hear Chelsie and her sister arguing from where I'm currently hiding like a fucking teenager in the bathroom. Luckily, my clothes are in here and dry too, which is a bonus, so I dress as quietly as possible. I'd rinsed them off last night when Chelsie didn't quite make it to the bathroom to be sick, and I hung the damp clothes to dry on the shower rod.

A door downstairs closes, and I chance a peek out the window to see Normandy slide into a limo, and it pulls away. Chelsie still hasn't said anything, and I've not heard any movement coming from the other side of the door, so I re-enter the bedroom and find her standing in the hallway, frozen in place, and her head in her hand.

"Everything okay?" I ask, knowing full well it's not. I heard everything said between the sisters. While it seemed like a typical sibling spat, I don't know their dynamic. It could be a big deal.

She finally notices me and glances up, her bloodshot eyes meeting mine with confusion. "What the hell happened last night? And why were you sleeping on the floor next to my bed?" Her tone isn't accusatory, and she just seems curious, which is a relief.

I notice she hasn't taken the ibuprofen I left for her on the nightstand, so I pick it up along with the glass of water I set out and take it to her. She probably didn't see it since she woke up in horror. She glares at me but takes the tablets and water. If how she felt last night is any indication, I'm sure her head has got to be killing her.

"How's your head?" We can get to her questions after I make sure she's okay.

After she swallows the pills and drains the entire water glass, she wipes her mouth with the back of her hand and studies me, I think, noticing my clothes and their current state. She squeezes her eyes shut and groans, which, in any other circumstance, would be totally hot. Right now, I think she's remembering last night.

"I am so sorry." Her face and neck are turning red, and while it's cute, she doesn't need to be embarrassed about anything. "I can't believe I...."

"Don't worry about it. We've all had too much to drink at some point." I take the glass from her since she looks like she's about to drop it or squeeze it into tiny shards. "I'm glad I was here to take care of you."

The disbelief and doubt in her expression are understandable but still hurt. I know I have a long way to go to prove to Chelsie I'm not the asshole I used to be, but I think I've taken some significant steps in that direction. She just hasn't noticed or taken the time to pay attention.

She realizes she's still in her pajamas and crosses her arms over her chest, and I do my best to avert my eyes.

"Did you do...?" she indicates her pajamas, probably wondering how they got on her body.

"No. That was all you. I swear."

I hate to admit it, but I've never seen someone so damned sexy in the morning. Chelsie's bedhead and camisole and pajama shorts are definitely becoming my kryptonite. I'm finding it extremely difficult to keep my hands to myself and not reach out to check if the skin on her bare shoulder is as soft as it looks.

"I need to get ready for work." She scowls and

pushes past me and into her bedroom, suddenly possessed and on a mission to search through every dresser drawer and closet.

I just stare; not sure what I'm supposed to do now. Do I order an Uber and leave? Wait for her to get ready and ask her to take me home? I have never been in this situation before, and I hope to God I never am again because this is awkward as fuck.

"So, should I wait? Or...?"

She stops her search and studies me as if noticing me in her presence for the first time. "I might be a while. Can you order a car?" Her shoulders slump in guilt at the request, but I understand. I don't want to make her any more uncomfortable than she already is.

"Not a problem," I say, looking down at the water glass still in my hand. "I'll just take this down...." I don't even finish and don't look at her before I go. Despite how well we got along last night, I'm afraid all that progress has vaporized since Chelsie probably doesn't remember any of it.

I didn't mind taking care of her last night, and as a matter of fact, I am glad I was able to be there for her when she needed me. Who knows how much her state was because of me? Probably a lot.

I don't know what the fuck I'm doing. Maybe I should try to find another job. The current one is fucking with my head and bringing up memories and feelings for Chelsie that are only causing more problems. We could both do without any of that. I resolve to at least keep looking for something else, but I won't quit this one until I find something, and even someone to replace me. Leaving Chelsie and Normandy high and dry without a head mechanic doesn't sit well with me.

What a fucking mess.

I take an Uber home, clean up, and take another Uber to work. I then spend the rest of the workday avoiding Chelsie the best I can. It's not hard to do since she's avoiding me too. At the end of the day, when I seek her out on purpose to see if she wants to go to Mrs. Bailey's house with me, I find her car is gone, and she's left for the day. So, I guess that answers that question. Loud and clear, too.

When I arrive at Mrs. Bailey's house to work on her lawn, she's initially disappointed Chelsie isn't with me but turns it into an opportunity to talk to me about her.

"So, Chelsie's a lovely girl. No?" She asks out of nowhere. I've finished cutting the grass patches and have joined her for an iced tea on the front porch to watch the sunset. Mrs. Bailey does make a wicked iced tea.

"Yeah, Chelsie is great," I deflect. She's fishing to

pry more out of me, but I don't even know what's happening between us, so I can't talk to anyone else about it.

I can feel the side-eye she gives me as it hits. "I know that look," she says, bobbing her head.

"What look?" I'm not looking any particular way. I made a point not to react at all for this very reason.

"The look of a man trying not to appear as though they care for somebody."

"Mrs. Bailey, with all due respect, I don't know what you're talking about." I'm trying my damnedest to avoid this conversation, but I can tell it's not working.

She doesn't say anything but keeps nodding, staring at the sunset. There's a small smile playing on her lips as if she knows so much more, and I'm just a silly fool. *Damn, she's good.*

"Okay, so maybe I might care about Chelsie a little bit, but there is a painful history between us that I don't think I can overcome. So, there's kind of no point in talking about it or entertaining that thought."

"Nothing is insurmountable if two people are willing to try." She meets my eyes pointedly and tilts her head. "Tell me about this history."

"I'm sure you don't want to hear...."

"Don't tell an old woman what she does or doesn't want to hear." Leaning over and patting my arm, she coos, "Believe it or not, I might just have some wisdom to share with you about it." Her smile is angelic but full of so much hope and confidence I can't deny her.

I tell her about everything that happened in high school and what's happened since I showed up at Mischief Motors looking for a job. When I finish and glance over at her, she's got a knowing smile I don't understand. It doesn't seem like an appropriate reaction to what I've told her.

"Mrs. Bailey? Why are you smiling?" It's getting a bit unnerving, actually.

"Oh, I was just thinking about Wayne," she waves a dismissive hand. "He was such a secret romantic...."

"And?" I don't understand what that has to do with anything.

"And nothing. Never mind." She takes a sip of her tea and sets it on the small table between us. "It sounds to me like you two need a sober talk. No beer or wine to 'grease your wheels' or whatever you kids call it. That's a bunch of hooey. If you can't talk to each other honestly while you're sober, you shouldn't be talking at all."

I don't disagree with any of that, but it's missing one major issue. "What about work? Chelsie's sister is adamant about no dating in the workplace. I don't think we'd get around that, and I'm not one to sneak around. I don't think Chelsie is either." I pause, considering any other options. "Plus, I've never dated anyone I worked with. I'm not sure it's the best idea."

"Why not? Wouldn't you want to spend more time with Chelsie?" Now she sounds offended.

"It's not that I wouldn't want to spend more time with her. But...." I don't want to say anymore. At least not to Mrs. Bailey. It just feels wrong somehow.

"But...? Come on, Noah. What is it?" She's turned away from the sunset and is focusing intently on me, as though this is the most crucial topic in the entire world. It's amazing how passionate she's being about it all.

I can sense the heat rising into my cheeks. "But....she's distracting." I can't help but shrug because it's the damned truth. Working with Chelsie in the general vicinity on any day is highly distracting. I'm often wondering where she's at in the depot, what she's doing, what she's wearing, what she'd look like naked, and it goes downhill from there. Every. Fucking. Day.

Mrs. Bailey also gets some color in her cheeks, but she smiles widely. "I see."

"So, yeah. It's not conducive to a productive work environment." I can't believe I'm having this conversation with an octogenarian. "Maybe I should find another job."

"Oh, heaven's no," she waves me off like the idea is ludicrous. "That's the last thing you should do. If you leave, then you two will never get anywhere."

I study her, trying to figure out why this is so important to her. "Why do you care if Chelsie and I are together or not? You hardly know us. Or me, at least."

She's still examining me closely, and it's starting to make me nervous. Something about the sharpness of her observations makes me uneasy.

"Because I've seen the two of you together, and it's meant to be." She is so matter-of-fact, I find it hard to doubt her, but I do.

"No offense, Mrs. Bailey...."

"Jeanette."

I sigh. "No offense, Jeanette, but you've seen us together a total of two times. I hardly think that's enough time to come to any conclusions, let alone that we're meant to be together."

"Believe me, Noah. I wouldn't say these things if I didn't believe them. I'm old, not dead. I know what I see between you two, whether you see it or not." She nods again to herself as if that settles the matter, and the argument is over. She's won.

And, she has. I can't argue with her. Despite my not believing her or anything she's saying, it doesn't knock my desire for it all to be true. I want to believe there could be something between Chelsie and me. But I know deep down it's not going to happen. Not if Chelsie has anything to say about it. And she's half of this, so her input is kind of crucial.

I beg off any more iced tea and say my goodbyes

with promises of returning next week with Chelsie to finish the car valuations. I don't know that Chelsie will want to come with me again after what happened last night, but I can hope. All I can do about anything with her is hope.

Chapter 17

Alone

Chelsie

Saturday morning, I get a call from Mrs. Bailey asking me to help her go through Wayne's clothes for a charity donation. I can't ever seem to be able to say no to her, so I arrange to stop by in the afternoon. I don't have anything else planned, so I'm happy to get out of the house and do something productive.

When I arrive at her house, she's waiting in the front doorway, clutching her necklace with an anxious look. I'm sure this will be a hard day for her. I hope I have enough emotional fortitude to help her without breaking down myself. At least it will distract me from my problems for a little while.

"Thank you so much for coming, Chelsie," she hugs me tightly. For such a petite woman, she is much stronger than she looks. "My friend Moira was going to help, but she's got her great grandbabies with her this weekend last minute, which left me in a bit of a pickle. Do you want some iced tea? It's a hot one today for it being so early in April."

Her string of topics tells me she's nervous and a little lost. My heart aches in an echo of her pain. After sixty-five years of marriage, trying to move on with your heart still intact has got to be near impossible.

"I would love some tea, thank you," I say, holding her at arm's length and giving her my warmest smile. There is no rush for anything to get done. I want her to know I'm here for her and can go at whatever pace she sets that's comfortable for her.

I follow her into the cozy kitchen, and she pours me an iced tea. She's still clutching at her necklace as though she needs assurance that it's still there. When she turns to hand me the glass, unshed tears are in her pale blue eyes, and my heart lurches some more.

"Here you go, dear."

I take it from her but set it carefully on the counter, pulling her into a big hug. She's so tiny, even to me, and I'm not very tall. Her grief seems to make her appear even smaller. It's then the levee breaks, and her tears start to flow freely, soaking into the shoulder of my t-shirt. I don't mind at all. There's no way for me to fathom how painful this entire experience must be for her. If all I can do is hold her while she cries, I'm happy to lend my shoulder for that purpose.

Miraculously, I can keep my tears at bay, although I do choke up. I know my role today is to be the strong one for her, and I won't lose sight of that.

Something brushes against the back of my calf, and I quickly release Mrs. Bailey and jump away with a screech, barely missing stepping on an enormous black cat.

"What the...? Where did that come from?" My heart is racing as I watch the cat weave in and out of Mrs. Bailey's legs, its tail twitching as it gazes up at her expectantly.

"Oh, this is Edsel," She sniffs, wiping residual tears from her cheeks. Bending down, the fat cat allows her to scoop it up. I'm surprised Mrs. Bailey has the strength to lift such a heavy animal. "Yugo should be around here somewhere too."

"I didn't know you had cats." I can't help but snicker at the cats' names, two of the worst cars in America's automotive history. "They didn't make an appearance when we were here before."

"Yeah, they're pretty reclusive and don't care too

much for people, especially strangers. Edsel here seems to have taken a shine to you, though. She doesn't normally like other females at all. That tells me a lot."

I get a strange sense of pride that the snobby cat likes me for some inexplicable reason. "Well, she's not too bad herself," I say, reaching out to pet her. She proceeds to hiss vehemently at me, and I yank my hand away, barely avoiding the swipe of her sharp claws. "Actually, I take that back." So much for my brief Dr. Doolittle moment.

"And that's why Wayne named them both the way he did," she chuckles, letting Edsel drop to the floor and scurry out of the room back to her hiding place. "Their manners leave a lot to be desired."

"I'm sure they're lovely with you."

"It took a long time for them to warm up to me, but they've been a great comfort with Wayne gone. I don't know what I'd do without them." She grabs her necklace again, her constant source of comfort that's always within reach.

"Should we start on your project?" I coax, not only changing the subject but also wanting to stay on track. It's easy to veer off course when Mrs. Bailey is involved.

She takes a deep breath, steeling herself against the upcoming wave of emotions undoubtedly on its way. "Yes. Let's go."

A few hours later, we completed going through Wayne's dresser. It's a stroll down their memory lane, and it's fascinating and heartbreaking at the same time. I'm told every story of every item of note, where things were acquired, fun or strange moments that happened when it was used, and conversations that were had. It's evident the two of them were still just as much in love this year as they were in their first. I try to tell myself I'm not jealous of that kind of love, but I know deep down I'll never have that kind of devotion from someone. It's an unattainable goal. People aren't built the same way anymore.

"So, what's going on with you and your Noah?" She asks as we take a quick tea break on the front porch.

I had a feeling this would come up, but it's been a few hours, so I thought I'd gotten out of it. Of course, I hadn't. I'm beginning to think this is Mrs. Bailey's specialty - meddling.

"There is no '*my Noah*,' and nothing's going on with us. He's my employee, nothing more."

She arches a bright white eyebrow that matches her short, cropped hair but doesn't say anything.

"I'm not kidding. Nothing is going on between us." I shrug to emphasize this for her.

"Well, when he was here last night cutting the

grass, he sure made it sound like he *wanted* there to be something between you two."

"Noah was here yesterday?" I don't know why this shocks me. I was here when he made plans to take care of her yard. Maybe I'm just surprised he would follow through. He's been cast as a villain in my head for so long, and even though my thoughts about him are shifting toward the positive, I'm still having a hard time reconciling him being a decent person. Deep down, I know he is. I can tell by how well he treats Mrs. Bailey. but my initial programmed responses still slide negative.

"Yes. We had a nice long talk." She smiles, but her brow furrows. "He's such a charming young man...." She puts a hand up to her chest, and I think she's just grabbing her necklace again, but her fingers are splayed, and her face is pained.

"Mrs. Bailey? Are you okay?" I sit up and put my iced tea on the table. Her skin has gone a pale ash color, and she does not look well. Something is terribly wrong.

She doesn't answer but grimaces, and I jump into action. I run into the house, grab my phone from my purse, and dial 911 at once. I stay on the line with them while waiting for the ambulance to come and reassure Mrs. Bailey that everything will be fine as best as I can. The hospital is luckily very close.

Once the paramedics arrive and have her on a gurney, she grabs for my hand. "I'm sorry, Chelsie."

Her voice is so weak and so unlike her. She's not a frail old woman. She's usually full of vigor and snark.

"Don't apologize, Mrs. Bailey. I'll follow the ambulance and be at the hospital waiting for you, okay?"

"Jeanette."

That makes me choke out a laugh underneath my sob. "Jeanette. I'll catch up with you shortly. Everything is going to be fine. I'll lock up here. Don't worry."

"Call Noah."

I don't hear anything else since the doors shut, and the ambulance takes off towards the hospital carrying the most precious cargo I can think of.

I don't think. I'm in automatic response mode. I dial Noah right away. Mrs. Bailey wants him at the hospital, and I will make that happen. I head into the house to grab her purse and keys to lock up the house while I wait for him to answer. After a few rings, I'm about to hang up and try later, but he answers.

"Hello?" He sounds hesitant. Maybe he doesn't know that this is my number. I'm not sure if I gave him my number. I put his in my phone while at work the other day, randomly thinking I might need it. The universe is creepy sometimes.

"Noah, it's Chelsie. Mrs. Bailey is on her way to the hospital, and she told me to call you, so I'm calling you. Can you meet me there?" I have to gasp air into my lungs; I just rushed everything out in a run-on sentence.

"Whoa. What? Chelsie?" He sounds surprised and concerned. "Which hospital?"

"St. Rose. I'll meet you there." I slam her front door shut and lock it behind me and run to my car.

Chapter 18

Do Ya Feel My Love?

Noah

I like to think of the speed limit as more of a guideline than a rule and use that reasoning to get to St. Rose's hospital faster than I ever thought possible. When Chelsie called, I had been with my brother checking out the progress on his house and left him there to fend for himself. He was okay with it, but I didn't think twice about it. The panic in Chelsie's voice propelled me into action so forcefully that I'd have driven across the fucking state if I had to.

When I step through the Emergency Room doors, I barely take two steps before Chelsie throws her arms around my waist and buries her face into my chest. I instinctively wrap my arms around her, kiss the top of her head, and stroke her hair. I'm again moving and acting without thinking. The only thing I'm actively thinking about is Mrs. Bailey.

"How is she? Have you seen her? What happened?"

"I don't know. They won't say anything other than they're running tests," she sniffles but doesn't let go of me. I realize then that we're holding each other in the middle of the emergency room, but I don't care and don't move away from her. "And they won't let me back to see her yet either."

"Okay, well, no news is good news." I can tell it's about to get awkward, so I preemptively take her hand and lead her to the seats in the waiting room. "Tell me what happened."

She tells me about Mrs. Bailey suddenly going pale, grabbing her chest, and the subsequent events, all the while holding my hand tightly. The fear emanating from her is palpable, and I wish I could do something to tear it away from her.

"I was so afraid she was going to die right in front of my eyes. I didn't know what to do."

I put an arm around her and pull her to me, letting her rest her head on my shoulder. "You did everything right. Don't even second guess that." It sounds like she was grace under pressure and handled everything perfectly. "She seemed fine last night when I was over to mow her lawn."

"Yeah, she said you were over." She pats my chest, and her touch sends sparks firing through me, even through my t-shirt. "Nice job with the yard, by the way. It looks great."

"Thanks." I wasn't expecting a compliment. Not from Chelsie. It leaves me tongue-tied. Not a sensation I'm used to.

"She seemed fine all day today. Not a single sign that she didn't feel well. It was so sudden."

"What were you two up to today?" I've been trying to figure out what Chelsie was doing at Mrs. Bailey's since I'd already taken care of the yard.

"She asked me to help her go through Wayne's stuff." She sits up and pulls her hand from me to rake through her own hair. The absence of her touching me leaves me cold, and I can't help the shiver that runs through me. "We didn't get very far...."

"Mr. Thompson?" A nurse shouts from the front desk.

Surprised to hear my name called, I jump to my feet and approach the desk.

"I'm Noah Thompson." For some reason, fear sinks its icy talons into my heart, and I prepare to be told the worst by this nurse. I swallow hard and reach for Chelsie's hand this time, and she's right next to me and takes it willingly. She's just as worried as I am, if not more.

"Oh good, you made it. She said you'd be quick. Mrs. Bailey is asking for you," she smiles at me and then glances at Chelsie. "You too, Ms. Blake."

A wave of relief rolls off Chelsie next to me, and I give her hand a squeeze as we head through the doors into the hospital proper to follow the nurse back to Mrs. Bailey's room.

When we enter, I'm surprised to find Mrs. Bailey sitting up, eating a sandwich, and sipping on a juice box. Chelsie and I glance at each other, confused.

"There he is," her face lights up as she sees me. "Didn't I tell you he was handsome?" she asks the nurse that led us here.

"You did," she smiles, and I can tell this nurse has heard some stories during her tenure here. I'm sure my apparent handsomeness is the least interesting of those stories.

"You look so much better," Chelsie declares, releasing me and going to the side of the bed. "What have the doctors said?"

"Oh, I'm fine," Mrs. Bailey waves a dismissive hand. "Don't worry about me. But they want to keep me overnight to pad their pockets with my insurance money."

The nurse laughs at this, taking the dig in stride. I'm sure she's heard this all before. "Mrs. Bailey suffered a bout of angina. The doctor wants to keep her here overnight for observation to ensure that's all it is."

"How damaging is angina?" Chelsie asks. "Isn't that basically a heart attack?"

"They're similar and can be just as painful, but they're not the same. Angina is temporarily reduced blood flow to the heart, not a complete blockage. But it still means that something's going on, and certain patients, who will remain nameless, should visit a cardiologist to have it checked out." She pointedly stares at Mrs. Bailey as she says this. Apparently, Mrs. Bailey is a stubborn patient. Imagine that.

"I'm fine, Missy. Thank you very much. You can go now," Mrs. Bailey says, waving her arms for the nurse to leave.

"Fine. I'll go, but your guests will need to leave soon. You need to move to your regular room for the night in a few minutes."

"Thank you," I call after her, not sure anyone has thanked her for her help today.

"I need to ask you two a favor," Mrs. Bailey says, leaning back and placing a hand over her heart as though it's giving her trouble again. I glance at the machines she's hooked up to, and nothing seems out of the ordinary. But then, I'm no doctor. No alerts are going off, at least. I can tell that much.

"Of course. Name it." Chelsie is eager to help, and it just endears her to me that much more.

"Do you have the keys to my house?" Now Mrs. Bailey seems a little breathless, and I'm starting to wonder if I should call the nurse back into the room.

Chelsie nods. "I need you two to stay at my house tonight. Edsel and Yugo have never spent the night alone before, and they'll be scared to death without me there."

"Who are Edsel and Yugo?" I can't contain the laugh, despite their possible distress. Those names are hilarious.

"Mrs. Bailey's cats."

"You have cats?" I didn't see a single pet or even a sign of one any of the times I was at her house. Of course, it's not been a lot, but still.

"I do, and you two will need to stay with them tonight while I'm stuck here." She clutches at her chest again and winces. My own heart lurches at the thought of her in pain.

"I can stay. No need to make Noah...." Chelsie sees her pained face and is eager to agree to the request.

"No, you saw how Edsel reacted to you. She doesn't like women, so Noah will have to stay too." They both switch their gazes to me in question.

I don't see a question here. As far as I can tell, we're being ordered to do this.

I shrug. "Sure, I can stay." My eyes lock with Chelsie's, and I want to believe I see relief or happiness in them at my answer.

Mrs. Bailey recovers swiftly and lets out a deep breath. "Good. You two get out of here before you're kicked out." She shoos us in the same fashion as the nurse a few minutes ago. "Can you pick me up tomorrow?"

"Sure," I say, holding a hand out to Chelsie, who takes it and rounds the bed to follow me. "We'll give our numbers to the front desk. They can call us when you're ready to go."

"You get some rest. Don't worry about your cats. We'll take excellent care of them." Chelsie gives her foot a quick squeeze and follows me into the hallway.

We find the nurse and leave our contact information for tomorrow.

When we're out in the parking lot, Chelsie finally drops my hand, and instantly the awkwardness between us is back.

"I need to stop at my house to grab some things, but I'll meet you there." Now she's back to avoiding my eyes, too. *Great.*

"Why don't you give me the keys since I'll head straight there." I hold my hand out, and she fishes in her purse for the keys and holds them up for me to grab.

"See you soon." She stiffly turns toward her car. I watch as she walks away, the evening dusk surrounding us, feeling the letdown of her drifting away from me again in more ways than one.

Chapter 19

The Way I Do

Chelsie

When I arrive at Mrs. Bailey's, I park behind Noah and stare at the house for a minute before getting out of the car. This is a choice. I'm choosing to spend the night in the same house as Noah. The last time doesn't count since I wasn't entirely in my right mind. Though, I'm beginning to question if I am now, either. What am I even doing here if the cats don't like women? I'm keeping my word. That's what. This is for Mrs. Bailey.

The sun has set, and Noah left the front porch light on for me. Its yellowish glow gets interrupted occasionally by the moths throwing themselves against it. They should be grateful for the glass between them and the hot light bulb inside. As I step onto the porch, I feel a strange kinship with them since I'm like a moth attracted to the flame that is Noah, right inside this house, ready to burn me any minute.

"We're off to a great start. I can only find one of the cats." Noah is in the doorway on the other side of the screen door, and I jump about ten feet in the air at the sound of his voice. I was so focused on the stupid moths I didn't notice him come to the door. "Sorry. Didn't mean to startle you." He opens the screen door and holds it open for me, and I need to squeeze past him to enter the house.

Even though I just hugged him about an hour ago at the hospital, for some reason, I have the need to keep my distance from him. I'm in danger of losing myself to Noah if I let him close. Despite everything that's happened between us, I can't deny our chemistry, but I have to find a way. It's not something that could ever work, so considering it is stupid.

"Which one did you find?" I ask, setting my overnight bag on a recliner.

"I don't know which one is which. I think it was a calico, but it was a blur as it ran into the back bedroom and under the bed."

"That must be Yugo," I nod, looking around the front room for any sign of a cat. "Edsel is all black."

"Okay, good to know. I haven't ventured upstairs yet, so the other one could be up there." He brushes past me to go into the kitchen, and his cologne lingers behind him, and I breathe deeply to take him in, making sure he doesn't catch me. "I can't tell if they've eaten already today or not. Their food bowls are empty. Do you think we should feed them just in case?"

He's in the doorway staring at me intently, waiting for my response to his question, and it takes my brain a second to travel from his scent to what he's said. I'm in trouble tonight. I can't believe I agreed to this.

"Chels?" He takes a step towards me, his voice full of concern. "You okay?"

"Feed them. Yes." I yank myself back to the here and now. "Maybe that will tempt Edsel out of wherever she's hiding." I flash a smile at him and nervously slide my hands into the back pockets of my jeans.

"Oh. You can take the bedroom. I don't mind the couch." His dark eyes travel over to the couch that is most definitely too small for him and probably very uncomfortable to sleep on. That brings to mind the piles of clothes and other items still littering Mrs. Bailey's bed and the stuff we never finished going through. I don't think I can sleep there.

"Well, we kind of left her bed in the middle of sorting Wayne's things." I shrug, unsure of what else to do. "I'd hate to mess it up until Mrs. Bailey finishes going through it all."

"Okay, well, then you take the couch. I'll figure something out." He glances at the stairway leading to the upper floor. "Any idea what's up there?"

I shake my head. "Nope."

He arches an eyebrow, and his lips twitch into a devious grin as he makes his way toward the stairs. "Shall we?" A hand is suddenly presented to me, and I automatically take it without thinking. His fingers are warm and dry, and the callouses tickle with friction as he leads me up the stairs.

There is a room on either side of the landing with a shared bathroom between them. We go into the room on the left first. Behind the door, we find shelves piled high with various car magazines and glass-paned cabinets with trophies and ribbons for achievements at different car shows. The walls are full of photos of Wayne and Mrs. Bailey in front of cars with their hoods open and holding a trophy or ribbon, with big smiles on display. There's also an overstuffed chair with a floor lamp behind it that is well-worn. Wayne must have spent a lot of time here going through the magazines.

Noah is in heaven, taking everything in, his eyes wide in wonder. He's careful with the magazines, treating them like they could crumble under his touch.

"Check it out. It's the Camaro from the garage,"

he points to a framed photo with the couple holding another trophy.

I step up next to him to get a better view of the photo, which doesn't look like it's too old, maybe from the 90s. Mrs. Bailey already had her bright white hair cropped close in a pixie cut. "She looks a little like Dame Judy Dench."

That gets a chuckle out of him. "She does. Don't tell her that, though. We might be ordered to call her 'Dame Jeanette.'"

"We can't even bring ourselves to call her 'Jeanette,' I highly doubt we'd do any better with 'Dame.'"

I wander across the landing to the other room, which is also full of bookshelves, but these actually hold books. Romance books. *Lots* of romance books. Who knew Mrs. Bailey was such a closet romance reader. She's got everything from Jane Austen to Danielle Steel and even more recent series like *Outlander.* There is also an overstuffed chair with a floor lamp behind it, so I grab *Pride and Prejudice,* turn on the light, and take a seat. As I'm scanning through the well-worn and well-read pages, I have the feeling I'm being watched, and the tiny hairs on the nape of my neck tickle. I glance up to find Noah, magazine in hand, watching me from across the hall while sitting in Wayne's chair.

A chill runs through me as I picture both of the Bailey's in their respective chairs, spending a quiet night reading and occasionally glancing up to smile at the other. What an incredible setup they had up here. I smile at Noah and give him a little wave, and he does the same. And then we both get back to our reading, just like an old married couple. It's kind of romantic.

It's sweet until it isn't. Until it scares the shit out of me, and I jump out of the chair. Noah must have the same thought because he does the same thing at the same time. I hastily put the book back, turn off the light, and shut the door before beating Noah down the stairs.

"So, I guess there are no hiding cats upstairs," he says, snapping his fingers and smacking a fist with the other hand nervously.

"Nope, I guess not," I say, equally nervous for some reason.

We stand there like idiots for what seems like an hour, afraid to look the other person in the eye. It's getting ridiculous, but I don't know what the heck to say or do. I'm still in Embarrassed Land from the other night, which we still haven't addressed. I swear, my common sense and reason jump out the nearest window whenever I'm around him.

"There's no TV."

I can't tell if that's disappointment in his voice or anxiety. Maybe it's both. I hadn't thought about what we would do while we were here. I didn't bring anything either, besides my phone.

"Oh...I hadn't noticed that...." Wow, this is going to be the most awkward evening in the history of evenings at this rate.

"Have you eaten?" He pulls his phone out of his back pocket. "I'm going to order pizza, I think."

"Is that all you ever eat? Pizza?"

He pauses as if he's considering. "It is the most perfect food, with all the major food groups. And yes, tomatoes are fruit, but put them near a fruit salad and it's pistols at dawn."

"I don't disagree," I laugh. "But variety is the spice of life. Here, let me order dinner for us." I pull out my phone and bring up a food delivery app. "Any food allergies I should be aware of?"

"Not that I know of."

Arching a brow at him, I say, "I'll take that as a *no*," and order some Thai food from one of my favorite restaurants nearby. "Okay, done and done. Let's see about getting some dinner for the cars."

"The cars?"

"The cats. Whose names are cars. They are the cars." *Eesh.*

After the cats are brave enough to come out to eat once they hear the can opener, and our food is delivered and eaten with an awkward conversation that sputters with fits and starts, we have absolutely nothing to do. We could each play on our phones, but that seems rude, which I never thought possible. For some reason, I care if I'm rude to Noah. I've seen such a different side of him since he's come back into my life, a decent side I think I've always known was there, that I'm being careful with how I act around him. Not that I'm acting, but I'm just...careful.

"Hey, look, I found a deck of cards in the utility drawer." He holds up a box of cards with a hole punched in the middle and the logo of the long-ago demolished Riviera casino. "Do you play?" He's got a mischievous smile playing on his lips, and I can't help but smile back at him.

"This is Vegas. Of course, I play cards." I qualify, "Not as well as Norm, the card queen, but I do okay."

"Have you ever played Kings in the Corner?" He's starting to clear the kitchen table of everything to make room for our game.

"No... what's that?" I've never heard of it. But then, there are probably a million card games I've never heard of.

"It's kind of a competitive solitaire game. I'll teach you." He then proceeds to explain the rules of the game. "But, the most important thing is the knock." He taps his knuckles on the tabletop a couple of times to demonstrate. "My grandmother taught me this game and was a stickler for the knock.

Once you knock, your turn is done, and you can't make another play until your next turn. There are no '*Wait a minute*' excuses. On the flip side, if you say your turn is over but don't knock, the table is technically still yours, and anything the next player does counts for you. But you can't withhold a knock on purpose, either. It's a fine line."

"I see. Your grandmother sounds like a lot of fun." A thought passes through my mind, and I have zero impulse control, so I blurt it out. "So, what are the stakes?" It comes out a little flirtier than I intended. Or maybe I did plan it to be, I don't know. Either way, it's too late to take it back now. And the blush that takes him over is totally worth my impulsiveness.

"That depends." Even though he's blushing, he doesn't back down and meets my gaze. His eyes smolder in the low lamp light of the kitchen, and my stomach clenches. "How much do you want to risk?"

"What are the options?" I ask, stalling as my mind races with possibilities. This could get interesting, but again, I need to be careful. "No losing any clothes. Hard limit."

"Hard limit?" He smirks and shakes his head. I get the feeling he knows where that's from. "Okay...How about Truth or Dare? The winner of each game gets to ask or dare. We'll play a couple rounds before it counts, so you get used to the game."

"Ok. Sounds good."

What the hell am I getting myself into? Agreeing to play Truth or Dare with Noah Thompson? Our troubles started in high school, and now it feels like we're back there. I must admit I'm intrigued, though. There are many things I'd like to ask him and make him do...

Damn. This could get interesting.

Chapter 20

No Sugar in My Coffee

Noah

What the hell is even happening? I can't believe I'm about to play a game where the consequences of losing are truth or dare with Chelsie fucking Blake. The fact that she agreed to it is even more mind-bending.

We play a few games to warm up and to give Chelsie a chance at understanding the rules, so it's a fair playing field. She catches on quickly and has even mastered the knock. I didn't doubt she would be good at this, and I may just have met my match.

"I think I may have underestimated you," I say

with a smirk, trying to sound more confident than I am. I might be in trouble.

"Most people do," she shrugs like it's no big deal. As if it's expected. She's not cocky about it. In fact, her words are edged with a sadness born from experience.

"Well, I won't be making that mistake."

"I should hope not." This time her tone is playful, and there's a glint in her eye that is so intriguing I can't tear my gaze away. As I shuffle the cards for our first real game, I study her while she's unaware. Her long dark hair is loose today and framing the perfect angles of her face. It matches the brown of her eyes that is so warm whenever she looks at me; I know she sees *Me*. The *real* me. Not that I've hidden from anyone before, but my past relationships have mostly been sailing on the surface of my emotions, not the depths of my soul. I know if I let it, a relationship with Chelsie would be the deepest experience of my life, probably in a soul-changing and profound way.

"Are you going to deal, or do you want me to?" Chelsie's head tilts in question, catching me in my examination of her.

"You're so eager to have your ass kicked. Be careful what you wish for."

"Oh, I'm careful." She arches one beautiful brow at me. "Bring it."

The first game is close, but I eke out a win, much

to Chelsie's dismay. But now the problem becomes what to ask or what to dare.

"So, truth or dare? Which is it going to be?" My mind starts racing with possibilities for either choice. I should have thought of this during the game, but I was too focused on not losing.

Chelsie is downright mortified, wringing her hands under the table and biting her bottom lip nervously. I can see the war going on behind her eyes as she chooses between a truth and a dare.

"Dare," she chooses with a nod as if convincing herself it's the correct choice.

My jaw drops in shock. "Really? A dare?" I can't help the dirty thoughts that start running around my brain. All the things that I could dare her to do, and she would have to do it.

Now she's panicked and is second-guessing her choice. "Wait!" Her cheeks grow red as she reads my mind. "Please. I'll take truth."

"Damn, I should have put in the knocking rule for this too." This can be even more dangerous than a dare. I need to take a second to reel my thoughts in and refocus on the new mission of finding out something honest about Chelsie. There are so many things I want to ask her, but I don't know where to start.

"Okay, if you were on a desert island and could only take one music album with you, which one would it be? And why?" I know it's a lame question, but we might want to ease into this whole thing.

She seems surprised by my question and probably the harmlessness of it. She was expecting a hard-hitting question right out of the gate, but hopefully, she sees that my intentions here are decent.

"One album? That's a tough one. I have a favorite album for every mood."

"Well, what kind of mood would you be in if you were stranded on a desert island?"

"I don't know. I've never been stranded on a desert island. I would have to assume I have the technology to play this, so maybe I have an entire resort to myself with power." She chuckles, and I can envision her enjoying an entire resort on the beach by herself, her earbuds in, and a playlist for every mood. "Well, I suppose if I'm stranded, I'm alone, which means I would be lonely. My go-to music when I'm sad or lonely is Adele or Billie Eilish.

"Interesting choices," I nod. "Okay, that's one question out of the way. Harmless enough."

"What about you? What would you listen to if you were stranded on a desert island?"

"Oddly enough, I think I would be in the same mindset as you, but I would go more with her brother Finneas than Billie."

I wasn't expecting to have the tables turned on me and my questions thrown back at me, so I say the first thing that pops into my head. She doesn't react other than slightly narrowing her eyes as she stares at me. That makes me wonder if I said the wrong thing. Too late now.

The second game goes my way again; it's an easy win this time. Chelsie seemed a little distracted this go round, and while I didn't mean to take advantage of the situation, I couldn't help myself. She knocked to end her turn on at least two occasions and left the board wide open for me. It would have been obvious if I had let it go.

"Okay, you know the drill. Truth or dare?" I hand her the deck of cards to shuffle for the next game. Our fingers touch as she takes them, but we don't pull away, letting our hands linger together for a moment.

"Truth." This time she knocks to confirm her choice, and I have to laugh.

"All right." This time I'm not going to go so easy on her. There are some things I want to know. "With what happened in high school, why did you hire me?"

Her attention is focused on the cards as she shuffles, and there's no reaction to my question, but it's clear she's considering her answer before giving it. I give her some time to think, and while waiting for her answer, an enormous black cat jumps onto my lap, and not graciously at all. It's a full-blown claw dug into the skin, hurling herself onto my lap situation. I can't help but cry out in pain.

"Holy tetanus shot, Batman, that fucking hurt!" I pull the cat closer, making sure it won't fall off my lap because I'm afraid in the process of falling, it would just dig its claws again.

"She likes you. All I got from her was a hiss and a swipe this afternoon. Mrs. Bailey says she doesn't like women." She seems put off by the cat's life choices.

"Well, from that greeting, I don't know if she likes me either." I pet the cat that is beginning to purr loudly as she pushes against my hand. I guess she's not all that bad. "And you're stalling, Blake. Why did you hire me?"

Chelsie sighs loudly, her shoulders sagging with the effort. "I didn't have a choice. Honestly, I wouldn't have hired you, but Normandy overruled me. Plus, it was pretty obvious you didn't know who the fuck I was."

While I'm not surprised by her answer, I am slightly hurt. I can't help it. But I do my best not to show it.

"I understand."

"I mean, don't get me wrong, I am glad Normandy overruled me. You're very good at your job; you're fantastic with the apprentices, and you're great at helping with stuff like we are with Mrs.

Bailey. I don't think many other mechanics would be able to do what you do. Or willing."

The follow-up to her answer is heartening and makes me feel better. I got the honesty I asked for, but I also got a little extra. It's that little extra causing me to smile.

"And... what were your thoughts once you figured out who I was?" Her voice is low now, almost timid. As if she's afraid of my answer. Worried that I'll hurt her again. That is the last fucking thing I want to do right now.

"Once I figured out who you were, and what I did to you in high school, and how that's affected you all this time, my thoughts have been nothing but regret for my actions, pain for whatever pain I put you through, and hope that I can make it up to you somehow. Chelsie, I do feel like shit for what I did to you back then. And I don't know if I've said it, but I *am* sorry. I went through a lot in high school, I think everybody does, but it is no excuse for how I treated you. Nobody deserves to be treated like that. Nobody."

I hope the passion in how I say the words comes across to her and shows I mean what I say. The last thing I want is for her to continue thinking she deserved that, or I think anything like it. Because that is the furthest thing from the truth.

Her eyes become shiny at my answer, and I hope to God she's not going to cry because I don't know what I'll do if she starts crying. I beat myself up enough over my past actions. I don't think I could take witnessing the destruction they caused right before my eyes.

"Thank you. Thanks for apologizing." While her smile is weak, I can see the strength it takes to show even that much. "Sometimes all people want to hear is the person who hurt them is sorry. And that's all I wanted to hear."

"Well, whenever you need it, just let me know. I'm happy to repeat myself."

The next game takes a while, with the victor uncertain until the very end. Chelsie somehow gets the right cards to finish with a sweeping win. The entire game is full of flirting and innuendo, and the energy in this kitchen is nearly crackling with electricity.

When I'm around Chelsie, I feel like I'm walking on quicksand, and I'll be pulled under at any moment or from even the slightest misstep. My body's instinctual awareness of hers is something I've never experienced before, and I'm not exactly sure what to do with it.

Edsel is now sleeping peacefully on my lap, only occasionally stretching and splaying her paws if she gets disturbed. Petting her has been a helpful distraction and something to keep my hands busy.

The devious smile on Chelsie's face as she asks,

"So what's it going to be this time? Are we sticking with the truth? Or are you feeling adventurous?"

I consider the options, but I feel feisty after all this flirting. "Dare." My tone is a challenge.

The surprise in her eyes is replaced with something else entirely. Something I have only dreamed of seeing and something I want more of.

"Kiss me."

This time the surprise is mine. After everything between us, I never thought we would be in a place where Chelsie Blake would be ordering me to kiss her, but I am not complaining.

However, I need to consider logistics now that I have a cat on my lap, and Chelsie is across the table from me. As much as I hate doing it, I wake up sleeping Edsel as I stand, letting her down gently. I grab Chelsie's hand and pull her up from the table, and she comes willingly. I frame her face with my hands, my calloused thumbs tracing her cheekbones as I gaze into her eyes. I should be nervous or hesitant, but the only emotion I can tap into is worry.

"Are you sure? Once we do this, there's no going back. Because what's about to happen between you and me can't be undone. So, I want to be absolutely sure you want me to do this." As much as every cell in my body wants to kiss this woman, with our history, the last thing I want is to hurt her ever again. I need to know we're clear on this.

She carefully studies my face, reading my intensity and intention, and nods. "I'm sure."

I lean in, wrapping a hand around her neck, and gently tug on her hair to tilt her face to mine. When our lips meet, it's not gentle or sweet. It's full of hunger and desire and want and lost years. It's overflowing with anger and regret, apologies and forgiveness, and it ends with us gasping for air.

When we pull apart, it's only a second before we're back at it; this time, other body parts become involved. Our groping fingers can't seem to find purchase on the other, and our tongues are more than happy to make each other's acquaintance. I'm driven to walk her slowly until her back is against the wall, and I'm pressing against her. The heat we're generating is making our clothing a problem, and soon it'll just be in the way. My hands have discovered her amazing breasts, and hers have found the bulge in my jeans. Her touch is electric, and my body catches fire at every touch. I can't seem to move close enough, and the thin barrier of our clothes puts metaphorical miles between us.

I want more. I *need* more. The taste and feel of her tongue against mine are quickly becoming addictive. The desperation that takes over for want of her is so foreign to me that I don't recognize myself or my reactions. I didn't know what I was missing until just now. I've been missing *her*. Chelsie. The girl I broke all those years ago is the one person in the world who can make me feel this good. It's insane. This has gone really far, really fast, and I have to yank myself away from her before this spins out of control.

"Jesus, Chelsie. This was more than a kiss." Words are hard at the moment, and they're not the only thing with that issue.

She's panting just as much as I am, still leaning against the wall. Her neck is flush with heat, and I want nothing more than to go back to kissing her. Touching her. And so much more.

Chapter 21

A Sound that Only You Can Hear

Chelsie

Well, this evening has surprisingly turned in a *very* interesting direction. My skin is so warm from where our bodies were touching that I'm about to catch fire. Part of me wants to ignite or internally combust just to make the sensation disappear quicker. I don't know what I expected when I dared him to kiss me, but it wasn't these emotions running through me at breakneck speed. It was just supposed to be a kiss. Nothing more. But damn if that wasn't just fucking everything.

By Noah's reaction and the desire reflected in his

eyes, I think he's feeling the same way, but I can't be sure. I never in a million dreams thought that was possible. My heart starts to ache for the years of kisses we've missed, even though they wouldn't have been the same or compared to the one we just shared. I don't think we would have had this kind of intensity without our lives as they were.

I press my back into the wall behind me, more for its solid form to hold up mine that is turning liquid the more I stare at Noah. His eyes haven't wavered since we separated, and I'm not sure what's happening between us. The weight of his gaze on me pushes against me with just as much urgency as his touch a second ago.

Once I catch my breath, I try to speak words but can only come up with one. "So...."

"Yeah...that happened." He's at an equal loss for words. Raking a hand through his hair, he leans back against the counter with a loud exhale. Edsel reappears from the shadows and weaves herself between his legs, her tail flicking as if she's claiming him and marking her territory. If I approached him now, I bet she would show me just how sharp her claws are. "To be fair, you did dare me to kiss you."

"I guess I should be careful what I wish for, huh?" I run a hand through my own hair, suddenly nervous again.

"Did you wish for it? Or dare me?" His face is

unreadable, but his tone is genuinely curious. A cocky corner of his mouth twitches.

I feel caught. Of course, I've wished for him to kiss me, but I'm not ready to admit it. "Does it matter?" My chin juts out in defiance of his confidence. I'm exposed. I thought I was playing the upper hand with the dare, controlling the narrative, but all it's done is reveal my inner self to him.

He continues his intense scrutiny for a few more long seconds before shrugging. "I guess not. We were probably always going to end up here."

I can't help but scoff at that. Now he's going too far. "I don't know where that's coming from. I wouldn't have bet on us kissing today. Not with our history." Pushing off the wall, I head back to the table and start cleaning up the cards, doing my best to play this whole thing as inconsequential. Even though my heart is still short-circuiting from our connection, I still need to protect it. Like I always do, I start laying the bricks between my emotions and Noah, one on top of the other until my feelings need to stand on tiptoe to see him.

"Fair point, but you have to admit there's been something sparking between us for a while now, despite our history." He's moved closer, and his breath fans across the back of my neck as he speaks. Soon his hands slide around my waist and pull me against him.

His firm body against my back does something to

my insides, and that ember in my core sparks again. My heart screams at me to turn around and retake possession of his mouth, but my head yells louder that it's a horrible idea. And then Normandy's phantom avatar pops up on my shoulder like a cartoon, shaking a finger at me and warning me about getting involved with an employee. I am completely torn to shreds on the inside from all of the warring factions using my heart as a battlefield.

"Noah," I groan, sinking into him for only a moment before reluctantly sliding away. I can instantly sense his absence and have to suppress a physical shudder. "We can't do this."

"Why can't we do what exactly? Honestly, I don't even know what we're doing." The hand is back through his hair. It must be a nervous habit, and the thought that he has little idiosyncrasies like that makes me want to completely ignore my sister and my own brain and go for my happiness for once.

I sigh. "I don't know either, but we can't take this any further, Noah. I'm your boss. It's not right. Normandy warned me off of you...."

"You and Normandy talked about me?" He crosses his arms over his chest, and I can feel this conversation and the entire situation slipping away from me and through my fingers like water. "What exactly was said?"

Shit. Of course, he would ask that. How honest do I want to be with him about this? He already knows about the whole high school ordeal, so he has to know it involves at least that. What he doesn't know is it also included my current feelings for him, which are surprising everyone, especially me.

"She just said not to even think about dating any of the employees because it could be a whole legal nightmare or something." While not the entire story, it's not a lie. She did say that.

"So, you've considered dating me then?" He closes the distance between us again, his hand reaches up, and he brushes my hair out of my eyes. As his rough fingers sweep across my cheek, I can't help but lean into his palm, relishing his caress.

When I open my eyes again to meet his, I don't find the heat or desire from a minute ago. Instead, I see concern and wonder I don't understand.

"Is that so far-fetched with what you know about me?" He must know it's at least crossed my mind with how we've interacted since he started. Plus, realizing how I felt about him in high school has to give him some indication of my current feelings.

"Nothing about you is far-fetched." He smiles, and it's tinged with sadness. My heart pounds at the bricks between us, trying to knock them down. "Chelsie, I asked if you were sure before I kissed you, and you said you were. What's changed in the minutes since then?"

The question goes straight through my soul. He's

right. He did ask, and I answered. For me to pull away now would be wrong on so many levels.

"I wasn't expecting to...feel anything," I admit, and I can't meet his eyes. I may be confused, but that doesn't mean I can't be honest with him. He deserves at least that much from me. "I didn't think I could."

A line creases between his brows. "Didn't think you could what? I don't understand." His thumb traces a lazy line down my neck and across my collarbone, sending low tremors through me.

I guess if I'm being honest with him, I may as well go all in. "I shut my emotions off a long time ago, Noah. I don't let anybody in, so I can't be hurt. And well, something's shifted with you. Something is different."

"That's a good thing, isn't it?" He leans in to catch my eye, and his crooked smile is comforting, but only so much.

"Noah, it scares me to death. *You* scare me to be more specific about it."

He closes his eyes, and his nostrils flare as he takes in and releases a deep breath. "Chelsie, I'm not the same...."

"I know you're not the same person you were years ago, but understand that when I see you, that's the person I see. My years-old pain sees you as the years-old reason."

"Ouch," he winces and clutches at his chest as though I've mortally wounded him.

"I know. So, besides the fact that I'm your boss, I still see high school Noah, ready to break my heart at every turn. But at the same time, I see you now, and I know deep down that you're not like that. I'm still reconciling the differences between the two in my brain and my heart. It's not easy for me. You scare me, Noah. You scare me to death. I'm afraid if I allow myself to be vulnerable with you, I'll end up even more shut off than I was before. I don't think I could survive getting hurt by you twice in one lifetime."

He nods his understanding and leans to rest his forehead against mine. "I get it, Chelsie. I really do. I know I'll need to work hard to earn your trust, and I'm willing to do whatever I need to." He runs a hand through his hair. "So where does that leave things? I can't ignore what's happening between us. I don't want to ignore it. Do I need to quit? Would that solve everything? Because I can hand you my resignation right this very second if that means I get to kiss you again."

The grin that spreads on my face is so genuine I couldn't stop it if I tried. He just offered to give up his job so he could kiss me again. This man is going to ruin me. It's just a fact at this point.

His question is valid, though. Would that solve everything? I doubt it. There are other issues besides my being his boss. If things didn't work out between us for whatever reason, I'd hate for him to leave his job because of me. We should be adult enough to deal with that outside of work.

"Don't quit your job," I laugh, hitting his chest playfully, reminding me how solid his body is and how close. "Let's take it slow and keep it quiet for now. I'll work on Normandy in the meantime and see if we can find a loophole. Who knows, I might quit."

"You can't quit; you're part owner. Goofball." He squeezes my side, tickling me and forcing me to collapse into him. His strong arms catch me and pull me closer.

As he kisses the top of my head, he whispers, "We'll figure it out. But just know I'm not giving you up. Not now."

I wrap my arms around his waist and listen to his heart beat in time with mine as I press an ear against his chest. I could become used to this. Now I need to figure out a way to keep it without risking my entire soul at the same time.

Chapter 22

Misty

Noah

Living down my past is going to be more complicated than I thought if Chelsie still sees me as the inconsiderate asshole I was in high school. I think I'm up to the challenge, and it sounds like she's at least willing to see where things go between us. That's a start and probably more than I could hope to ask for.

When we turn in for the night, Chelsie takes the couch, and I take the floor in front of it. This is the second time I find myself sleeping on the floor next to her this week, and I hope it doesn't become a trend. My back and neck will be none too happy come morning despite the pile of blankets we scavenged to put on the floor under me. As it is, it's nearly impossible to fall asleep with my thoughts consumed by everything Chelsie, interspersed with worry for Mrs. Bailey. It hasn't escaped me why we're here in the first place. Of course, the dense weight of Edsel sleeping on my chest is a persistent reminder.

Warm fingers suddenly start running through my hair, and I open my eyes to discover Chelsie gazing down at me as she hangs an arm down from the couch to touch me. I must jump at the contact because Edsel digs her murderous talons into my chest and uses me as a springboard to dive into the room's shadows.

"Ah... fuck, that hurt." I clutch at my chest, where I swear I'm now carrying wounds that will cause me to bleed to death. I'm going to leave here with so many scars.

"Oh, shit, I'm sorry," Chelsie whispers, leaning more to place her hand over mine on my chest, and I can't help but gently take hold of her arm and pull until she slides off the couch and rolls onto me. "Hey!" The squeal of protest is half-hearted and morphs into giggles as I clutch her tighter against me, nuzzling against her neck with my stubble.

Now that I've tasted her kiss, I can't get enough of her. My thoughts are swirling with memories of her tongue dancing with mine and her hands all over me. I want more. But we're taking things slow. I need to respect that. This means I must somehow squash every carnal instinct that goes haywire whenever I'm around her, like now.

I shift so we're lying side by side, facing each other, and she doesn't move to go back to the couch. In the darkness of the night, with only faint moonlight making its way into the room, my eyes have adjusted enough to make out her face and her bright eyes staring back at me. I could get lost in those eyes. There always seems to be a question behind her gaze and a worry. It's an insecurity I hate to see because I know I'm at least part of the cause of it. Seeing it makes me want to do whatever is necessary to change it to confidence and security with me.

The magic that's been cast on us keeps me silent. I don't want to break the spell keeping this euphoria alive. Words don't seem important right now. Holding her against me is what is important, keeping her close. Letting her know I'm here and not going anywhere is my priority.

She must sense the magic, too, and she snuggles into me, wrapping her arm around my waist and tucking her head underneath my chin. The scent of her hair and the warmth of her body against me is comforting beyond measure, and after only a few minutes, I can feel myself drift asleep. I don't think I've ever experienced this level of contentment, and it's so strange that I don't know if I can get used to it. Part of me hopes I never do, so I can realize it anew every time it hits.

Chelsie's breathing eventually slows and evens out, so I know she's fallen asleep, but she doesn't loosen her grip on me. I like the thought that even in dreamland, she's comfortable enough with me to want me close. The idea relaxes me, and I soon sync up with her quiet breaths and join her in sleep.

When I wake the following day, my arms are empty, but I can hear Chelsie negotiating a truce with Edsel in the kitchen. It doesn't sound as though peace between them is on the horizon.

"I swear I'm a good person, Edsel. That food is fresh out of the can." There's a pause as Edsel mewls sharply in response. "Well, you saw me open it, so I don't know what to tell you."

From where I lean in the doorway to listen to the conversation, their earnestness makes me wonder if they don't actually understand what the other is saying. It's an unnervingly realistic conversation.

"I can vouch for her, Edsel. She wouldn't poison you. On purpose." I grin as they both stop their standoff to stare at me in surprise. Even their expressions are similar. Edsel meows in what can only be a snarky comment toward Chelsie and rushes over to weave herself between my feet in greeting. "At least one of you is happy to see me this morning." I bend down to pet the black cat but smile up to Chelsie. "Did you sleep okay?"

She's standing with her arms folded across her chest now, eyes narrowed. "You didn't even give me a chance to acknowledge that you were awake. Not fair." The pretense of annoyance fades, and a bright smile takes her over. "Yes, I slept *very* well. Thank you. How about you?"

A grin of my own rises up. "I did too. Is that coffee I smell?" The aroma wafting through the kitchen smells like how I imagine heaven.

"It is, indeed. How do you take it?" The domestic scene playing between us is so comfortable I'm not sure how to react.

"Um, lots of milk, little sugar." Watching Chelsie maneuver around the kitchen as though it were her own is an interesting side of her. She's a bit of a chameleon, able to fit in wherever she goes and whatever situation she's put in. The ability to be so adaptable to circumstances is something I don't think I have. At least not to the extent that she does.

She hands me a steaming mug and reaches up on tiptoes to kiss my cheek. "Good morning." Her lingering smile is infectious, and I automatically smile back. "Are you ready to get some work done today?"

This throws me off. "Work? It's Saturday." I was not planning on working today.

"Not real work, or at the depot, but here. I figured we could finish the car inspections while we wait for a call from Mrs. Bailey."

"Jeanette."

"Oh my gosh, yes, *Jeanette*."

It's a good idea. We may as well get something productive done while we wait to hear from her. However, my dirty mind had other ideas of how we could pass the time. *We're taking it slow. So, take it slow, pervert.*

"Sure. Sounds good." I am a man of few words until the coffee kicks in, and I just started.

She holds her hand out for the keys to the garage, and I pat around my pockets but come up empty. I can't remember where I put them.

"Oh no. You didn't lose the keys, did you?" Her brows raise in anxious surprise. "Shit, Noah."

"No, I didn't lose them. I just don't remember where I put them. There's a difference." *There is, isn't there?*

"Well, we'd better find them. Help me search."

It takes about ten minutes and a lot of swearing on my part for being so careless, but we eventually find them under the couch. They must have fallen out of my pocket and somehow walked beneath the sofa. As keys are known to do, obviously.

"How the fuck...?" I can't understand how they got so far deep under there.

"Don't question it. Just be glad we found them." Chelsie doesn't seem too perturbed at the magically moving keys like I am. There she goes, adjusting flawlessly to the situation again. "C'mon, let's get busy."

I follow her to the garage, and as we step inside, I instinctively reach for a light switch to illuminate the area. When my hand finds a switch and flips it, my heart stutters for a second. There's a fucking light switch in the garage. I glance up and discover a series of small fluorescents that don't appear to be working. I flip the switch some more just to double-check.

"Holy shit."

"What is it?" Chelsie turns and sees what I'm doing. "Is that a light switch?"

"It is." I start looking around for a fuse box along the garage's walls. "It seems we've been played by sweet old Jeanette."

"Oh my God. I can't believe her." She shakes her head, but her smile grows at Mrs. Bailey's ploy.

I find the fuse box, and sure enough, the main breaker is off. I switch it back on, and the entire garage lights up brighter than the Strip, the cars gleaming in their radiance.

"Well, I feel like a total idiot now," I say, looking around at the cars, my hands on my hips. "How did we not look up before? Or notice the switch on the wall?"

Chelsie shrugs. "I have no idea."

I can't believe Mrs. Bailey would be so sneaky. If she hadn't, though, we would have finished our assessment that first night and never returned. Well, I wouldn't have since there'd be no need for me to. And if we hadn't returned, Chelsie and I wouldn't be where we are now, would we? Is there some way Mrs. Bailey orchestrated this whole thing? It's too far-fetched. But the gnawing sensation in my gut tells me it's as close to the truth as you can get.

Thanks, Mrs. Bailey. Sorry, Jeanette.

Chapter 23

Stand For Myself

Chelsie

As we finish going over the last of the cars for valuation, Noah gets a call from his brother Theo asking for help with his car, which has broken down. I stay at Mrs. Bailey's to clean up and wait for the call to pick her up from the hospital. Once I finally receive that call, I don't waste any time making my way to get to her.

Mrs. Bailey is as chipper as ever when I walk into her room. She's flanked by two nurses listening to her finish a story. When she sees me, her face brightens, and her eyes light up.

"There she is." Her smile is part happiness and part mischievous. "The woman of the hour."

The nurses turn to me with knowing smiles I don't understand.

"Oh? Why's that?" I arch a skeptical brow.

"She was just telling us about your Noah," the closest one says. "He sounds like a keeper."

"*My* Noah, huh?" I can't help but scoff a little. "Did she also tell you how she lied to us and tricked us into spending time together? She may appear innocent, but I assure you this woman is far from it."

Mrs. Bailey raises a hand to her chest in demure shock, her cheeks now rosy. "Little old me?" She even bats her eyelashes for good measure.

The nurses laugh at her antics and proceed to give me instructions on Mrs. Bailey's care for the next few days before sending us on our way. In the car, she starts in with questions about how the rest of yesterday went.

"So, how did the cats do without me?" At least she starts innocuously enough.

"They were okay. Noah's going to have a few scars, but nothing too serious. I think they missed you."

"Noah stayed the night too?" It's an innocent enough question, but how she asks it makes her seem very pleased with herself. She totally planned for us to be together, so she shouldn't be surprised.

"Yes...he did." I glance over at her; sure enough,

she's got a smug little smile. "Wasn't that your intention? For us to spend the night together?"

"My intention was merely for the cats not to be lonely. That's all."

"And by the way, Noah fixed the nonexistent lights in the garage."

She lets out a long sigh accompanied by a giggle. "Okay, so I may have told a fib here or there to put the two of you together...Did it work?" The dreamy expression of hope in her eyes is too much.

"Maybe...." I don't want to feed her matchmaker ego, but I can't stop my mouth from twitching up into a smile at the thought of Noah kissing me last night against the kitchen wall and falling asleep in his arms. Heat rises on my face, which I'm sure is a dead giveaway.

"Ooh, I like the sound of that." She rubs her hands together like a dastardly villain in a cartoon, but she's so slight that she makes it adorable. "Care to share any details?"

"No, I would not."

"You're no fun," she grumbles with a pout. She's actually *pouting*. Unbelievable.

"Mrs. Bailey...."

"Jeanette."

I sigh. "*Jeanette*. There's a not-so-great history between Noah and myself that you don't know anything about. Whatever is happening between us is still tentative."

"I like that you used the words *'happening'* and *'us'* in the same sentence. That's a good start, isn't it?"

My insecurities have been rising all day since Noah and I parted ways earlier this afternoon. Not that I need constant validation from him, but a little would be nice. The negative side of my brain keeps coming up with hypotheticals about his intentions and trying to convince me this is all a cruel joke. Any minute he'll laugh in my face and say, 'April Fool's.' It's an effort to keep those thoughts at bay and to take him at his word.

"It's a start of *something*. Not sure what yet...."

"You'll figure it out." She reaches over and pats my hand. "I have faith in you two."

At least one of us does.

We spent the rest of the afternoon going through the piles of Wayne's belongings on her bed. If I didn't just pick her up from the hospital, I'd never know she was just there. She spends a lot of time interrogating me about what Noah and I did last night. I'm happy to tell her about the card game 'Kings in the Corner' he taught me; surprisingly, she knows it. After a light dinner, we play a few games. I have to teach her Noah's grandmother's knocking rule, which she gets a kick out of and is very good at using strategically. She's pretty diabolical when it comes to cards.

After our third game, her mood shifts, and she turns sober. "Now that you and Noah have finished with the cars, would you mind terribly if I invited you two over once in a while to visit? Maybe for dinner sometime?"

"What do you mean? We're not finished." The loneliness buried in her question claws at me. I'm starting to grow attached to this woman, and I can't imagine us disappearing from her life. "We still need to have the valuations completed, and then I'll need to see what Mischief Motors wants to do, if anything, with them. And if we're going to sell any to outside buyers, we'll need to handle that too. You can't be rid of us that easily."

"Oh, well, when you put it like that, I guess I'll see a lot of you." The relief is evident in the relaxing of her shoulders, and my heart constricts a little bit more. It's got to be so horrible for her to live alone after being with her husband for so many years. She has her cats, but that's not enough. The melancholy behind her small smile is so heartbreaking I just want to wrap her in a giant hug.

"Yup. You're going to end up sick of us in no time."

"Well, I look forward to getting sick of you."

"Oh, and don't forget Noah kind of has his heart set to stay on as your permanent landscaper, too."

"You two are so kind and so good to me. I don't know what I'd do without you." Her eyes fill up with tears, and I give in and pull her into a hug. She feels so tiny and frail. So fragile she could break with a deep breath.

"Don't even think about it." I rub her back lightly as she pulls herself together. "We're here for you. Whatever you need."

Chapter 24

Peer Pressure

Noah

The rest of the weekend, Chelsie continued helping Mrs. Bailey go through her late husband's things. Honestly, that task seemed to be a little too rife with emotions for me to deal with, so I kept my distance. That doesn't mean we don't continue our flirtatious banter. On the contrary, we seem to have kicked things up a notch or two.

CHELSIE: So, what are you wearing?

ME: Working on my brother's car, so very sexy coveralls.

CHELSIE: I think the name alone calls you a liar on the sexy part.

ME: Oh honey, I'm sexy in everything I wear.

CHELSIE: Honey? Have we reached the pet name phase of the relationship? I think we skipped something.

ME: What? You don't like Honey? What would you rather I call you? And yes, we're at pet names. Adopting actual pets together comes much later.

CHELSIE: I don't mind Honey, but it's a little tame.

ME: So, you're saying you're too wild for Honey? I may need to run some tests...

CHELSIE: I didn't say that. You did. I guess you'll just need to find out.

ME: I intend to, don't worry. But will you still have me if I'm in coveralls? I'm so unworthy.

CHELSIE: It's what's underneath that I care about. 😉

ME: Daaaaaaammmmmmnnnnnnnn woman. You're killing me.

CHELSIE: Oh, just you wait...

Come Monday at work, it's nearly impossible to stay professional when I see Chelsie throughout the day. She knows how torturous it is to be around her and not be able to touch her because she's doing everything in her power to drive me wild. The sway of her hips when she walks is exaggerated for my benefit, the lower lip biting and hair twirling are amped up when we talk, and the leaning over my desk, giving me a clear view of her beautiful cleavage, is almost more than I can take.

By the end of the day, as I wait for her in the parking lot, it's all I can do to keep from pouncing on her when she walks out of the garage. The sly smile on her gorgeous lips as she approaches me leaning against my car, tells me she knows exactly what she's doing. And she is very good at it.

"You really are trying to kill me, aren't you?" I ask as she gets close. I hook my fingers through the belt loops of her jeans and tug her against me. "Or get me fired. One of the two."

I sweep her hair off one shoulder and drag my mouth along the skin of her exposed neck, relishing the shiver that runs through her under my hands. Her breath escapes sharply through her teeth, and I'm instantly hard.

"Noah...." She groans softly as my kisses make their way along her jawline and find her mouth. The taste of her only ramps up my desire, and I turn us, so her back is against the car, and my hands pull her hips to grind against me. It's exquisite torture.

I could quickly lose my sense of where we are if I let myself, but I find the strength to pull myself away. I realize the middle of our work parking lot isn't the most romantic of locations.

"Chelsie, you're driving me crazy here. Any chance you'd want to come by my place?" I'm pretty sure my brother won't be home until late today, so we would have the apartment to ourselves for a little while, at least. I pepper languid kisses along her collarbone to further entice her. I think it might be working from how she rocks against me in response.

"I can't tonight." There's at least disappointment in her voice, but my heart still sinks at her answer. "I'm going to my sister's for dinner since her husband is out of town. I've already promised I'd go." Her hands are gripping the front of my shirt in tight fists, letting me know she's just as aroused as I am. I take a little comfort in the fact our feelings are mutual.

I force myself to stop the torture and press my forehead against hers, giving my body a minute to catch up to the change of plans it was working up to. The smell of her intoxicating perfume lingering around us isn't helping matters. I take one last deep breath, committing all these sensations to memory before taking a step back.

"That's fine. Rain check?" I keep the disappointment out of my voice, even though my body screams in protest. I can be patient if I need to be. Things with Chelsie are different than they've been with anyone else. When we are together for the first time, I want it to be perfect. Not rushed or hurried. I want to take my time with her.

She nods. "Yes. Definitely a rain check. There's always tomorrow." She smirks and yanks on my shirt to drag me down into a deep kiss that makes me want to cash that check. Fuck, this woman is going to undo me. When we separate, her sly smile is back. It's obvious she's having way too much fun torturing me.

Words fail me, and I can only shake my head as I watch her stroll provocatively to her car. Her hair sways with her movement, and picturing my fingers tangled in its length is almost too much. I have to tear my gaze away from her and switch my thoughts to something utterly unsexy, like filling out tax forms just to be able to fold myself into my car without pain.

Chelsie Blake is definitely going to be my undoing.

Chapter 25

River

Chelsie

At Normandy's house that evening, I do my best to try to put Noah out of my mind, but of course, my half-sister has other plans.

"So how is Noah working out as our new Head Mechanic? I haven't been at the depot much since he started." She's tossing a large salad for dinner on the vast marble island in her gourmet kitchen. Being married to a billionaire has its perks.

"He's doing okay." I shrug noncommittally, trying to be nonchalant in my answer, but I doubt I'm entirely successful.

"Just, okay?" She frowns, a crease deepening

between her brows. "That doesn't sound too encouraging. Shouldn't we be aiming for fantastic? Not just, okay?"

"Okay, he's doing fantastic. I don't know, Norm. He does his job. What do you want me to say?" I can hear the defensive edge of my tone and hope she doesn't notice. But of course, she does.

She narrows her eyes at me, examining me. The flush I can feel rising in my cheeks will betray me immediately. Normandy is too astute to miss anything so glaringly obvious.

"What is going on with you and Noah?" When I don't answer right away, she latches onto the thought like a dog with a bone. "Something is going on with you two, isn't there?"

"Norm...." I can't bring myself to answer honestly, and a non-answer isn't a lie.

Her exhale is loud and deep, expressing just how upset she is by the idea of Noah and I having 'something going on.'

"Chelsie, I thought we talked about this. Getting involved with employees is a big no-no. The legal ramifications and liability we'd face if something were to go wrong between you two could be astronomical. Especially with Brandon's wealth. I've got to consider him in all this too, you know."

"What does your husband have to do with anything?" I ask, confused as to why my involvement with an employee would concern him at all.

"If Noah were to sue for harassment or something, Brandon has much deeper pockets than either of us. He'd be an obvious peripheral target of any litigation against us." The stern expression on her face tells me she's seriously concerned about the possibility. The two of them are so protective of each other that it makes me half perturbed and half jealous.

I don't admit anything but ask her, "What about you and Brandon? Wasn't he a client when you two got together? Didn't your policy include clients?"

She blushes a little but tries to deflect. "That was different."

"How was that different?" She can't believe I'd really buy that excuse. "Just because you ended up married doesn't mean it's different. Is it because Brandon has money, and Noah doesn't? I didn't think you were such a snob, Norm."

"What?" A hand flies to her throat in surprise at my statement. I admit it was a low blow, but she's not being fair about any of this. There can't be a double standard for the two of us where this is concerned. "Chelsie, I am *not* a snob. I'm trying to...."

"Well, you're kind of acting like one." I cross my arms over my chest, standing my ground. We own this business equally, so we should have rules and policies applied similarly.

"I'm trying to protect both of us and the company." She shakes her head. "We just started being profitable after the mess Dad left. I don't want anything to happen to set that progress back. It's not selfish at all. I'm thinking about your future."

That makes me scoff. It sure doesn't feel like it's for my benefit when it's denying me something I want. Never mind that it's something I've wanted desperately for *years*.

"Yeah, well, I don't need you interfering in my personal life, either."

This gets me an arched brow in question. "What exactly is going on with you two, Chelsie? Has this ship already sailed?"

I simply shrug with a smirk. "I'm not confirming or denying anything. Plausible deniability for you. That's a thing, right? You're welcome."

By the time I see Noah again the next day, my thoughts of him have amped up my libido beyond recognition. The idea that our relationship is taboo entices me to dive head first into it. The rebel inside me bristles at being told who I can or can't have a relationship with. As a matter of fact, as soon as I see him, I order him to follow me to the supply room.

With the click of the door shutting behind him, I can't keep my hands off his body, and he doesn't resist. My palms press heavily against his chest, and my mouth takes command of his as I force him back until we're against a desk, and I lean into him, thrilling in the sensation of his hard muscles against me. His strong hands cup my face gently, and then his fingers deftly weave into my hair, grabbing it in fistfuls as our kiss deepens.

I lift his shirt and run my hands across his abs; the sensation of his skin underneath my touch is electric, sending shockwaves through my bloodstream. He mirrors my movements and slides a hand under my blouse, his touch gentle. When he moves my bra to take hold of my breast, his calloused thumb snags on my taut nipple, causing the ache between my thighs to feel him inside me to multiply to the point of near pain. I can't help the deep moan that escapes from deep in my throat.

His erection presses against me, and I know he's just as eager to take this further as I am. Slipping a hand into the waistband of his pants, I barely graze my fingers across his silky length, and he shudders against me, groaning into my mouth. We're reaching a point where decisions will need to be made, and from the looks of things, we're coming to the same conclusions. This hunger between us needs to be fed because I am starving.

"Chelsie..." Noah's voice is soft and reluctant as his hands wrap around my waist, and he pushes us apart gently. "Not here. If we're going to do this, and just so we're perfectly clear, I want to do this. I don't want it to be in some dusty old supply room. I want to do it right."

While I like everything he's saying, my body is mounting a revolution against his words. His hands are still on my bare waist beneath my blouse, and the sensation of his rough skin against mine is like heaven. I'm aching to be with him in a way I've never felt before, and I want to satisfy that ache right now.

"Are you sure...?" I whisper into his ear, finding his ear lobe, and I can't help but take a little nip. I don't think I've ever been this sexually forward with a guy, and I have to admit I kind of like it. "It could be fun."

"Fuuuuuuuck, Chelsie." He growls, pulling me against him roughly. He cups the back of my neck and drags me into the most passionate kiss of my life. The emotion and desire packed into that one kiss are dizzying, and when we pull apart, I have to grab onto his shoulders to stop from falling over.

"Whoa." Real words have escaped my brain in a mass exodus.

"Well put," he chuckles, pressing his forehead against mine again. I love when he does that.

"Care to cash in that rain check tonight?" I grin. I knew that thing would come in handy. I just didn't expect it to do so the very next day.

"Grrrrr. I just promised Mrs. Bailey I'd head over there after work to help with a few things. But I can call her back and reschedule...."

"No, no. Don't do that." I run my fingers through his dark hair, straightening the mess I made. "There's always tomorrow."

"That's what you said yesterday."

"And I was right. Here we are today." I poke a finger at his chest to prove my point. I can wait one more day. *I think.*

Chapter 26

You'll Be Fine

Noah

By the time I arrive at Mrs. Bailey's that evening, my nerves are so on edge, and I'm so damned irritable, I'm afraid I'll accidentally say something to offend her. She must notice something wrong when she opens the door for me because her face grows concerned.

"What is it, Noah? Is everything alright? Are you not feeling well?" She reaches up and places the back of her hand on my forehead in search of a fever. "You don't feel warm."

"I'm fine. I'm not sick." I deftly swerve away from her outstretched hand, avoiding further contact.

Any touch right now would be too much and make me even more of a monster than I already can feel myself becoming.

"Alright then. Have you eaten dinner yet? I made way too much stew today...."

"No dinner for me, thanks." I'm being short with Mrs. Bailey, and I cringe inwardly at what an asshole I'm being. It's so not like me. I'm just so twisted inside, physically and mentally, and every thought I have is consumed by Chelsie. "You said you had a list of things that needed tending to?"

"Oh. Of course." She can't cover her disappointment because it's not only in her voice but also on her face. I really am a jerk.

"Sorry, Mrs. Bailey. I don't mean to be short with you. It's just been a weird day."

She pats my arm and gives it a slight squeeze. "Don't worry about it, Noah. We all have good days and bad days. It's a part of life." Her understanding smile guts me. "Let me find that list for you."

As she shuffles off to the kitchen, my gaze slides to the spot on the floor in front of the couch where Chelsie and I fell asleep in each other's arms just the other day. Memories of her head on my chest flood through me, and my yearning for her grows that much more. I want to experience that feeling again. Soon.

"Here we are." Mrs. Bailey's voice breaks through my reverie, bringing me back to the present.

"The main thing is the thermostat. It's always been on the fritz, and Wayne always worked his magic on it, but it never lasted very long. And sure enough, it's back to being persnickety."

"Okay, I'll take a look at it." I'm not an electrician, but I have enough theory training to figure out most systems. A thermostat should be simple enough to fix. "You go put your feet up and relax."

"You're a good man, Noah."

"Coming from you, that is very high praise, indeed." I force a smile for her that I only partially feel and head to the hallway and the busted thermostat.

While working, I listen to Mrs. Bailey humming softly as she putters around the kitchen. From the sounds of it, she's packing up the stew and cleaning dishes. She has a pleasant and melodic voice, but I don't recognize any of the songs, though they sound vaguely familiar.

When I take the thermostat apart, I find corrosion at the junction of the wires and the corresponding terminals that might be part of the problem. I head out to my car to grab my toolbox and stop behind the attached garage to check the HVAC system. After a thorough examination, I don't see any problems with the unit and head back inside.

As I finish cleaning the terminals and rewiring the thermostat, it dawns on me that I don't hear Mrs.

Bailey humming anymore. In fact, I don't notice her puttering around, either. The hair on the nape of my neck stands on end, and a sudden chill runs through me.

"Mrs. Bailey?" I call out to the silent house and get no response. The chill in me deepens. "Jeanette?" When I enter the kitchen, I find her laying on the floor, her skin pale white. I slide onto my knees next to her. Feeling for a pulse and finding none, I immediately pull out my phone, call 911 and start CPR. "No. No. No. We're not doing this today, Jeanette. Sorry for swearing, but not fucking today."

After several rounds of chest compressions and breath exhalations, I detect a pulse. It's shallow and weak, but it's there. Her chest is rising and falling with her own breathing, too, thank God. There's a little color back in her cheeks, and her eyelids flutter open, her gaze locking on mine.

"Hey there, lady," I force a smile, squeezing her hand. My pulse is racing through the fucking roof of this house, and I can feel my back slick with sweat. Adrenaline is spiking and coursing through my veins. I somehow keep my cool on the outside for her sake. "Sleeping on the job, huh?"

Her eyes are the palest blue as if the color is draining from them. And they're full of so much fear that my heart clenches as though I feel that same fear because I feel at least part of it. I was afraid she was about to die in my arms on this cold tile floor. The relief of her being alive hasn't even sunk in yet. My brain is currently running in slow motion.

I hear a sharp pounding and glance down to find her frail fist hitting the ceramic tile next to her. Her eyes fill with tears when I look back at her in question. She still hasn't spoken, and I wonder if she's had a stroke and can't talk.

"I don't understand, Mrs. Bailey." What the fuck is she trying to tell me? It seems extremely important to her, but I can't figure it out. *God damn it.*

She knocks on the floor again, this time with her knuckles. *She fucking knocks.*

My eyes snap to hers, and there is a pleading in her now I don't think was there before.

"No," I say, swallowing hard, trying desperately not to lose my shit. "No. Your turn is not over. Not yet. We've got too much to do yet." I wipe my eyes with the back of my hand, not caring if I'm a blubbering idiot. "You've got a whole list of stuff to do and everything, remember? So, no. I don't accept your knock. New rule - knocks can be denied. Okay? So, I deny it."

Her lips twitch briefly, and I think her head nods, but I can't be sure. Good. At least that much is sorted.

The ambulance arrives soon after that, and the paramedics take over. I tell them the situation and what little I know of her medical history. I call

Chelsie to help fill in what blanks she can for them and make plans to meet at the hospital.

Before they wheel her gurney out of the kitchen, I grab Mrs. Bailey's hand. "Remember, no knocks allowed."

"I remember." She nods, her voice a small rasp.

After I watch the ambulance pull away, I double over, plant my shaky hands on my knees, and let out a soul-wrenching primal scream to release all the built-up tension from the last fifteen minutes of having someone's life teetering on the brink in my hands. I have never been so scared in my fucking life. I never want to go through that again. *Ever*.

Chapter 27

Rescue My Heart

Chelsie

Mackenzie drives me to the hospital since we were out to dinner when Noah called. She comes into the hospital with me, but I run into his arms as soon as I spot Noah. He holds me tightly, and I think I detect a slight tremor radiating from his bones. He must be so upset.

"Thank God you were there," I say, wiping my wet cheeks. "What happened?"

He walks us through the series of events at Mrs. Bailey's house and how it took his performing CPR to bring her back. No wonder he's shaking. There isn't anything more emotionally intense than bringing someone back from the dead.

"Holy shit, Noah, you saved her life." Mackenzie sounds impressed, but Noah shrugs and shakes his head like it's not a big deal. I can tell by his playing it down that it is a big deal to him, just not one he wants to celebrate for some reason. I would think he'd be over the moon.

His dark eyes turn to me with a sadness I've never seen in him, and my heart lurches in response. "She knocked, Chels. After I brought her back. She knocked to end her turn." He leans forward with his elbows on his knees and drops his face into his hands as emotion takes him over.

After the magnitude of what he said settles over me, I rub his back. "And you told her that was bullshit, right?"

"What does that mean? She knocked?" Mackenzie appears confused. "I'm a bit lost."

"It's from a card game we've been playing. It's how you announce your turn is over," I explain.

"Oh, shit." She tugs on one of her long violet braids nervously. "That's heavy."

"Yeah, she's not going to get any better if she's giving up." I turn to Noah, still rubbing his back. "Did she say anything after that?" I need to hear Mrs. Bailey hasn't completely given up on life. I've heard so many stories of people deteriorating after a spouse of many years dies. I don't want to believe that is what's happening here now.

He shakes his head again, still hanging low with his hands twined behind his neck. "I just told her that knocking isn't allowed in this, and she said she gets it. I don't know." He bursts out of his seat and starts pacing in front of us. He's radiating frustration, and it's starting to seep into my mood. "She just felt so small and frail when I was administering CPR. Like she'd break in half with a strong wind. I'm afraid I may have broken something in the process. Nobody can really be that fragile, right?" He runs a shaky hand through his hair, and his anxiety is overpowering. It's taking him over.

I stand and grab his hands, forcing him to stop moving and focus only on me. He's starting to spiral out of control, and he needs to calm down before he has a full-blown panic attack.

"Noah, you didn't do anything wrong. In fact, you did everything right." He's not meeting my eyes, so I know he still teetering on the edge. "You saved her life, Noah. Even if she does have a cracked rib or something, which I doubt she does, *you* brought her back. *You* got her heart started again. *You* breathed life back into her. And you should be so proud of that. I know I am."

He sits down, letting out a long breath, rubbing his hands down the thighs of his jeans. But just as quickly as he sat down, he's up and pacing again, the worry in his eyes painting dark circles underneath.

"I need to leave for a little while," he says, pulling his car keys out of his pockets. "I'll be back. Text me if something happens?"

It's obvious he needs to do something. He's got too much pent-up energy to sit here in the waiting room for news that's taking forever. Maybe getting out of here for a while will do him some good.

"Of course." I grab his free hand and walk out to the parking lot with him, the evening's chill starting to settle on the night. "Are you going to be okay?" We stop, and I sweep his dark hair out of his eyes to see his expression better. He's so distraught I'm not sure what I can say to make him feel better. I don't think there is anything.

Grabbing my waist, he pulls me to him and wraps his arms around me tightly. He doesn't say a word but holds me close, and I let him stand with me like that for as long as he needs to. I try to take some of his pain and worry from him by hugging him back just as ferociously, but I don't know if it works.

Eventually, he pulls away, flashes a weak smile, and squeezes my hand. "Thanks for that." He walks backward a few steps, and it looks like he's going to say something else, but he turns and goes to his car without another word.

I wish more than anything I could take whatever it is that's bothering him away and make it my own.

Seeing him so anxious and upset after he was so heroic just doesn't make a lot of sense to me, but then I've never had to deal with something so massive. This could be a normal reaction for a hero. What do I know?

"Chels, they're looking for you two," Mackenzie calls from the sliding doors to the Emergency Room. I nod at her and turn to call Noah back, but he's already pulling out of the parking lot and driving out of sight. I could text him to come back, but I think he needs a little while to himself to sort out whatever's going on with him. I can give him that much.

When I return to the ER, a cherubic-faced nurse, whose name badge reads, *'NEIL, I'm the first thing you'll see after saying: "Hold my beer!"'* greets me with a tired but genuine smile. "You must be Chelsie, the inamorata of today's hero. I've heard so much about you."

I raise a curious brow as I start to follow him. He walks especially fast. "Oh, really?"

"Oh yes. Jeanette told us all about her matchmaking prowess. She even tried to get Doctor Sylvan and me together while running her EKG. I told her I don't think my husband would appreciate my taking a lover." He fans himself dramatically. "Though, to be fair, Doctor Sylvan *is* hot." He turns into an open sliding glass door to Mrs. Bailey's room. "Here we are. I found half of your power couple, Jeanette."

"Noah just went out for a... minute." My words catch as Neil steps aside, and I see Mrs. Bailey for the first time. She's almost unrecognizable. Her skin is pale, and the fluorescent lights make her even more ashen. Her cheeks and eyes are sunken, lending her an even stronger skeletal appearance. I have to try very hard not to let my internal reaction show on the outside.

Neil checks the machines attached to Mrs. Bailey, then leaves, saying, "I'll give you two beautiful young ladies a few minutes to catch up. Doctor Sylvan should be by in a few minutes to get you up to speed."

"Thank you, Neil," Mrs. Bailey croaks, her voice dry and brittle.

"Anything for you, Jeanette." And in a whirl of curtains and sliding doors, Neil disappears like he's in a magic act.

"Wow, I wish I had his energy," I say, glancing at the curtain, still swaying in the remaining breeze.

"He's a sweetheart, but he's no Noah."

"I hear Doctor Sylvan is quite the catch..." I smirk, moving around to the side of her bed to check the machines she's hooked up to. There are a lot.

"Oh, he's not for you." She waves a dismissive hand at me. "He plays for the other team. That's why I thought Neil would be a great fit."

"The other team, huh?" That makes me chuckle.

"You just can't stay out of people's love lives, can you?"

"Oh, nonsense." She pushes her fists into the bed to sit up straighter, and Noah was right; she looks very fragile. "It worked with you and Noah, didn't it? Where is he, by the way? I thought he was in the waiting room."

"He was," I say, biting the inside of my cheek as I try to think of what to say to explain what's going on with him. But I don't have the first clue. "He just...."

"Just took a quick drive. But I'm here now." Noah's deep voice announces from the doorway. When I glance up and meet his gaze, it's clear that whatever made him crazy a little while ago is gone. He seems much calmer, but exhaustion still emanates from him. We share a quick second between us, communicating without words, and I know he's okay now. "How are you feeling, Mrs. Bailey?"

Her eyes become watery when she sees Noah, and she holds out a hand to him. "There's my knight in shining armor. Come here."

His cheeks turn red at the compliment, but he stays silent and steps up to the opposite side of the bed to take her hand into his. A swelling of pride bursts in my chest as I watch the two of them interact, knowing that he just saved her life. It's incredible.

"I hate to ask you two for anything more since

you've been so generous with your time already." She breaks off into a coughing fit that seems to rack her entire body. Noah and I both freeze, unsure if we need to fetch help or let it run its course.

Noah reacts first, still in hero mode, and pours her some water from a pitcher on her tray table. "Here, drink some of this."

She takes the cup from him with two shaky hands and sips it carefully. I can't believe how much she's deteriorated in the days since I last saw her. There's a lump starting to form in my throat full of emotion I need to keep inside, and I swallow hard to push it down. I need to be strong now. Like Noah is.

"Thank you." She pats her chest briefly to compose herself again. "What I was going to say was that I need to ask another favor. I know two youngsters like yourselves have more fun things to do, but I just worry so much about Edsel and Yugo."

"I'll stay with them, don't worry," Noah offers before she can even get the question out. Damn, this man is reinventing chivalry for my generation, and I am all about it.

"You are an angel. An absolute angel," she says, her eyes getting misty again as she gazes up at him with so much admiration it hurts. She turns her gaze to me. "You better marry this one, Chelsie. Or I will. I'm sure Wayne would understand."

I can't help the laugh that erupts from me, and I can't tell if it's at the ludicrous idea of me marrying

Noah or her doing the same thing. Either way, it's hilarious, and it's only when I notice the two of them aren't laughing that I halt immediately.

"What? That was funny...." She couldn't have been serious, could she? And why is Noah looking at me like it's the sanest proposal he's ever heard?

Mrs. Bailey tsks her tongue at me with a head shake and says to Noah, "The kitties will still need their evening food." Ignoring me completely.

"I'll make sure they're fed. Don't worry." He pats her hand that he's still holding.

The sense that I just missed a sign, made an inappropriate joke or committed some major social faux pax builds inside me. I can't believe that wasn't a joke to either of them. Noah and I married. Come on. It's only been a few weeks, if that. It's way too early to think about something like that.

Isn't it?

Chapter 28

Hymnal

Noah

How the fuck did I end up here? In just a few weeks, I quit my job, found a new job, started a crazy relationship with my predecessor's widow, and a budding romance with my boss, which just might be serious. Add on top of that the fact I just had to resuscitate said widow, and things have gone from weird to insane. I think I might be on the brink of a breakdown or something because I'm having a hard time dealing with it properly. I'm going through the motions of what I think are the right things to do, but fuck knows if they are.

Mrs. Bailey, who just told Chelsie to marry me, putting all kinds of thoughts in my already messed up head, needs her cats kept company yet again. I don't know when I became a pet sitter, but here I am, dropping off Chelsie on my way to Mrs. Bailey's so she can gather some things and will meet me there later. I stop at my apartment for a brief shower and head back out right away.

When I enter Mrs. Bailey's house, I'm reminded that I left when the ambulance did. Just locked up and took off without thinking. Now, as I walk into the kitchen, I find the scattered remnants of today's events. There are medical wrappers for various implements, what's left of a roll of gauze stained from the spots of blood it's sitting in, and a broken mug. I don't remember hearing anything break, but it might have happened while I was in the garage. And the blood...reminds me she must have fallen too, on top of whatever was happening with her heart. I had been so focused on getting her heart going I didn't notice anything else.

I stare at it all, the trash, the blood, the broken ceramic pieces, and I catch Edsel and Yugo huddled together in the corner, watching intently. Thinking about the cats having to step on shards of broken pottery gets my ass moving. As much as I'd love to ignore that any of this happened or that I could probably leave all this for Chelsie without it being an issue, I start cleaning up. The entire time, my mind keeps flashing back to only a few hours ago, kneeling in this very spot, yelling at Mrs. Bailey not to die, and it's all I can do to not break down.

"Let me help you," Chelsie's voice cuts through, and she kneels next to me and starts picking up pieces of shattered ceramic. I was so far down in my own head I didn't hear her come into the house or the kitchen.

"Be careful," I say without thinking. Everything seems to be on autopilot at the moment. Not just my thoughts but my actions and words are too.

She pauses and glances up at me, taking time to study me. "Noah, I can handle all this. If you want to go home, it's not a big deal...."

"I gave my word that I'd stay." My tone is way too harsh, and I can feel Chelsie wince in response.

"Okay...Noah," her voice is super calm, like someone talking a jumper off the window ledge of a skyrise. "Let me do the cleaning up, at least. You don't need to do all of this. You've done more than enough today. You need to chill out. You've earned it. Go hang out in the front room for a while. Maybe set up the blankets again?"

It's working. What she's saying is getting through to me and making sense. I do need to chill the fuck out. It takes me a second, but I finally nod and get up from the floor, tossing broken bits of the mug into the trash can before heading out to the living room without a word.

Chelsie's voice carries into the living room as she talks to the cats while she finishes up and feeds them. "I know it's been a very stressful day for you, with all the excitement, but you still need to eat."

A duo of replying meows calls back to her, making me smile. They're back to sounding like they're having a real conversation. It's precisely the distraction I need.

"Well, we can debate all night about the virtues of tuna versus salmon, but I'm afraid all we have is tuna. You'll need to adjust your expectations accordingly."

Again, the cats respond in tandem, apparently letting their feelings about tuna known. Then a second later, they all go quiet, and it sounds as though the two felines have been persuaded that tuna will do after all. After a few moments, Chelsie appears and snuggles next to me on the couch.

When she lays her head on my shoulder, I'm instantly grounded. The weight of the day still encroaches on my thoughts but having her presence next to me is soothing to my frayed nerves; I don't ever want to separate from her. I suddenly need to be with her all the time, which is crazy. The scent of her perfume reaches me, and it smells like home, or what I envision home to be like. Not an apartment, or house, or even a building, but a feeling. Chelsie *is* home to me. Wherever she is, I'm safe.

My masculine alpha side bristles at the thought

of feeling safe because of a woman, but it's not physical safety. It's an emotional one. I know I can rely on her to light my way during the darkest times. When I'm on the edge, she'll talk me down. Just basically need her for anything; she'll be there. She's proven this much to me. If I start kicking myself for what happened in high school and regretting the wasted years without her, I will be in big trouble.

With my arm around her shoulders, I kiss the top of her head, breathing her in. "Thank you," I say. I have so much to thank her for. Too much.

"For what? I didn't do anything." She lifts her head to meet my eyes, and hers blow me away. Her gaze has so much emotion and expression it's hard to comprehend. The concern and worry, the caring and passion, and the curiosity and amusement are all wrapped into one look. It floors me.

That's the minute it happens. I fall in love with her while sitting on this couch with my arm around her, staring into her bright eyes. There's no particular reason. Neither of us said anything spectacularly profound or life-altering. Nothing special at all happened, which is why it's perfect. Why it's totally Chelsie. Why it's totally *us*. It's random. It's out of nowhere. But it's typical for the two of us.

I'm about to say the words, but I catch myself. This is way too soon to be saying shit like that. She will think I've completely lost my god-damned mind, and I might not argue the point. Maybe I have.

Perhaps I should rethink this. I could just be reacting to today's events and not thinking clearly. I need to give this time to make sure I really love her before I profess it aloud.

"But you did." I pull my fingers through her silky hair, letting the long strands glide against my skin, making me shiver. "You showed up. You didn't have to, but you did."

"Of course, I showed up," she scoffs, tapping my chest with the palm of her hand. "How could I not show up after what happened?"

"Well, I don't know when the two of us adopted Mrs. Bailey to be our honorary family, but it seems like we have, doesn't it?" I pull her close and press my lips to her forehead. "Not that I mind, but it's weird how we have. And in such a short time, too."

"I don't think we had much choice in the matter," she giggles, playing aimlessly with a button of my shirt. "Mrs. Bailey always finds a way to get what she wants." I can sense her smile and join her, thinking of how surprisingly powerful such a petite woman can be. It's impressive. "Matchmaking included."

"True." I can't argue with that. My thoughts then stray to how frail and fragile she can be, and my mood is instantly dragged down. I was doing great for a little while there, not picturing her...

"Hey, don't do that." Chelsie must sense my emotional shift, and she reaches up to turn my face to hers. Her brow is furrowed, and the empathy pouring out of her is palpable. "Don't dwell on the negative. Focus on the positive stuff. Like the fact she's alive now because of you. That's what is important in all of this."

I search her eyes, wanting with all my being to be able to do just that, ignore the bad and embrace the positive. But my mind doesn't seem to work that way. Letting myself exist in Chelsie's presence for another minute, I go back to feeling like I'm home again. I just need to keep doing that. Repeatedly.

For the rest of my life.

Chapter 29

Sleep Baby Sleep

Chelsie

Noah looks me directly in the eyes in a way I've never seen him do before. As though he's suddenly noticed something there that he hadn't realized before. It's like he's staring into my soul.

I like it.

What are we even doing here? My forehead still tingles from where he kissed me. How on earth can something so simple feel so good? Being here, curled up with his fingers sliding through my hair, is so natural. A part of me still can't believe it. How many times, back in high school, did I dream about this exact situation?

Until he decided to humiliate me.

No. I can't keep thinking about that. He's changed. He's different. Yet, there's still a part of that boy I remember inside him. The way he snapped at me just then brings back a whole pile of memories. But he's different now. He stops. He listens to me when I call him out. He *wants* to be a better person. I'm different now too. I don't let it fluster me. I've grown strong enough to call him out. Not only that, I trust he'll listen when I do.

That's when I realize this is what makes me want to be with Noah so much. He's still that angry boy I crushed on as a teenager, only now he's learned to be vulnerable. That pride is still there. That need to be in control. But he's learned to accept when both of those things are threatened rather than lash out.

Then, suddenly, he's kissing me.

I hadn't even noticed his hand slide around to the back of my head to gently pull me in. I'd been just as caught up in his eyes as he had been in mine. But the when doesn't matter. Only the now. I close my eyes and focus on the sensation of his lips against mine. Part of me expects him to be rough, but instead, he holds me in place with a gentle strength, just enough to keep me pressed to him without making me powerless.

I immediately lean into him, moaning softly.

Taking his face in my hands, I press myself against him, and it's the most natural thing in the world. This is *right*. There are no more thoughts about who the two of us used to be. No more doubts about what we have become. There is only the moment, and the understood admission of what we both want so badly.

Rolling towards him, I slide my leg over his and sit on his lap. For a split second, I wonder if he thinks I'm too forward, but when his hands slide up my back, it's clear he wants me there. Did he worry I would pull away? Well, no chance of that now. His lips part and my tongue eagerly meets his. His hands slip under my top, and his palms against my skin are electric. I fumble with his shirt buttons, my hands working automatically as we kiss. I can sense him hardening beneath me, his cock pressing against me through his pants, and I realize I can't remember the last time I wanted someone as much as I want him right now.

Finally getting his shirt open, I pull away from the kiss and peer down at his firm chest. Biting my lip, I slide my hands across his skin, drinking in the feel of his body. I slide my thumbs over his nipples, and he makes a noise that's half sigh, half gasp. When I glance up, the expression on his face is a mixture of excitement and joy I don't think I've seen on a man's face before.

"Let's make this fair," he grins, grabbing my top

and pulling it gently over my head. I raise my arms, but as soon as it's around my head, Noah sits up and presses his mouth into the flesh of my breasts, hungrily kissing my cleavage and up towards my throat. I actually shudder when his lips hit my neck. A whole honest-to-goodness body shake. His hands deftly unhook my bra with a quick, practiced flick of his fingers. I let it slide down my arms, and as I toss it aside, he lowers his mouth to my breast with a groan of hunger. *God, his mouth feels incredible.* I hold his head to me, running my fingers through his hair as he gently sucks my right nipple, then the left, swapping between them as his hands softly massage.

I let my head fall back, closing my eyes and letting the sensations run through my body, which moves without thinking about it. I begin to grind on the rock-hard length beneath me as if my hips have a life of their own. Right now, they do. I don't know if I could stop myself if I tried. I am far past the point of no return. I want him. *Dear God, do I want him.* And clearly, the feeling is mutual. I can feel his bulge straining in his jeans. It has to be uncomfortable.

Well, I guess I can do something about that.

Leaning forward, I pull his face to mine and kiss him hungrily. At the same time, I reach down and start fumbling with his fly buttons. I can feel his smile against my own, then his cock is in my hands, all but vibrating against my palm. He groans as I start to stroke it up and down, but he immediately gets his revenge by sliding his hand into my open jeans and running a fingertip across my clit through my underwear. My entire body jumps as pleasure simultaneously shoots through what seems like every nerve ending in my body.

Frustratingly, we both know we need to detach if we want this to go any further. This is the bit they never show in movies. The awkward rolling off each other and tossing around on your back to pull off your pants. But we're both too excited to care about looking sensual at this point. I manage to pull mine off, then scramble to where I left my bag to grab protection. Turning back to see Noah toss his jeans aside, I take a moment to admire his body, then straddle him once again, putting the condom into his hands and kissing him. This time, our mouths are wide open with hunger and lust. I can't keep my body still. But then he's ready, and I reach down and glide him into me as I lower myself on top of him.

I feel so perfectly full. For a moment, we don't move. Any more pleasure at this point would be too much for me to take.

"Give me a sec," I whisper. I want to enjoy this. I want us both to enjoy this. We stay still and simply stare into each other's eyes. Communicating without words.

I love him. The realization hits me all at once. I think I knew it already. I just hadn't been able to acknowledge it to myself. I didn't want to admit that vulnerability. Because it is one. I'm exposing myself to a whole lot of pain. But with Noah, I think it will be worth it. I hope to God I'm not wrong about him this time.

I lean forward and kiss him, soft and passionate, drinking in this moment so it will stay in my memory forever. His hands run up my back, his fingers tracing my spine. Then I begin to rock my hips, feeling him inside me. Our kiss deepens as our movements build in tempo. He cups my breasts in his hands, sucking on my nipples like they are the only things in the world. I grab his shoulders, holding myself up as I continue to grind on him. He moves his mouth to my neck, clearly remembering the response this had last time and getting it. A moan escapes my lips, and I involuntarily dig my fingernails into his back. When he grabs my ass, at first, he's content to simply knead the ample flesh, but then he begins to use this grip to push me back and forth on his cock in time with his thrusts. He grunts with each one, a masculine, animal noise that trips some instinctual switch inside me. It's the most erotic sound I've ever heard.

My orgasm comes with almost no warning. One moment, I'm focusing on moving my body in time with his, kissing his neck, and reveling in the sounds he's making. Then the next, I'm convulsing around him in an almost agonizing feeling of pleasure, and I'm saying his name over and over. I expect him to stop moving, satisfied that he's succeeded in bringing me to orgasm as well as his own. But instead, he keeps moving, maintaining precisely the same movement and speed that tipped me over the edge, so my climax keeps going. I've never had a man do this before. All I can do is ride out the explosion as best I can and simmer in the aftershocks.

After a blissful eternity, I realize I'm being lifted into the air. I wrap my legs around Noah as he grabs my ass and lifts me like I weigh nothing before laying me on my back, never once allowing himself to leave my body. My climax has passed its glorious peak, but this new position finds a whole new swathe of nerve endings. I hook my ankles together and reach behind him to grab his sexy ass. His mouth is by my ear, nearly growling. Each thrust inside me is harder than the last, and I can tell he's reaching the point of no return.

With a wordless cry, I feel him slam his body into mine and explode. I hold him tight, letting him buck and ride out what has to be an insanely intense orgasm. Then, eventually, he carefully collapses on top of me, his comforting weight holding me in place, his cock twitching inside me.

"I love you," I whisper, almost without thinking.

He's still for a moment, and I swear he's holding his breath too. He pushes up on his elbows to meet my gaze, the sweat on our skin shimmers in the room's low light. He searches my eyes, and I think he's examining my face for a sign of doubt, something to tell him I don't mean what I said. He doesn't find anything. I meant it.

"You don't have to say it back...." I say quickly. I don't want him to feel obligated to feel or say anything. I just needed to tell him what I was feeling because I've never felt this way and I wanted to tell someone. Especially him.

"I love you too," he replies, interrupting anything else I was about to say, and brushing the hair sticking to my forehead aside. Then he plants his lips firmly there in a soft kiss. Tears are in my eyes again as I hold him to me like I never want to let him go. Because I won't. Now that I have this, I don't ever want to lose it.

Chapter 30

All These Things That I've Done

Noah

After the incredible events of last night, when we wake the next day, Chelsie and I agree I should be the one to go to the hospital to await Mrs. Bailey's release while she goes to the depot to work. We need to keep up the appearances of professionalism when it comes to Mischief Motors since Normandy is so dead-set against us being together while working alongside each other. I can do that. Probably.

When I get to the hospital, I find Neil, the nurse on duty last night, who has apparently worked a very long overnight shift. You'd never be able to tell, though, with his bubbly attitude. He sees me heading to Mrs. Bailey's room and arches an eyebrow at me.

"And, what are you doing here, Mr. Knight in Shining Armor? No distressed damsels in the outside world today?" His snark is laced with humor.

"Nah, I thought I'd take the day off from new damsel saving and check on the previously saved." After last night, my own attitude can be nothing but positive. It's a god-damned beautiful day, and no amount of snark can ruin it for me. "Why? Should I not be here? Is Mrs. Bailey not being released today?" I can't imagine why he would question my being here.

"Oh, no. She is." He hesitates, and an uneasy feeling starts to grow in my stomach. "But there's a daughter here now?" He scrunches his face in obvious distaste for the person. "She appears to have taken over Jeanette's care. Quite forcefully, I might add."

"Whoa. A daughter? I thought they didn't have any children?" I am thoroughly confused. I'm half elated at the discovery of this news since whoever they are will now be able to handle all of this, and half suspicious. There has been zero evidence of the existence of children or any offspring.

Neil leans in conspiratorially and whispers, "Apparently, Jeanette's late husband wasn't so true to her in the beginning." He shrugs his shoulders. "She said she always suspected something but didn't have proof until today when the woman walked out of the ether."

"You make her sound like a monster." I'm starting to dislike this person before I even meet them.

"Those are your words, sir. Not mine." His grin is devilish, as is the chuckle that accompanies it. He pats my arm and turns. "Now, if you'll excuse me, Sir Knight, I'm sure there's somebody here that needs help only I can provide."

I shake my head and continue down the hallway to Mrs. Bailey's room. When I enter, I find a woman about my mother's age in her mid-fifties, with wispy blonde hair and no waist to speak of. She has almost no shape; she's all hard angles and rough edges. She's fussing over Mrs. Bailey's pillows, complaining about their firmness, or lack thereof, and Mrs. Bailey is apprehensively allowing it. I can see the hesitation all over her face, but she also seems resigned to whatever fate this situation brings her.

Her eyes light up when she sees me enter the room. "There's my hero. Heather, this is the young man I was telling you about, Noah. He's the one who rescued me and got my old ticker back to working order." She gives me a wary smile and indicates to the other woman, "This is Heather Cunningham. She's apparently Wayne's daughter." The expression on her face tells me she's both not sure about this fact and not happy about it.

I hold out a hand to the woman to shake, and she takes it firmly, leveling me with a stare. "Nice to meet you, Noah." Her voice is a little stiff, but then she's probably feeling just as awkward as everyone else in the room. "Yes, I recently learned of Wayne...my dad's passing, so I thought I would at least come to pay my respects, even though I didn't know him at all." Her eyes start to tear up, and she turns away to blow her nose. Behind her back, Mrs. Bailey rolls her eyes at me, and I need to stifle a laugh. I'm glad to see she's back to her old self.

"Well, I'm sorry for your loss. I understand Wayne was a remarkable person." I have zero clue what to say to this woman. Sorry the dad you never knew died? I'm sure there's a greeting card for this somewhere.

"Thank you, but I'm upset because the man I thought was my father my whole life died a few months ago. I didn't learn about Wayne until recently from my mother, who said it was time I learned the truth." She sighs heavily, and I can tell she's been on her own emotional rollercoaster.

"Oh, wow. So, everyone is getting surprises." Again, no idea what's an appropriate response to this.

"You can say that again," Mrs. Bailey chimes in. "I about died again when she told me who she was."

"There'll be no more of that, young lady," I say, still trying to wrap my head around this entire situation. I can't imagine Wayne would do something like that to his wife, but I didn't know him at all. "Did Wayne ever tell you about him having a child?

"Oh, heaven's no. We always were under the impression he couldn't have children due to a bad case of the mumps when he was a child. At least, that's what the doctors told us. But miracles do happen, I guess." She forces a smile for Heather's sake, and my heart breaks for Mrs. Bailey. This must have been a shock for her, learning her husband fathered a child outside their marriage. Something it sounds like she may have wanted for herself but never had.

Heather gives me another weak smile, and everyone is awkward all over again. I can't get a read on this woman. "So, anyway. I'm here, and I'm going to be staying with Jeanette, so I'll be able to take her home from here and take care of things."

"Oh, wow. Okay then. Are you sure? I don't mind helping out." I guess I'm being dismissed. My knight duties are over. I have mixed emotions about that.

"Yes, Noah. You should go to work or whatever else you had planned for today," Mrs. Bailey says. I study her closely, making sure it's what she really wants, and it seems like it is. "I'm sure I'm in good hands with Heather. You go on." She shoos at me to leave, and I can take a hint.

"Okay, fine. I know when I'm not wanted." I feign hurt and clutch at my chest in mock pain. That gets a laugh out of both. "Call me if you need anything, alright?"

"I will. Thank you, Noah." Mrs. Bailey's smile is genuine and aims straight for my soul. It's almost as though since I saved her life, we're connected somehow. Bound by some cosmic force. It's a strange feeling.

"It was nice to meet you, Noah." Heather's smile differs from Mrs. Bailey's, but I couldn't say how. But then, I haven't saved Heather's life, so we don't have any connection whatsoever. I shouldn't expect anything supernatural.

"You too," I say with a slight wave as I exit the room.

I don't make it ten feet before Neil is sidling up to me and walking alongside, the aura of conspiracy shrouding him.

"So, what do you think of the interloper?" He's holding a hand up to his mouth but projecting with a stage whisper. "Do you think she's legit?"

I eye him sideways, "I guess so. Mrs. Bailey thinks she is, so I can't disagree with her judgment. She would know better than anyone what her late husband was capable of, right?" I'm not going to argue with Mrs. Bailey. If she thinks Heather is who she says she is, who am I to disagree with that? I barely know either of them, least of all, Heather.

He lets out a long dramatic breath. "I guess. I don't know. Something is rotten in the state of Denmark."

"Well, it's a good thing we don't live in Denmark, then." I slap his shoulder as I veer off to the exit doors. "Take care, Neil."

He waves and watches me for a few seconds before returning to work. I wonder what that was all about. He sure seems awfully interested in the relationship between Heather and the Baileys for some reason. Other than the plain awkwardness of the situation, I didn't get any bad vibes from her. She seems sincerely interested in caring for Mrs. Bailey, and far be it from me to interfere with anyone's family business.

So, outside of selling Mrs. Bailey's cars, there isn't much need for me to be involved anymore. The thought tugs at my heartstrings. I was getting used to that feeling of being needed. There really isn't anything like it. But then I remember being with Chelsie last night, and that kind of being needed is much more my speed. I wouldn't mind getting used to that kind. Not at all.

Chapter 31

Deep End

Chelsie

I'm staring at Noah from across my desk with my jaw dropped open. "She's Wayne's what?" I can't believe this. There's no way this Heather person is Wayne's kid. Surely Mrs. Bailey would have said something about her by now if she knew. And how could she not know? She and Wayne were so in love with each other. I can't believe he would do something like that to her.

"She says she's his daughter, and her whole life, she thought someone else was her real dad." The more I think about that, the more it must really suck to have that information dropped on you when a parent dies. "It wasn't until he died recently that her mother told her the truth. Maybe Wayne didn't even know about it. I don't know."

I nod. That might be the case. I don't want to believe Wayne was the sort of person that would abandon a child like that. The tiny hairs on the back of my neck prickle at the entire story as though my spidey senses are sending up an alert. I don't like this. I can't say why exactly, but something just feels off.

"I don't believe it," I say, getting up from my desk and brushing past Noah to close the blinds at the window between my office and the garage. I make sure to exaggerate my movements around him, giving him all the best angles to view. Until now, the only thing on my mind is how amazing last night was between us. I can't push him or his body out of my mind. This news, however, might be the only thing that could distract me from that.

"I didn't think you would, to be honest. But it is what it is." He smirks, wraps his arms around my waist, and pulls me onto his lap. His rough hands on my bare arms cause a fire to instantly ignite inside me, and I can't stop myself from taking his mouth with mine until we both need to pull apart forcefully. Hands had started searching and grabbing and feeling way too good for the middle of a workday and the middle of my office.

"I hate that saying," I smile up at him, rubbing

his nose playfully with mine. It's hard to think seriously when I only want to rip his clothes off right here and now. I do hate that saying, though. It's so apathetic.

"Only you could smile while saying you hate something and make it sexy." He laughs but then nips on my bottom lip sending a spike of desire through me that makes me squirm.

"Oh, I can make everything I say sound sexy," I say, turning the heat up in my voice that much more. Leaning in to brush my lips against the shell of his ear, I purr, "I'll have a double cheeseburger...and fries...."

"Fuck, woman," His tone is husky and full of grit as he pulls me into a kiss that could definitely lead to something else if we let it. I glance up to check if my office door has a lock, and it doesn't look like it does. I need to change that.

"That's the idea." This is too much fun.

"Okay, I need to work." He stands up quickly, basically throwing me off his lap in his hurry to separate himself from me. I like that I have this strong effect on him, but eesh, it's a good thing I can balance on high heels like a pro.

"Fine. Get out of my office," I laugh, enjoying his uncomfortableness too much. "I'll see what I can dig up in Wayne's file. Maybe there's a mention of a beneficiary somewhere we all missed."

"Good idea." He hesitates in the doorway with a

look that completely undresses me. I can almost feel my clothes coming off piece by piece with that gaze, and damn, I don't mind him being hungry for me at all. He just shakes his head and growls, "Fuuuuuuck." And he's gone.

I drop into my desk chair and let out a long frustrated breath. Working with Noah is going to be a lot harder than I thought. Maybe Normandy is correct, and it's a bad idea to work with someone you're involved with. It's definitely a distraction. And that right there is the understatement of the century. After the emotional explosion of last night, I think I'm too far gone with Noah to back out now. I'm stuck. In the best possible way, I'm stuck with him.

Seven years ago, when he devastated me beyond what I thought could ever be repaired, I swore to myself I wouldn't let myself be hurt like that again. I never in my wildest dreams could have imagined the guy that forced me to build the walls around my heart in the first place, and in such a public and dramatic fashion, would also be the one that tears them down. Nobody would have my heart so entirely without knowing for sure it was returned. And here we are now, not only repairing that hurt but building another bridge to each other, more substantial and secure than anything I've ever known.

"And where did you float off to?" Normandy's words cut through my daydream about Noah, surprising me. She stands in the doorway to my office, rubbing her slowly burgeoning pregnant belly, probably without thinking about it. It seems like something that's a habit.

"Huh? Oh, sorry. I'm just exhausted today. It was another late night with Mrs. Bailey at the hospital."

"Oh, no, what happened? Is she okay?" She steps in and sits in a chair across from me. I explain the previous night's events with Mrs. Bailey and Noah's heroics, carefully dancing around the details of the rest of our evening together. The last thing I need is another lecture from her about the dangers of getting involved with an employee.

"Noah said she's going to be fine, but when he went to see her today, there was a woman there claiming to be Wayne's daughter. Can you believe that? Did you know he had a child?"

"What? No way. That can't be right." A crease deepens between her brows. "I would have seen something in his insurance files about it. But then again, maybe not since his child would have been grown up, and his wife was still alive. There's no reason to list adult children on anything, really."

"I hadn't thought of that. Do you still have Wayne's file? Maybe I should go through it again and see if I can find anything." Suddenly, I'm determined to get to the bottom of this. I don't know what's going on with this Heather person, but it seems suspicious she just showed up out of the blue like this.

"I'll find the file and bring it to you. It might be in my office at home, but I'll take a gander and let you know." She pauses and gives me a curious look, raising a pale eyebrow at me. "You really have taken a shine to Mrs. Bailey, haven't you? Spending a lot of time over there and going above and beyond the call of duty with all the hospital and medical emergencies. Not to mention babysitting her cats for her while she's gone. What's going on with that?" The way she asks this makes it sound like this is out of my character to do something nice for someone, and I'm kind of offended.

"Why is it so hard for you to believe I would do something kind for someone else? Do you think so little of me?" I can't control the hurt and anger in my words, which are much sharper than I intended. I think. Maybe I do want to hurt back, I don't know. Normandy and I didn't grow up together, so we're not used to spending time together. We're still brand new in this working together thing and dealing with each other at all. "You may think I'm a selfish brat because I'm younger than you, but you don't know me, Norm. You don't know who I am."

She jerks back as though I've struck her, surprised I would lash out at her like that. My reaction now does seem disproportionate to her question, but I didn't know what else to say. Part of me is proud to stand up for myself. I don't always do that with Normandy. Another part is sorry for my words. I don't apologize but hold my ground stubbornly. As my mom says, *'If you can't stand by your own words, shut up.'*

Normandy studies me and nods, and I'd swear I see approval in her eyes. I wasn't looking for that, but it's encouraging to see. "You're right. I'm sorry. I didn't mean to insinuate you're not a kind person. Of course, you are." She turns to the door to leave. "I've never seen you this way, so it's a new side to you that I'm discovering. I like it." She gives me a wide smile before leaving my office.

There are many sides to me that a lot of people haven't seen yet. That just makes me human.

Chapter 32

All on My Mind

Noah

Suspicion isn't in my nature, but I can understand why Chelsie would be suspicious of Wayne's daughter Heather popping up out of the blue. If I'm honest, it is strange, but if I'm even more honest with myself, I'm glad to have someone else responsible for Mrs. Bailey. That makes me sound like a horrible person, but I didn't sign up to be anybody's Knight in Shining Armor. And my nerves are still on edge from saving Mrs. Bailey yesterday. I don't know how long that's going to last, but hopefully, it will go away soon. While last night with Chelsie was terrific, it didn't keep my nightmares of the earlier events at bay. I'm not sure what could since it's seared into my mind.

"Hey stranger," Chelsie purrs from behind, her arms wrapping around my waist. Luckily, we're in the supply room where nobody can find us. Still, it's bold of her to be affectionate here while Normandy is around.

I turn in her arms to face her. "Hey yourself." I kiss the top of her head as she leans into my chest. "Do you hug strangers a lot? Should I be worried?"

"Only if they're handsome," she chuckles. "And you, sir, are extremely handsome."

I can feel my face flush at the compliment. I'm not used to getting those, or at least such blatant ones. If I get anything, it's typically just an extended gaze of admiration, but even then, I don't usually pay attention. I like how open Chelsie is. It's refreshing.

"Well, then, it's okay. Hug away." We sway a little as we hold each other, her hands slowly running up and down my back and mine doing the same with hers. It's innocent until I take a finger and trace it along the length of her spine, making her shiver.

She tilts her head up to me, her eyes closed, and her long lashes fanned. Her lips are so inviting I can't resist leaning in to brush mine against hers, tasting them as my tongue strokes hers. Her hot breath against my mouth isn't enough. I want it on my neck, on my chest, everywhere. What starts out tame starts to build in intensity.

I have no thought of anything but Chelsie right here, and right now, with her body pressed against me and her lips on mine. My hands reach under her blouse and skim across her bare skin. Just the feel of her under my fingers drives me insane. I'm starting to get overwhelmed by her taste, perfume, and touch. It's almost too much. But it's not enough either. I walk her back into the shelves behind her, pressing against her as she grinds into me.

"Chelsie. I need you," I groan into her ear, my voice barely a whisper since she's stolen the air from my lungs. She arches into me in response, fingers raking through my hair, and then she grabs it in fistfuls to pull our kiss deeper. I need to be inside her now. The desire to hike up her skirt and take her right here is so overpowering I start to lean down to find the bottom of her hem.

"Chelsie?" A female voice questions from behind. Normandy. *Fuck.* This is not good. *Fuck. Fuck. Fuck.*

I freeze, and Chelsie slides out from under my arm. I'm not about to turn to face her sister with a raging erection. This is bad enough; thank you very much. *Shit. I'm about to be fired.*

"What's up, Norm?" Chelsie's tone is professional and calm as if she was not just dry humping my leg or kissing me like it was about to be banned forever.

Her question is met with silence, and I have the awkward feeling Normandy and Chelsie are having a staring contest. Showdown at the OK Corral style. I can't keep my back turned. The two of us are in this together, whatever this is, and I need to face it with her.

When I finally face Normandy, I see I am right; they are caught in an intense but silent war. I clear my throat in an effort to break them out of it as subtly as possible, but I'm not about to speak first and interrupt them. This is clearly a sister or family thing, and I have no business getting in the middle.

"Is that Wayne's file?" Chelsie holds a hand out to take the folder Normandy is holding. It takes a minute, but Normandy obliges and gives it to her.

"Yes," she says stiffly, careful to keep her eyes on Chelsie and not in my direction. Shit. That can't be good if she won't look at me.

"Thank you." There is a power struggle of some kind going on here, and I'm right in the fucking middle of it. "Is there anything else?" Chelsie raises a single brow in challenge.

Normandy finally turns my way, her gaze piercing through me. There's judgment going on here that I don't understand, but I don't react. I just take it. If I have to, I'll stand up for myself and Chelsie, but they need to sort out whatever that energy is about. But if Normandy thinks I'm going to back down or stop seeing Chelsie, she's got another thing coming. That is not happening.

She must recognize the determination in my stance since she shakes her head at Cheslie in answer to her question.

"I'm going to have our lawyers draw up some sort of liability release for you two to sign for whatever this..." she waves at the two of us, "...is. Okay? I'm really not trying to be the bad guy here. I'm trying to be practical."

"Sure," I say with a nod, and Chelsie nods too.

Normandy stares at us for a long moment, then leaves without another word. Once the door shuts behind her, both Chelsie and I let out long sighs of relief.

"Wow, I thought that was going to go so much worse than it did," Chelsie lets out a small laugh.

"Worse than that?" I scoff. Other than yelling at each other, I don't know how it could have been much worse. Sometimes silence is worse than aggression.

"Yeah, I thought for sure she'd try to fire you or something."

"Whoa. Fire me? Really? That bad?" It had crossed my mind as a possibility but not a truly practical one. Maybe I did just dodge a bullet I didn't even know was heading my way.

"Norm was fairly adamant about the no dating thing," she shrugs. "I guess she's getting over it."

"Getting over it?" Now she's taking this a little too lightly. Especially if I could have really been fired. "Chels, getting fired isn't an option for me. I'd rather not have to find another job again so soon."

She steps up to me and places her palms flat on my chest, tilting her face up to me with a smile. She's luminescent when she smiles like that at me. "I wouldn't let that happen, Noah. Don't worry."

I examine her closely and see that she means it. Whether she has that kind of power here or not, I don't know. I assume the sisters each own fifty percent of the company, but I don't know that for sure. All I can do is trust that she's right. And as I lose myself in her warm brown eyes, I'd believe anything she said right now.

Chapter 33

Trouble's Coming

Chelsie

After the faceoff with Normandy, I also need space to gather my bearings. I force myself to go back to my office and away from the temptation of Noah so I can go through Wayne's files. That was intense. While we weren't close growing up since we lived in different households, we've started to make a real sisterly connection ever since our dad died. That relationship was tested when Normandy walked in on Noah and me in the supply room. The fact she's agreed to some kind of legal release is perhaps proof she might be giving in to my way of things when it comes to Noah.

Grabbing a fresh cup of coffee, I close myself in my office to review Wayne's employee records. If there's anything to be found, I'm determined to find it. I have a terrible feeling about Heather, and I need to figure out why, considering I haven't even met the woman yet.

An hour and a half later, my eyes are crossing from going through every piece of paper in his file. Wayne had been with Mischief Motors since my dad started the company years ago, so there's a lot of documents. And there is nothing here about any children or other beneficiaries outside of Jeanette. This just adds to my unease about this random woman suddenly in Mrs. Bailey's life. With nothing in the file to go on, I run a quick internet search. I check the usual social media sites, and while there are several Heather Cunninghams, none look like Noah described or were in the same age range. The search is fruitless. I'm going to have to go and see for myself.

I check my watch, and it's about time to leave, so now is as good a time as any. Before I go, however, an idea strikes me. Normandy's office door is open, so I knock lightly before stepping in. She glances up from her laptop but continues typing away.

"What's up?" Her tone is normal. Not a hint that she walked in on a hot and heavy make-out session between an employee and me.

"I need a favor."

"Go on..." Now there's suspicion in her tone, which I can deal with.

"Any chance you could have Taylor check into this Heather Cunningham?" Taylor is the head of her and her husband's security team, and he can find out just about anything about anyone. If Heather Cunningham has something to hide, he'll find it.

"Already on it," she says, still not taking a break from typing. "As soon as you mentioned her, I gave her info to Taylor. I should have heard back from him on it by now, actually."

"Oh wow. Why'd you do that?" I'm not complaining, but I'm curious as to why she did it.

"Same as why you're probably asking. I don't like it." She shrugs one shoulder. "Just a feeling."

"Huh. Okay, well, cool. Thanks." I start backing out of the office. "I'm going to head over to Mrs. Bailey's to check things out in person. Let me know when you hear back from Taylor, okay?"

"Will do." Still with the typing and not looking up. I'm unsure what to make of her response, but I let it all go. I can deal with Normandy any time. Right now, I need to focus on Mrs. Bailey.

When I told Noah I would check on Mrs. Bailey and Heather, he told me I was overreacting and should let it be. I can't do that. There's an alarm deep in my bones that is screaming red alert. I asked him to join me, but he has plans with his friend River, so I'm on this mission alone. I don't call ahead since somehow, I think the element of surprise will expose Heather, but even I know it's a foolish notion.

I was surprised to learn earlier that Mrs. Bailey was sent home so soon after her incident yesterday, but I'm no doctor, so I don't question it. Maybe it wasn't all that serious. Pulling up to the house, I notice a car with a California license plate. That must be Heather's car. As I think about it, I don't know anything about this woman other than her name and story. I start to question my doubt of her as I think about her driving all the way from California to be here. You don't come all this way on a guess about your parentage. She must be sure about Wayne being her father.

As I step onto the front porch, the front door opens, and a tall blonde woman frowns at me from behind the screen door. The scowl on her face could scare away random visitors, but I'm not a door-to-door salesperson. I'm a friend.

"Who are you?" she barks, defiantly crossing her arms over her chest. Those red alerts in my bones are now going into frenzied haywire.

"You must be Heather," I say, forcing a smile I don't feel. "I'm Chelsie Blake. I'm a friend of Mrs. Bailey...Jeanette."

No response, just a continued glare. Her silence demanding a further explanation of my visit. What the hell?

"I came to check on her after what happened yesterday." I shift to peer into the house behind her, but it's dark with no lights visible. And it's eerily quiet. "Can I see her?" The question is plain enough, but there's an edge to expressing to her I'm not going anywhere until I do.

Her demeanor morphs into that of a tired caregiver, full of sympathy, and the change is so drastic it almost makes me dizzy.

"I'm so sorry; she's resting right now. Maybe you can come by another day?" The sweetness in her new tone is saccharine and jarring. There's also an undercurrent of rage vibrating through her for some reason. "You should call first next time...to make sure she's able to receive you." Her face pinches into a regretful smile I know she's putting on for me. I don't believe this woman has a sympathetic bone in her body.

I stare at her for a long minute, trying to gauge her and her shift in mood. There's nothing I can do about anything. I'm not family. I'm barely a friend. I have no standing other than I care what happens to Mrs. Bailey. I can't break the feeling that I need to burst through the door and see with my own eyes she's okay. If Mrs. Bailey is resting, though, the last thing I want to do is disturb her.

This is crazy. I'm overreacting and seeing things that aren't there. Maybe Noah is right, and I should give this woman the benefit of the doubt. She did come a long way to be here and has been through her own turmoil regarding her father's status. She could just be emotionally exhausted, which would be understandable. Even though it goes against every particle of my being, I nod.

"I'll call tomorrow and maybe stop by?"

"Sure," she answers harshly and steps back, shutting the door.

I stare at the closed door for a moment, and a chill washes over me so cold I shiver. I was almost willing to give her the benefit of the doubt, but that was rude. No amount of exhaustion can excuse her erratic behavior in the last five minutes. I could try to rationalize it, but even I wouldn't believe me. There is something off about this woman, and now I'm more determined than ever to find out what it is. I hope Taylor can come through with information to explain this woman's presence here because the one she gave isn't ringing true for me.

Chapter 34

Rage or Romance

Noah

My buddy River has been hounding me to meet him for a couple of beers, so I had made plans for it tonight. I hadn't planned on my world blowing up or nabbing a girlfriend in the meantime, but I haven't seen or talked to him since the night at the Murderous Crows show, so we have some catching up to do. We hit the Island for the typical pizza and hockey, and I'm reminded of Chelsie getting a little too tipsy the last time I was here. I can't hold back the smile as I remember her face the next morning when she realized what had happened.

"You can't be that happy to be here. We're playing Tampa Bay," River jokes as he comes up beside me in line for pizza. "Unless you're a glutton for punishment."

"Ah, but I am. That's why I'm a hockey fan at all." We grab our food and find a table on the enclosed patio where we can see the giant screen easily.

I bring him up to speed on all the events that have happened since the last time I saw him, including my saving Mrs. Bailey and Chelsie and I becoming an item. Heather's new insertion into Mrs. Bailey's life. It's a bit much to digest at once.

"Man, it's only been a couple of weeks since I saw you. If that. What the hell?" He scoffs in disbelief. "And don't you have a phone? Your fingers aren't broken." He grabs at my hand and pretends to examine my fingers. "You could have texted me or something. Geez. Thanks a lot."

"Sorry," I say, shrugging. "As you've heard, I've been a little busy."

"So, what do you think about this new lady? Do you think she's legit?" He takes a bite of his pizza. "It sounds like Chelsie disagrees with you."

I consider that for a second but dismiss it at once. "I think she's legit. Not only did she seem honest, but Mrs. Bailey accepted her at face value. I don't think she would have done that if she didn't believe it. She may be old, but she's not dumb or gullible. Quite the opposite. She's too clever herself to be tricked." I realize I'm getting irritated. I think I'm just sick of talking about the whole situation.

He runs a hand through his long blonde hair. "Alright, chill. You know what you're talking about. I'm just an innocent bystander here."

He drops the subject, and we watch the rest of the hockey game without another word about Mrs. Bailey, Heather, or Chelsie mentioned. And for a couple of seconds, I can breathe. I didn't realize how high-strung I had gotten until I unwound. River is right. It is a lot to deal with in such a short time.

The following day, Chelsie and I meet with the assessor who is giving us a valuation of Mrs. Bailey's car collection. Surprisingly, Normandy and her husband, famous billionaire Brandon Carmichael join the meeting. He's nice enough and shakes my hand when we are introduced. With him being here, I start to worry the cost of these cars may just have skyrocketed. That could outprice potential buyers and leave Mrs. Bailey with a long waiting game ahead of her until someone with deep enough pockets showed interest.

The assessor is an older man with a full head of steel gray hair and a crooked smile. He fidgets nervously once he meets Brandon, not expecting him today either. But he carries on the meeting as scheduled, sitting at the head of the table with Chelsie next to me and Brandon and Normandy seated across from us.

"I've looked at all the photos and read all the specifications and notes you've put together. Thank you, Noah and Chelsie, for creating quite a portfolio to work with." He nods in appreciation. "I've taken the liberty to value each car individually...."

"Would it be possible to get an appraisal for the whole lot?" Brandon interrupts, but in a friendly way, as though he just wants to help get to the point. I admire the skill that took. But he didn't become a billionaire by waiting for things to happen.

"The entire lot as one transaction?" The assessor asks, unsure he heard the question correctly. Someone buying the entire collection wasn't something he considered.

"Are you thinking of buying the collection?" I ask, impressed if he is. It won't be cheap by any means.

Brandon glances at his wife but then smiles as though he's getting away with something he shouldn't. "Yes. Depending on the price, I might just do that. Of course, I'd be willing to negotiate with Mischief Motors if any cars were on their shopping list." He defers to Chelsie and Normandy, who glance at each other, then at Brandon, stunned at this development.

"What do you mean you might buy the whole lot of cars?" Normandy is incredulous, and it's suddenly very awkward in this conference room as we all witness the beginning of a marital spat. "I think we probably should have discussed that. Where exactly would we put ten classic cars? We don't have a garage that big."

The hard swallow Brandon takes is audible from across the table. He's gone a little pale too. I don't blame him. Both Chelsie and Normandy have a whole 'if looks could kill' vibe going on that intimidates me too.

"Why do you think I'm here if not to buy the cars?" he scoffs, as though it's obvious. I thought he was here perhaps to bankroll any of Normandy's purchases, not make any of his own, let alone the whole shebang.

"I thought you were here for support." Normandy is still not happy with this turn of events but softening some.

"I'm *being* supportive. I've already said Mischief can have first dibs on the cars."

Chelsie and I, and even the appraiser, watch the two as though they're playing a tennis match. The back and forth is rather entertaining. I have the urge to reach under the table and grab Chelsie's hand but stop myself. Things are tense enough in the room.

There's a break in their discussion, and Normandy crosses her arms with a defeated huff. She's apparently lost the argument.

"Right. So, to value the entire collection," The assessor continues without skipping a beat, "including all ten cars, would be $1.32 million, give or take. I have a few questions about aftermarket modifications I noticed that were not in the reports I received. But the overall price wouldn't change much either way."

Chelsie and I stare at each other in complete shock, our eyebrows raised, and jaws dropped. Normandy glares at Brandon, who is nodding but appears deep in thought. Maybe he's weighing how much he really enjoys being married, or at least I hope he is because his wife does not look happy.

"Mrs. Bailey is going to freak out." Chelsie brings us back down to Earth and reminds us of who this sale will benefit. She turns to me with a huge smile lighting up her face. "I can't wait to tell her."

As soon as she says those words, her smile falters, and her face falls. Her brow furrows, and a deep crease forms on her forehead as she worries about something.

"What's the matter?" I ask, placing a hand on her arm automatically in concern. That was a sudden shift in mood.

"I don't want to tell her," she mutters, glancing at

Normandy, and they share an unreadable look. "Not until we know Heather is who she says she is."

That makes me laugh. She absolutely needs to let that entire situation go. It's starting to get out of hand. "Chelsie, come on. That's Mrs. Bailey's business, not ours. She's an adult who can take care of herself. We need to let her do that."

"How can you say that?" Chelsie is getting angry now, too. "You, of all people, should know how vulnerable she is since you had to bring her back from the freaking dead the other day."

My face reddens at the mention of the other night. I didn't do it for praise in front of people, especially Chelsie's family. "That just makes her old, Chelsie, not stupid. If she wants to claim a relationship with Heather Cunningham, she has every right to do that." I can't believe I'm arguing with her like this in front of other people. This is not how I operate. "Let's talk about this later." I shift uncomfortably in my seat and avoid the gazes of everyone else in the room, which are firmly planted on the spectacle of the two of us fighting. Public displays of affection, for the most part, I'm okay with that. Public fights? No. Not my style at all.

"Noah, we have a responsibility to Mrs. Bailey..." she starts, but I don't want to keep discussing this. And, she's wrong.

"No. We don't. End of argument. We aren't

responsible for her, and we never were. We just happened to be around when she needed us."

Chelsie leans away, pulling her arm out from under my hand, and glares daggers at me. Her eyes narrow, and she studies me like she's seeing me for the first time. I do not like how she's scrutinizing me all of a sudden. Is she really reacting like this just because I disagree with her?

"Oh. Okay. Noah has spoken everybody. That means that's the end of the argument. We can move on with our lives now. Thank God." The sarcasm drips from her words like venom, and I can feel my face flush even deeper, but this time it's more anger than embarrassment.

"Chelsie, that's not fair," I say, trying to keep my voice steady, but it's getting damned hard.

"Not fair?" she scoffs. "Noah, you can't tell me who I can or can't feel responsible for or when an argument is over. That's not how relationships work. That's not how this is going to work between us. I should have known you couldn't care about anyone but yourself or whatever everyone else thinks. That's what's always been most important to you."

There it is. Everything finally swung around to us as I knew it would. Of course, my asshole past makes a special appearance too. Glad she didn't forget to drag that back up conveniently. Her words hit me straight in the chest like a blow. I think something in me expected this to be the outcome once I saw we disagreed on Heather's involvement with Mrs. Bailey, but I hoped Chelsie would see reason. I guess that's not going to happen after all.

I stare into Chelsie's brown eyes that now look at me with so much disappointment and indignation I almost don't recognize her. It's not a look I ever wanted to see from her. Not directed at me. This can't be happening. She's slipping through my fingers, but I have no idea how to catch her. I can't apologize for how I truly feel, and I'm not going to. And that kills me because I know not apologizing will lose me the woman I've been falling desperately in love with.

Am I doing the right thing? Should I apologize, even though I disagree? I can't bring myself to do it. It's wrong. On the same token, I wouldn't want Chelsie to apologize or yield for anything she believed in, either. Like now. I just didn't think this issue was the life-or-death subject for our relationship that it has become. I can see in her eyes this chasm between us is quickly becoming an ocean so vast and deep that neither of us can cross it. It's not even a slow death. It's a suicide bomb we're both wielding, and neither of us can or will give way.

After a few moments more of studying Chelsie one last time, I realize she's not seeing *me*. She doesn't *want* to see me. I nod my understanding to her and push my chair back loudly as I stand.

"Since I'm not needed here, let me know if I can

assist with whatever you decide," I say, nodding at everyone but Chelsie, and I hurry out of the office, slamming the door behind me.

If my thoughts or feelings about anything don't count or matter, I don't need to be involved with Mischief Motors or Chelsie.

Fuck this.

Chapter 35

Fools Gold

Chelsie

After Noah storms out of the meeting, I'm unsure what to do with myself. I want to go after him and fix this, but at the same time, I don't. He's being so coldhearted about Mrs. Bailey all of a sudden, I don't know what's gotten into him. The other day he said we basically adopted her, and now he's washed his hands of her entirely since Heather came into the picture. It doesn't make any sense to me.

We finish the meeting with Brandon officially wanting to put in an offer to Mrs. Bailey for $1.3 million, which I'll take to her this afternoon.

Normandy and I will go through the cars more closely and see if there are any we want specifically for Mischief. We'll also ask to lease Mrs. Bailey's garage from her to keep the cars for now. I'm hopeful it's a good enough offer for her. I don't think she knew she was sitting on such a gold mine.

Nothing is said by anyone about Noah or our argument, thank God. I wouldn't know what to say if they did. I'm still shocked by the whole thing and so hurt. I never imagined Noah could be so distant and cold, even with our history. I suppose, like I said, I should have known he was so uncaring. Tigers can't change their stripes, or whatever that saying is. I guess Noah can't change either. God, I'd hoped he was different.

I spend the rest of the morning preparing the offer for Mrs. Bailey and avoiding Noah like the plague. I only saw him once in the lunchroom, but he left as soon as I entered, leaving his coffee brewing in the machine. I was half tempted to take it to him once it finished but I thought better of it and took great joy in dumping it down the sink. Okay, not great joy. Mild satisfaction.

As I'm about to leave, I run into Normandy, heading out at the same time.

"You doing okay?" She puts an arm around my shoulders. It's odd for her to be affectionate with me, but it's welcome. I could use a sister right now.

Hot tears are waiting to just let loose, but I keep

them at bay. "I'll be fine, thanks for asking." I'm waiting for the *'I told you so,'* which I'm sure is right on the tip of her tongue, but it doesn't come.

"How about you?" I'm not the only one who had a relationship meltdown this morning, but she lives with her adversary. I noticed Brandon didn't stick around too long after the meeting and was in a hurry to leave. Can't say I blame him. Normandy is not someone you want to piss off.

"I'll be fine. We'll be fine." She sighs. "I was surprised by his buying all the cars since we didn't talk about it. But of course, he did it to help us, not for selfish reasons. It just took me a little while to figure that out. I should have known that, so that's on me. I've got some apologizing to do when I get home."

"Well, you have fun with that," I laugh. "Do you want a ride home? I don't mind going out of the way."

She stops abruptly and pulls her arm off my shoulders. "Crap. I just remembered something I forgot to send to Sorah, our accountant, for this quarter's taxes. Pregnancy brain for the win. Thanks for the offer, but I need to stay a bit longer. Tell Mrs. Bailey congratulations from me, okay?"

I leave her and head to my car. As I drive through the lot, I catch Noah watching me from the doorway of the main garage with no expression whatsoever. Everything in me wants to stop the car and run into his arms, but that stern expression on his face tells me that would be foolish. But then, I am usually a fool. Just not at this moment.

This time when I get to Mrs. Bailey's house and declare my intentions for the visit, Heather welcomes me in with open arms. As I knew she would. When I see Mrs. Bailey in her recliner, she doesn't appear at all like herself. Her hair hasn't been brushed, and her clothes are wrinkled as though she's been wearing them for days. The shadows under her bloodshot eyes clearly indicate she's not been resting. She's a shell of the person she was just a few days ago. I somehow suppress the gasp that wants to escape when I see her.

She gives me the weakest smile I've ever seen, and I know I'm looking into the eyes of someone who has given up. The guilt that racks through me at not insisting I see her last time I was here is overwhelming. It's my fault she's like this.

I plaster on a smile and move to Mrs. Bailey's side, taking her hand into mine. "How are you doing? Are you feeling okay?" Her fingers are cold and frail, and there's no strength when she attempts to squeeze mine in response.

"I'm just tired. I haven't been sleeping well." This poor woman. Her voice is even tired.

"What's been going on with your sleep? Is there anything I can do?"

Heather pipes in, a complaint at the ready. "She needs a new couch. I'm sure it's not very comfortable for her, it's so old. Definitely not good enough to sleep on."

I turn on her, "Why is she sleeping on the couch? She has a perfectly good bed?"

"Heather wouldn't fit on the couch, she's too tall, so I gave her my bed. It's not a problem," Mrs. Bailey explains. Thoughts of Noah and I, together on the blankets just feet away, try to invade my thoughts, but I'm too mad about this new situation to think about being mad about the other one.

"Yeah, but you just got out of the hospital. You need your rest to recover." I glare over my shoulder at Heather. "She can get a hotel room. This city does have over a hundred and fifty thousand of them."

She seems offended at this suggestion, and a hand flies to her throat as if shocked. "I didn't drive all this way to stay at a sterile hotel."

I shift to face her head-on. "Why are you here exactly? Your father is gone. If Wayne was, in fact, your father at all. It doesn't seem like there's any real purpose to your visit." I am not in the mood for this today. Not after what I went through with Noah earlier. I know something is off with this chick, and I may just have ruined the best thing in my life because of that belief.

My confrontation is met now with anger; she's no longer playing coy. She stands and puts her fists on her hips, trying to intimidate me with her height. I stand, my three-inch heels getting me eye to eye with her. She was not expecting me to stand up for myself since I backed down yesterday and left when she told me to. *Not today, lady. Not today.*

She must realize her situation as Mrs. Bailey and me both stare her down, waiting for her answer. Her demeanor switches abruptly, and tears start streaming down her cheeks. I was not expecting that at all. I thought for sure she was going to throw down and fight me or something. Tears weren't even on my radar with her.

"I just came here to learn about my real father since I knew nothing about him. I wanted to get an idea of what kind of man he was and find out why he would abandon my mother and me like he did." She looks around and finds a box of tissue, taking one to wipe the mascara from under her eyes. My heart tugs at me to ease up on her and makes me question my first impression of her. Maybe she's not that bad and really is hurting after losing two fathers in as many months.

"I didn't mean to come off so harsh...." I start.

"Oh no. I don't blame you at all. I'd be suspicious

of me too. Don't worry." She laughs a little, still wiping her eyes.

"Well, if you're okay, how about I jump to the reason for my visit?" I ask, trying to lighten the mood. It was getting too heavy there for a second.

"Yes, please," Heather says excitedly, sitting on one end of the couch and patting the cushion next to her for me to sit, so I do.

I pull out the folder I brought with Brandon's offer and hand it over to Mrs. Bailey. I only have one other copy, which was going to be mine to read, but I hand it to Heather. Her eyes grow wide when she sees the dollar amounts, and I swear her lip twitches, almost a smile, but not quite.

"So, Normandy's husband, Brandon, would like to offer you $1.3 million for the complete collection of cars and would also like to temporarily lease the garage for storage at a rate of two thousand per month until they can find other arrangements." I glance at Mrs. Bailey, trying to gauge her reaction, but she's studiously reading the documents I gave her, reading glasses perched on her nose.

"Obviously, she'll accept," Heather says in her place. "Isn't that right, Jeanette? You'll take the money?" She practically shouts at Mrs. Bailey as though she's deaf. She is many things, but she is not hard of hearing. She then turns to me, as if in confidence, "She'll take it, I'm sure. It would be silly not to, right?"

I shrug since I don't know what Mrs. Bailey thinks about that kind of money. It's definitely a lot, and probably much more than she ever expected.

"I think I need to consider the offer for a while," Mrs. Bailey says, taking off her glasses and leaning back, obviously exhausted.

"Let me make some tea, and we can talk through it." Heather stands and makes her way into the kitchen.

Once she's out of the room, I arch a silent eyebrow at Mrs. Bailey in question. Something is bothering her, but she could just be tired. I need to know what she's thinking about everything.

Her only response is a long exhale, a slight shake of her head, and a dismissive wave. Yup, Mrs. Bailey has had enough of everyone's shit. I can't blame her. She's had a hell of a week.

I get up to use the restroom, and as I pass the kitchen, I see Heather, shoulders hunched over, texting furiously on her phone. I'm tempted to ask if everything is okay since she looks so intense, but I decide to leave her be. I don't want to interfere in her business on top of everybody else's I seem to be involved in.

When I return from the restroom, I find Heather pouring tea with a sweet smile and notice Mrs. Bailey's hair has been brushed. They also seem to be reconfiguring the sleeping arrangements.

"Well, no, Chelsie was right. You should sleep in

your own bed. You need better rest than I do. I can rough it for a few more days. It was rude of me to take it in the first place." Heather appears to be contrite, and again my heart tugs for her. This entire situation can't be easy for her.

We spend about another hour chatting about Wayne, and Mrs. Bailey perks up given a chance to talk about her late husband. Heather seems genuinely interested in learning about him, too, and that puts my mind at ease for the most part. I'm starting to feel horrible for ever doubting her. Even the cats have come out of hiding and are at least in the same room as us women.

I've been able to dodge any questions about Noah that Mrs. Bailey throws at me and deflect them to other things, but I think she's catching on that something might be wrong in that department. Little does she know the size of the apology I will need to come up with to make amends with him. If he'll even listen to me after the way I treated him today.

A sudden pounding on the front door makes us jump, and the cats scatter. I didn't hear a car pull up or footsteps on the porch. I peek out the front window on the way to answer it and see a police car in the drive, along with Noah's car. What the heck?

When I open the door, I first notice how pale Noah is. He's holding a folder with a Citadel Security logo, Taylor's company. *Oh no. My initial instincts were right.* Heather is trouble of some kind.

I step back to let him in and see that Heather isn't in the living room.

"She's running," I shout. "She must be going out the back." I head toward the kitchen to chase while Noah and the officer turn to cut her off. She looked athletic, but I doubt she's any match for Noah and the police. No matter my skills, running in heels is not recommended for a reason. By the time I make it out of the back kitchen door, the officer has Heather in handcuffs and is explaining her Miranda rights while escorting her to the patrol car. That was incredibly fast.

As I reach the front of the house, the officer is back, thanking Noah.

"That was one hell of a move, sliding across the hood like that to grab her. You should look into law enforcement if you're looking for a new job." He shakes his hand and pats him on the shoulder. "If you all could wait here, I have backup coming in just a few minutes that will need to interview everyone, but I need to get the suspect down to the station. This woman is wanted in a few states, so we'll have a hell of a time figuring out who gets her first. Officer Foley over there will wait for backup here." He points to another officer standing at the corner of the house, keeping a lookout. "Feds might come poking around too. Who knows."

I can see Heather through the patrol car window, glowering and mad at the world. She did this to herself and has no one else to blame. *Maybe you shouldn't prey on old ladies, bitch.*

"Thank you, officer." Noah nods, picks up the papers strewn across the yard, and then turns toward the house, avoiding me altogether.

"Noah...?" I don't know what I'm feeling at the moment. So much just happened, and I have no clue what's going on.

"I need to check on Mrs. Bailey," he says coldly, eyes trained on the house as he moves. He deliberately avoids looking at me, but I see more guilt than anything else. He's going to beat himself up over this now. Of course, he is. That's who Noah is. The knight in shining armor is feeling tarnished, and I don't know how to react to that.

His complete avoidance now hurts. But I guess that's how it's going to be now. *Perfect.*

Chapter 36

Glasgow

Noah

Looking Mrs. Bailey in the eye when I see her is one of the most challenging things I've ever done. Not only does she appear physically put through the wringer, but I could swear there is hurt in her pale eyes. Knowing what I know now, leaving her in the hospital and in Heather's care after that is something I don't think I'll ever forgive myself for, and I can't even bring myself to ask for it from her either. All I can do is make up for it in any way possible.

Sitting on the couch, I open the folder Normandy gave me from Taylor's security company and reorganize the pages that were disheveled after I gave chase. I jump right into it because I couldn't make small talk if I tried. My brain is racing too fast for minutiae.

"Heather Cunningham is actually Lauren Wagner, a con artist from Reno. She has a partner, Troy Winslow, who is on the run now. From what Taylor uncovered, Lauren saw the obituary for Wayne, saw where he worked, and made the connection to Brandon Carmichael. There might also be a connection to the vehicle appraiser, but they're still looking into that." I take a deep breath, trying to ignore the shakiness of the exhale. "Her pattern is to show up as a long-lost relative of the deceased, particularly to widows and widowers who have no other family, and persuade them to leave everything to her. Or, she'll petition probate courts to claim assets as a forgotten beneficiary. It's quite the racket she and her partner have got going. She's done this in several states." I glance up at Mrs. Bailey, afraid the next part might frighten her. "She also has been known to use violence to intimidate and get her way." I cringe inside, imagining all the things that could have gone wrong.

"She never...?" I lead the question, not wanting to come right out and ask if she was abusive.

"Oh no, honey," she replies, her expression softening. "Nothing like that."

I can't help but sigh. "Good."

"Well, I'm glad she was caught," Mrs. Bailey says. "But she wouldn't have gotten a penny from me. I've prepaid my funeral and everything, so my affairs are in order. Heather, Lauren, or whoever she is was never a part of that. And honestly, even if she was Wayne's daughter, she wasn't family. He never knew her. I'm ashamed I ever thought Wayne would have done that to me. I should have known better." She puts a hand to her heart, and a flash of grief crosses her features. "I can't believe I ever doubted him."

"You aren't the only one who was wrong about her, so don't feel too alone in that." I glance at Chelsie standing in the doorway, listening in, making sure not to meet her eyes. While yes, I was wrong about Heather, I might have been wrong about Chelsie too. How she treated me in the meeting in front of her family and a stranger isn't something I'll forget anytime soon. Despite my obvious errors in judgment, I didn't deserve that humiliation. Not unless she was looking to even the humiliation score between us. I place the folder on the coffee table and stand.

"You're not leaving, are you?" Mrs. Bailey asks, disappointment in her eyes.

"No. We all need to give statements to the police when they get here, which should be any minute. I'm just going to stretch my legs for a bit." I try to force a smile but I know I don't pull it off. I am not in a smiling mood, even though I did just catch an inheritance hijacker and fraud. It doesn't make me feel any better about anything. "I've still got adrenaline from the chase to work off."

I go out the back door to avoid interacting with or passing Chelsie; luckily, she doesn't follow me. The last thing I need is for her to come at me with the '*I told you so*' that I know is on my horizon. I could really do without that at the moment.

Making a circuit around the large garage out back, I let my mind wander and punish at the same time. How could I have been so wrong? So able to relinquish responsibility to a complete stranger, even Mrs. Bailey didn't know? Was I that anxious to run away from accountability? That desperate to hand everything over to somebody else to take care of? I was. And it makes me sick. To think that I put Mrs. Bailey in such danger makes me nauseous. I wouldn't have been able to live with myself if something had happened to her due to my idiocy.

When I emerge from the back of the garage, I notice two police cars pull in front of the house, so I make my way to them to give my statement. Not leaving the front yard, it takes about a half hour to tell the entire story as far as I know it. When we finish, I let them know Taylor's file is inside for them to use as they see fit.

"So, you really did jump over the car to catch the suspect?" One of the detectives asks. The exaggeration makes me cringe. "That's what Officer Coltraine told us when he called us in."

"No, I didn't jump a car," I say, rolling my eyes, my impatience getting the better of me. "I merely slid across one that was too close to the back of another. See?" I point to Chelsie's car right behind what I assume is Heather or Lauren's. "There wasn't a lot of room to run, so I... improvised."

I am not a hero in this. Far from it. And I don't want to go through the whole knight in tin foil armor bullshit again, either. My part in all of this is done.

I need to go. The adrenaline is still coursing through me with no sign of relenting any time soon. I turn to Chelsie, who is still in the doorway of the house, but watching us talk in the front yard intently.

"Tell Mrs. Bailey I'll check on her tomorrow," I call to her.

She doesn't say anything or even nod. She just stares at me with an unreadable expression on her face that is hard to see through the screen door to begin with. I'm sure it's not friendly anyway.

Great. So, we're not being cordial with each other or speaking whatsoever. Noted. I should find another job. Law enforcement? No way. Just the thought makes me shudder. If this is how you feel when you catch a suspect, it's definitely not for me because I just feel empty inside. And that's no way to live.

Working around Chelsie day in and day out is

going to be nearly impossible. Seeing her causes my heart to skip beats and my skin itch to feel hers against mine. Going through this every single day is a nightmare I can't imagine living through daily.

I had surprisingly found the woman of my dreams, someone I stupidly hurt and overlooked years ago, but she forgave me for that enough to want to be together. She showed me what real love looks like. It was the most remarkable thing ever to happen to me. Now we're staring down the barrel of a future where we are not together, where this love burning inside me goes unanswered. And I don't know what the fuck I'm doing. I don't know how to react or respond to anything. And I sure as hell don't have a single clue how to fix any of it.

Chapter 37

Lost It All

Chelsie

After the detectives leave, having asked every question known to man, Mrs. Bailey is drained of energy and downright weary. And since Heather/Lauren said she hasn't been sleeping in her own bed, it's no wonder she's so tired. The poor woman just got out of the hospital after a harrowing experience and was forced to sleep on an old lumpy couch. She deserves some rest. But of course, in true Mrs. Bailey style, she wants to talk about Noah and me. I can't think of a decent enough excuse not to either, so I'm going to have to. I remake us some tea, and we settle into opposite ends of the couch with our steaming mugs to chat.

"Tell me everything," she orders. Not beating around the bush or warming up to anything, just straight for the throat. And not even specific, so I'll need to start from the beginning.

"Are you sure? You could use some rest, no?" I can't believe she wants to talk about my problems after everything that's happened to her. "I don't want to bore you with my silly troubles."

"Nonsense. You should know by now I couldn't mind my own business even if I had a business to mind. Go ahead, start talking."

And I do. I tell her everything. Well, almost everything. I leave out the bits about making love for the first time on the floor right in front of us. While I'm sure she wouldn't care, I can't bring myself to get *that* open with her.

"So, what happened today when he was here?" She asks. "Did you two talk?"

I'm reminded of how Noah barely looked in my general direction the entire time he was here earlier, and my heart clenches just thinking about it. I wanted nothing more than to tell him how much I cared about him. That we're being silly, not talking to each other like the adults we are. I honestly love him and know we can move past all the hurt we're both going through. But my brain and mouth weren't cooperating with each other at all. In fact, they were arguing with each other too. Keeping me from saying or doing anything to resolve our issues.

"No," I finally say. "I couldn't bring myself to say anything to him. I think I was too shocked by everything he told us to compute what he was saying. Thoughts about us didn't even cross my mind until he was leaving. I was more concerned about you at the time."

"Oh, honey. You don't need to worry about me." She smiles over her mug at me. A pensive expression crosses her face. "I think our Noah is scared."

"Scared?" I love how she calls him 'our Noah.' "Why would you say that? What does he have to be afraid of?"

"You, of course." Not only is she still smiling, but she actually winks at me. She's definitely feeling better.

"Me? Why would I scare him?" The idea is preposterous.

"Maybe scared isn't the right word. Intimidated? Does that fit better? Try it on."

"Intimidated...." I think about it but I can't see how I could possibly intimidate anyone. "Nope. Sorry Mrs. B., but I am not a frightening person. At least I don't think I am."

"Look at it from his perspective for a minute. When he sees you, he's constantly reminded of a time when he deeply hurt you in the past that he didn't even remember. So, you just existing reminds him of his failures."

"Great. I'm a walking bad reminder." I can't help the small grunt of agreement that comes out.

"You know what I mean. I'm sure it's not all the time, but it has to be a thought of his at some point now and then."

"Okay, but how does that scare him?" I'm still not getting the point of this.

"You also stood up to him and were brave enough to disagree with him." She pauses, taking a sip of tea. "But I must tell you, I think you went about that wrong."

I nod my head. I know where she's going with this. "I know. I should have waited to talk to him privately about Heather, or Lauren. Can we just call her Heather? Once I hear a certain name, my brain rebels switching to another."

She laughs. "I'm the same way. Heather it is."

"Anyway. Yes, I probably should have talked to him outside of the meeting, and away from other people. But I can't imagine that would scare him off like this."

"You also have to consider where his head is at right now. I gave him my own scare, remember? Much bigger than yours too."

"This isn't a competition, you know," I smirk.

"Well, if you recall from our card games, I do like to win." She straightens her shoulders with pride. She is very good at cards, I'll have to give her that.

"You are a card shark." I consider that idea. Maybe his having to save Mrs. Bailey the way he did would have some sort of adverse effect on him. I hadn't thought of that, but I can see it now. "There was a change in him after that happened. It was subtle but definitely there. Do you think that's why he's been so sensitive about everything?"

She nods her head from side to side. "It could be. He's been through a lot in a short amount of time. And you need to remember one more thing."

"What's that?"

"Back to when he hurt you back in high school. Yes, it was a long time ago, but he did it, and he knows it. And now he's probably so scared to death he's going to do it again that he doesn't even realize he's done it again. Do you understand that maze of words?"

"I do." I reach across the couch and pat her knee. "Thank you."

"I didn't do anything but babble on."

"Oh, but you did." She doesn't realize how just having a calm conversation like this is clearing my head. I don't have Normandy threatening me with the potential legal action that can be taken against the company and me because I'm involved with Noah. I don't have Mackenzie poisoning my thoughts with what happened in high school. Mrs.

Bailey doesn't have those concerns. In fact, it was her who brought us together. Whether it was on purpose or not, I don't think she'll ever say, but I have a feeling she had a very purposeful hand in Noah and me becoming a couple. And now, she's our biggest cheerleader. I love that.

I don't believe in coincidence. I think everything happens for a reason. It can take a long fucking time to figure it out, but it eventually reveals itself. Sometimes that reason can even be that you're just really stupid and make bad choices. That might be the case here. History has proven that I am the consummate dumbass when it comes to love.

When we graduated high school, my best friend Mackenzie wrote a quote in my yearbook from a nineties movie we repeatedly watched about two women going to a high school reunion, "If we're not married by the time we're thirty, ask me again." I still laugh when I think about it. Who knows, the way my love life is going, I might just do that if I'm not married in five years.

It's been a few days since the Heather incident and arrest, and Mackenzie and I meet for Sunday brunch. We never do this, but she's of the opinion we're getting to a 'certain age' where brunch should be a regular thing. We're barely twenty-five. I think she's just looking for an excuse to drink champagne for breakfast.

"So, when did brunch become some sort of rite of passage?" I ask, taking a sip of my mimosa and pursing my lips as the cool acidity hits my mouth. "I never took you for a brunch type of person. You're all rock 'n roll, and anarchy and stuff. This seems way out of character for you."

She tugs on a long dark purple braid and frowns. "That's precisely the reason why we're here. We're disrupting the norm. Breaking the mold. They'd never expect a purple-haired, tattooed, boot-wearing, foul-mouthed woman here. Especially one with such superior intelligence. But, here I am." She spreads her arms wide in greeting to the other people in the restaurant who barely acknowledge us.

I'm not embarrassed. It takes a hell of a lot for Mac to embarrass me, but she sure does try. I've gotten used to her antics and have come to expect them, to be honest. This is tame for her. And she's not lying. She is super intelligent. She took every AP class and made every honor roll ever invented. Colleges and universities were begging to give her scholarships, but she turned them all down. Her love is music and the music business. I think she's insane, but she's a cool kind of crazy and a very loyal friend.

After we order our food, she dives right in. "So, what's up with the asshole? I mean, Noah?" She makes a face when she says his name, as though his name tastes terrible in her mouth. "Have you guys talked yet?"

I can't help but roll my eyes. I don't think she's ever going to forgive Noah for high school. If I can get over it, she should too. I appreciate the sentiment, though.

"No, not yet. As soon as we enter the same room, we kind of scatter like cockroaches in the light."

"Wow, great visual right before our food comes. Thanks so much for that."

I grin. "Anytime."

"So, what are you going to do? You can't work like that forever. Or is that your plan? Do nothing?" She refills her champagne flute and levels me with a stare. "Or are you considering making up with him?" As if that would be the worst idea in the world.

"What if I did? Make up with him?" I arch a brow at her, challenging her opinion. "Would you be mad at me if I did?"

"Of course not." She is becoming defensive. "You are free to fuck up your life as much as you want and in any way you can. I just need to know what type of glue I will need to put you back together when he breaks your heart. Again."

That shuts me up. She has a point. I was devastated back then, and what's going on now between Noah and me hasn't even hit yet. The longer our silence goes on, the more obvious it will be it's over between us. I don't know if I'm prepared to face that.

Mac leans over and grabs my hand. "Girl, this man has put you through hell, and he didn't even realize it last time. And how he's acting now...I don't think he's learned anything."

"I think you're wrong."

"Why? What has he done this time that makes you think he's changed?" She lets go of me and crosses her arms, confident she's right in her opinion.

I consider my answer carefully. There are a lot of ways Noah has changed since high school. Lots of good ways. Ways I can't even begin to explain out loud with words because I just suck at that.

"I love him, Mac." There I said it. I hadn't gotten the nerve to tell her that part. "And he's told me he loves me too. There's an entirely new level that we've reached, and I can't believe a little argument like this could be the end of it."

Now it's her turn to arch a brow. "Really, Chels?" She leans in, arms on the table, studying me. There's curiosity in her eyes, not judgment. "Do you really love him? Or are you in lust with him because he's so fucking hot?"

I can't contain the laugh that erupts from me at the second half of her question. "It's love. It's definitely love. I've never felt this way. Nobody has ever *made* me feel this way."

"Okay. I'm *almost* sold. What exactly are these

'feelings' like? Is it the butterflies? Is it your heart racing?" She bats her eyelids with as much snark as she can put into it. I know she's being sarcastic, and I get it. We've both been of the mind that true love isn't real, but I think I'm now a convert. I just need to convince her now.

"Do you realize how hard it is to describe? Yes, there are butterflies and racing hearts, but it's much more than that." I take a second or two to gather my thoughts. Trying to put this into words is going to be near impossible. At least words that are accurate enough to explain this. "It's complete chaos, but with a feeling of so much safety and security that you thrive in it. It's like that part in The Wizard of Oz when it switches from black and white to color, and you've never even seen colors before. Everything and everyone before him pale in comparison. And when we're together, I feel like I won the biggest damn lottery jackpot ever. And even now, with us not talking, I only want the absolute best for him. Whether that includes me or not."

I take a deep breath. I hadn't meant to talk so much about it, but once I got started, I couldn't stop. I glance up to check Mackenzie's reaction, and she's got tears in her eyes. That is not what I expected.

"Wow." The snark is gone from her face and replaced by wonder and awe. I don't think I've ever seen her like this. "You do love him."

"Duh. That's what I've been trying to tell you." I

shake my head at her but can't help a grin. "For a Mensa genius, you can be pretty dumb when it comes to stuff like this."

"I won't argue with you there." She wipes her eyes to catch the tears before they fall and ruin her perfect makeup. "So, what are you going to do about it? You obviously have to do something to fix this if you're so in love with him."

"I don't know what to do. So much time has passed, and I wouldn't even know where to start. Besides, he probably hates me now with how poorly I treated him. And I wouldn't blame him."

"Talk to the man. It can't be that hard."

That's so much easier said than done. I've composed and deleted so many texts over the last few days, but I'm afraid. I've been rejected by him before, and it nearly broke me for good. I don't think I would survive it again. I'm barely hanging on now as it is. If I put myself out there and expose my feelings and emotions, I'm not confident they won't be utterly crushed.

I have some cars to check out this week outside the depot, so I'll be in and out of the office. I'll take a few days to see how things go. Maybe these feelings will go away with time on their own. If they don't, then I know I'll need to talk to him.

I can only pray he's feeling the same way.

Chapter 38

Time Is Running Out

Noah

A solid week goes by of Chelsie and I doing our best to avoid each other. If one sees the other, we instantly turn and walk the other way. I want to talk to her so badly and tell her I was wrong. That I was a fucking idiot. But I know from her stubbornness that those words would fall on deaf ears. She's already forgiven me once for my past transgressions; there's no way I can expect her to do it again now. I need to learn how to let her go, but I don't know how.

Everything changed for me when I realized I was in love with her. How I saw the world changed. Shit, how I saw *myself* changed. And it's all because of her. She wants me to be a better person, and I failed epically at that. I'm not a better person. If anything, I'm worse because of how I reacted to our disagreement.

Late on Friday, after almost everyone has gone for the evening, I'm checking work on the brakes of an old Range Rover when the garage door squeaks open and shut. It must be my apprentice, Mick, returning for something he forgot. I swear he'd lose his head if it wasn't attached.

"What did you forget this time?" I chuckle and turn towards the door.

It's not Mick.

It's Chelsie.

She. Is. Beautiful. I've been trying so hard not to look at her directly this entire time that it almost escaped me how absolutely gorgeous she is. Her long brown hair frames her face and features perfectly. And her outfit accentuates every single delectable curve stunningly. It might just be me, but I think she's the most beautiful woman in the world, and seeing her now makes my breath catch. I want to freeze time right this second so I can stare at her like this forever.

For a moment, we simply gaze at each other. *God, I miss her.* Obviously, physically, but not just that. It was always the emotional closeness that made our physical connection so intense. I miss the world we were creating together. The one that reminded me of the jerk I had been in high school, but through that, how much I've changed. When I had Chelsie in my arms, it was a reminder that I hadn't merely grown as a person, leaving behind who I had been back then, but that I had done so to the point where Chelsie, the one person who I least deserve to forgive me, could actually *love* me.

Falling in love with Chelsie had been the best thing to ever happen to me. This falling out with her has been the most stupid. The fact I let myself lose that, even temporarily, is heartbreaking.

But now she's here. With me. Alone. And as much as I want to apologize, to tell her how much I miss her, need her, and want her, I know I can't.

But it's precisely because I know I can't that I know I have to.

"Chelsie, I'm sorry..." I begin.

She moves, and suddenly we close the distance between us, and we're kissing, clutching at each other like we can't bear to be apart. Her mouth is open, and my tongue meets hers. I have no idea who kissed who. Just as I have no idea whether I'm the one who pressed her up against the wall or if she pulled me there. All I know is that we are here, my hands on her waist and her arms around my neck, and I have no plans of ever letting go. I feel like a man lost in the desert who has found a source of fresh water.

Stepping between her legs, I press myself into her, and she pushes back. Yes, she wants me as much as I want her. A small part of me, a voice in the back of my mind, keeps saying this isn't a healthy response. We need to sit down and talk about what happened and what getting back together means for us both before we have sex again. But I pay it no attention. I don't think I could if I even wanted to. Touching and tasting her again has set something off inside my soul. I need her, and I can't stop until I've had her.

It takes a moment, but I realize where we are. We're alone, but if someone walks in on us, we are going to be caught. And stopping isn't an option. Grabbing her hands, I pull her towards the storage room, kick the door open, and drag her through.

The shelves rattle as we fall against them, crushing our mouths together. She moans into my mouth as I run my hands down her body. I can't stop. Her soft throat, her full, luscious breasts, the curves of her hips as they glide around to her fantastic ass. It's all too much for me. Without making any conscious decision, I begin to hike up her skirt. She doesn't stop me.

On the contrary, she begins to undo the buttons of my jeans. She reaches inside, and her fingers are red hot against my cock. I almost finish there, but as she caresses me, I melt into the movements. When I was younger, I thought the man had to take the lead during sex. What a fucking idiot I was. Nothing is hotter than knowing that Chelsie wants me and is willing to take what she wants as much as I am.

As she begins to stroke me harder, I take a moment to caress her perfect ass before grabbing her lacey underwear and pushing it down so they fall and puddle around her ankles. Then I spin us around, watching her brace herself with her hands on the shelves opposite as I step up behind her and slowly push myself inside her.

If she moans, I don't hear it over the growl of pleasure that escapes me. For a second, we just stand there, pausing at the moment of penetration. She told me she needs a moment after I enter her for her body to process how amazing it feels. But the truth is, I need that moment just as much as she does. Her body around mine this way is different from any other woman I've been with. As if we were perfectly sized for each other. Just entering her is a moment of pure bliss I want to enjoy.

The moment doesn't last long, however. Both of us are too riled up for that. Pushing her skirt all the way up around her waist, I take hold of her hips and begin to thrust deep inside her. The scent of her excitement fills the small storeroom, wafting into my nostrils and driving me into an even deeper state of lust. Chelsie pushes back against me, the sound of our bodies connecting loud in my ears.

I lean forward, reaching around and pulling her

body back to reach her mouth with mine. As our tongues glide against each other, my hands roam her body. Her nipples are hard, poking through her top's fabric and pressing into my palms. However, the only problem with this position is that I'm unable to thrust as deeply, and she clearly wants more. Leaning forward once again, she grabs the shelves and arches her back.

This is very different from before. Last time, it had been more like making love. Beautiful. Passionate, yet controlled and focused. This is a lust that's built up during our time apart. A desire we've been unable to consummate. That small part of my mind still reminds me that there would need to be a conversation about our relationship after this. We need more than sex to reconcile what we had. But before doing any of that, we have to let what we are feeling physically burn out.

Suddenly, Chelsie pulls away. Falling out of her is almost painful, and I must fight the urge to pull her back into the same position. But I don't need to worry. She has no more desire to stop what we're doing than I do. Turning to face me, she reaches above her head and grabs hold of the shelves, smirking at me. I smile, realizing what she intends. Stepping into her, I kiss her while grabbing her thighs and lifting her up. She pulls with her arms, taking some of the weight while hooking her legs around me. I groan as she lowers herself onto my twitching shaft and see the glint in her eye as I do so. I begin to fuck her against the shelves. With gravity helping us, I push deeper inside her than I ever have been. This position makes kissing awkward, so instead, we stare at each other. Seeing my own lust reflected in her eyes is one of the most exciting things I have ever experienced. I haven't done anything like this before, sharing the intimacy of looking into a partner's eyes while we fuck. She's biting her lip so hard I worry she might draw blood, and I growl with pleasure so intense I almost can't bear it.

When we come, we come together, and we come hard. I don't know if it's a coincidence or something about the connection we're sharing, but the second I explode inside her, her entire body spasms, and her head falls back in a silent scream.

Fighting to keep my legs from collapsing under me, I lower her slowly until her own legs can support her. Then, slowly, her arms wrap around my neck, and she kisses me softly and lovingly. I sigh into the kiss, placing my hands on her arms. We have burned away the desperate physical need hanging between us, leaving only the intimacy and love we've been craving.

At that moment, I swear I'll never do something as stupid as allowing myself to lose her ever again.

"We need to talk, Chelsie," I rasp, finally catching my breath. My elation at being with her again in any capacity is overpowering, but this was totally unexpected. I never even considered this a possibility with all that's happening between us. "This was amazing, but I have some things to say to you."

She nods, her eyes intense. "And I have some things to say to you too." Sweeping my hair out of my eyes, she says, "Meet me at my house? We can order food and talk."

"It's a date."

About an hour later, I pull up to Chelsie's house, surprised to find a security guard at the gate. He looks over the car, checks my I.D., and then lets me through. I didn't realize she had her own security detail. When I brought her home drunk a few weeks ago, there wasn't any here. At least, not that I remember. After her sister's kidnapping by some crime family not so long ago that was all over the news, I guess they've taken steps to protect themselves even more. I hadn't even considered Chelsie might be in danger. Maybe I should have.

I was instructed to go to the back door, and Chelsie is in the doorway as I approach, gorgeous as ever. I'm tempted to slide my hand under her shirt and continue where we left off, but I restrain myself. We're here to talk, so talk we shall.

"Hey," I say with a smile, stepping up to her and pulling her into a kiss. While I know it's not why I'm here, I can't help stealing what I can.

She returns the smile when we pull apart. "Hey yourself. Come on in."

"What's with the security at the gate? Did something happen?" I'm worried there's some kind of threat to Chelsie I don't know about. The urge to protect her myself floods through me.

"Oh, yeah. Normandy and Brandon kind of freaked out with the Heather thing. I guess her partner is still on the run, so they're just being cautious." She dismisses it like it's no big deal, but my antennae go up on full alert. "Do you want a beer or something?"

"I should stay with you. Or you should come to stay at my apartment. Until they're caught, I mean." It's not a request. At least, not really.

She turns and eyes me curiously, "I have security. I'll be fine," she scoffs. "I doubt I'm the target on anybody's hit list."

"Regardless. I need to make sure you're okay." That came out way too honest. But I guess that's why I'm here, so I may as well dive in head first. "If it's even an inkling of a thought of a possibility that you might be in danger, I can't let anything happen to you."

The warm smile that greets me this time when she turns to me could melt icebergs. It's the sweetest thing I've ever seen. She's changed from her business attire into shorts and an oversized sweatshirt with a ripped neckline. Her hair is pulled into a loose ponytail, exposing her long neck. She may be sweet, but she looks downright delicious.

"Careful; your testosterone is showing." The sweet smile turns into a smirk, and it's all the more enticing. "Seriously. I'll be fine. I'm not worried." She opens a drawer and pulls out a stack of take-out menus.

While I appreciate that she's not worried about her safety, it still bothers me. It's obvious, though, that she wants to drop the subject. Now is not the time to push my feelings onto her, even if it's for her benefit, so I let it go for now.

We order food, and she pours us some wine while we wait for it to be delivered. Moving to the living room, we sit on the couch. I take off my shoes, and we face each other with bent legs, playing footsie with our stocking feet. The energy between us is relaxed, as though we've passed whatever initial hurdle was in our way, and we're heading downhill now. I need to navigate carefully. I don't want to blow this.

"So, about what happened between us...." I start. One of us has to get this conversation going. It may as well be me. Her response is only to blink, anticipating my following words. No pressure. "I'm sorry for how I reacted to you. I should have taken the time to listen to your reasoning about Heather. Lord knows I'm kicking myself as it is for believing her. I can't believe I did that...."

"You had no way of knowing she was a fraud. She was very convincing when she wanted to be. And like you said, even Mrs. Bailey went along with it, so there was no reason for you not to." She's being very gracious about this.

"Yes, but obviously, I missed something huge or even something small. I missed something. And it could have been catastrophic if you didn't follow up on your hunch about her. You're the hero now." I poke at her with a foot, making her giggle.

"I'm no hero," she shrugs and takes a sip of her wine. "I'm just a nosey bitch with impeccable intuition." She squints her eyes and points a warning finger at me. "Just remember that. I can sense disturbances in the Force."

"Okay. Good to know."

Her voice quiets, and she gets serious again. "I'm sorry too, Noah. I shouldn't have spoken like that to you in front of other people, especially strangers or my family. It was rude of me."

"Well, I deserved it."

"No. At least not like that; you didn't."

We both go silent. The only sound is the ticking of a grandfather clock in the corner. It's not a weighted silence but more of a thoughtful one. We each take our time to think about our actions and consequences. And with that, rehashing the apologies we've received, absorbing the healing energy from them.

After a little while, we gaze at each other, studying the other for long minutes. I see a freckle on her neck I hadn't noticed before, and I wonder how I missed it. I want to press my lips onto her skin and feel it beneath my kisses. But more than anything, I just want to hold her. I need to feel confirmation we're going to be okay.

I sit up and put my wine on the coffee table. I grab her glass and do the same thing. Then I take her hands, pull her up, and spin her, so her back is against my chest. Wrapping my arms around her, I lean back and twine my fingers with hers across her stomach. We stay like that, not saying a single word. Just reveling in and enjoying each other's presence until the food arrives. It's pure heaven after a nightmare week of separation.

It isn't until now that I realize my heart is full. While apart, she was missing from me, and I was empty. I was just a shell or a shadow without her.

I don't ever want to feel that way again.

Three weeks later
We finally get word that Heather's accomplice is

caught and arrested somewhere in Michigan, so Brandon can call off the hounds of security he's put in place for everyone, including Mrs. Bailey. I get the honor of telling her about the good news since everyone else is busy, and I am a bit surprised at her reaction.

"I'm a little disappointed in this because I liked the company and having someone to talk to and fuss over daily. I haven't had regular fusses like that in a long time." She smiles sadly. "I was just getting Boris to open up about his family too. I won't get to hear his stories."

My heart clenches as she continues to speak. She has nothing to say about the bad actors that were out to harm her and only wants to talk about the lovely people she met because of it. True Mrs. Bailey form.

"You're something else, you know that?" I say, interrupting her and taking her by surprise.

She stares at me, startled. Her pale blue eyes sparkling. She is so shocked she can't even speak, which is something for the record books.

"I mean it. Not only are you the sweetest person I've ever met, but I wouldn't have Chelsie if it weren't for you."

Snapping out of it, she taps my arm, "Oh, stop it. That's not true. If you're destined to be together, you'll be together. It had nothing to do with me." She waves the thought away like it's a nuisance.

"Thank you, anyway."

Meeting my gaze with all seriousness, we share a moment. A moment where we share the knowledge that forces are in motion in the universe that work in strange ways and nudge the smallest of things one way or another, changing the course of a life. And sometimes, altering the course of many lives. Like this. This chance meeting with Mrs. Bailey was arranged somehow by a really fucked up universe that has changed my life irrevocably for the better.

Chapter 39

Cold Water

Chelsie

Three Months Later

Noah and I have spent almost every day together for the last three months. Actually, I don't think we've missed a day yet. And we're still not sick of each other. If anything, we're closer than ever since our initial hiccup. I didn't think it was possible to be this much in love with someone, but even Mackenzie is convinced now that true love is a real thing. She's even formed a friendship with Noah I never saw coming. He's been trying his darndest to get her interested in his friend River, but there are zero sparks between those two.

The four of us are out to dinner when I get a call from Normandy. She's just over eight months pregnant, so when she calls, I answer quickly on the off chance she's going into labor early. I'm excited to become an aunt and of a girl, no less. I will spoil the ever-loving shit out of her when she comes.

"Hey Norm, you would go into labor as soon as we sit down for dinner, wouldn't you?" I laugh and give Noah a quick wink as he squeezes my thigh under the table. He knows how anxious I am about the baby.

"I'm not in labor, Chels," she hesitates. Her tone is way too serious. The hairs on my arms rise with goosebumps as I straighten in my seat.

"Norm, you're scaring me. What's wrong?" Everyone at the table stops talking at once and turns their attention to me. The weight of their gazes is oppressive.

"Can you come by the house after your dinner?" Now she sounds fake, like she's pretending everything is alright. This only ramps my concern even higher.

"Just tell me what's going on, Normandy. Cut the bullshit already."

She lets out a shaky breath but finally says, "Mrs. Bailey passed away a little while ago."

Everything inside of me goes numb, and my breath leaves me. I couldn't have heard her correctly.

"No..." Tears well up in my eyes, and I'm starting

to shake uncontrollably. I can only push the one syllable out with the bit of air left in my lungs.

"Her friend Moira found her. She said it looked like it was peaceful."

I don't hear anything she said. Or I hear it, but I'm not listening. My mind flashes back to the last time I saw Mrs. Bailey, just this Sunday with Noah for dinner and cards. We'd started doing that about once or twice a month. She looked healthy at the time and even stronger than she had been back when we first met.

"Are you sure?" This could all be a misunderstanding of some kind. This can't be true. She can't be dead. *She can't be dead.* "Norm, don't say stuff like that unless you're sure. It's not funny."

"What is it, babe?" Noah frowns with concern. I hold a finger up to him to wait a second. He grabs that hand with both of his while he waits. That just makes me cry harder.

"I wouldn't joke about this, Chels, you know that. I'm so sorry. I know you were all close."

"One sec," I say quickly, handing my phone roughly to Noah and waving my arms in a 'don't talk to me right now' warning to River and Mackenzie. My face falls into my hands as a sob bursts from me, my shoulders shaking from the violence of it. I can barely hear Noah talking to Normandy, getting the news himself. His body tenses next to mine when he learns, and the next thing I know, his arms are wrapping around me, and he's pulling me to him. I lean my head into his chest and cry like I haven't cried since I was a little girl. Harder than when my dad died not long ago, even.

"It'll be okay, Chels." His voice is a warm and soothing whisper against my ear. "I'm so sorry." He's being strong for me. I can feel it. Holding me so tightly, I know how much this hurts him too, but he's choosing to comfort me instead.

He lets Mac and River know what's going on and walks me out of the restaurant. I don't remember the walk or getting in the car. I don't remember the drive to my sister's house either, but here we are, approaching her front door, and I'm hanging onto Noah for dear life. I need to feel him, hold his hand, or make any contact as if my life depends on it. He's my grounding rod. Without him, I would be curled up in a ball under the table back at the restaurant.

When Normandy opens the door, Noah carefully transfers me to her arms, and I go willingly. Things between my sister and me have improved since she realized I wouldn't give up Noah, and he wouldn't quit. She also has more important things to think about, like her fast-approaching daughter, than to worry about my love life.

"I'm so sorry, honey." She pulls back to give me a smile edged with sadness. "It's going to be okay. She had a remarkable life. And just think, she's with

Wayne again. You know what a die-hard romantic she was. She's probably thrilled to pieces."

That does give me some comfort, but not enough to feel better yet. As this all sinks in, I'm sure it will all make more sense. Right now, life just seems hugely unfair.

I nod. "I know. I know." I glance around and find Noah, and it's as if it's the first time I'm seeing him since we heard the news about Mrs. Bailey. His posture is slumped, and he's not his usual confident self. I can clearly see the massive amount of pain behind his eyes that he's hiding from everyone else. My knees almost buckle as it crashes into me how much this affects him too. I've been so selfish, letting myself drown in my grief, I haven't considered his. "I'm sorry, Noah. I know you loved her too."

Pulling him into my arms, he lays his head on my shoulder, but he doesn't cry. His hands clutch my back as he trembles and buries his face into my neck. I want to take this pain away and carry it for him. I'll gladly hurt more if it means he doesn't hurt at all. I run my fingers through his hair and rub his back lightly, trying to be the rock he needs *me* to be. It's my turn to be here for him now.

"I'll go make you guys some coffee," Normandy whispers, leaving us in the front room.

"I'm so sorry. I've been so wrapped up in my grief I didn't realize I was ignoring you and yours," I say to Noah. I can't believe I could be so rude. I really have not been thinking straight.

"Chelsie, you didn't ignore me, and I didn't feel ignored." He rests his forehead against mine, staring intently into my eyes. "This is hard for both of us, and we're each going to react differently, and it's okay. I'm here for you however you need me to be. And I know you're here for me. Okay?" He gently wipes away my tears that haven't stopped with his thumbs. I close my eyes and nod, then lean into his palm, needing the warmth of his skin against me, even if it's just that slightest bit.

"Okay. Thank you."

"You don't have to thank me, Chelsie. I've got you. It's what people do when they love someone, and you know I love you more than anything, right?"

I nod.

That's apparently not enough. "Right?"

"Right."

"We're going to get through this. Yes, this absolutely sucks, and it's going to suck for an extremely long time, but it will get easier to live with." He wraps me in his arms again, and I breathe in his spicy cologne, calming aromatherapy for my nerves. "You've had to deal with this too much lately, but I'm here for you this time."

I don't know how I got so lucky. Actually, I do. Mrs. Bailey.

I miss her so much already.

Chapter 40

Nature Girl

Noah

After a night of holding each other and wiping away tears, Chelsie and I meet Moira at Mrs. Bailey's house the next day. She's about the same age as her and has just as much spunk, if not more. It's evident she's been crying, but despite that, she's holding herself together pretty well.

Moira is a stout woman with a loud voice that carries to find you wherever you are. I could be in Arizona, and if she wanted to tell me something, all she would have to do is say it normally, and I'd hear it. It's almost magical because it's not exactly *loud*; it's just effective.

When she sees us, she pulls us both into a group hug. "You kids really brightened Jeanette's life after Wayne passed. I don't know what she would have done without you two."

"That's very kind of you to say, thank you." I love hearing we made a small difference in Mrs. Bailey's life. "I don't know what we would have done without her, to be honest." I glance at Chelsie and can't help the smile that grows as I take her in. "She was kind of instrumental in us getting together."

Moira steps back and waves a dismissive hand at us. "Oh, I know all about you two *and* her matchmaking abilities. Trust me." She takes a seat at the kitchen table and indicates for us to sit across from her. "Jeanette is the one who introduced me to my late Lawrence; rest his soul. I lost him about five years ago, but Jeanette got us to go on a blind double date with her and Wayne when they were still dating. Larry was a friend of Wayne's, so the four of us became just about inseparable." A shadow crosses over her features briefly, but just as quickly as it appears, it fades. "It was just awful they couldn't have kids. Poor Jeanette was heartbroken, but she never let Wayne know that, but I think he knew. I know they would have been the best parents. They were such fantastic human beings."

We are getting the abridged version of Mrs.

Bailey's life, and it's fascinating to hear. Especially from the perspective of someone who loved her and witnessed it. We'd listened to some of these stories during our dinners here, but to hear them from Moira is a special treat since she has such a sharp sense of humor. She goes on to tell us several hours' worth of stories about her, with a few crying jags in between for her and for Chelsie. I refill the tea during those episodes. Not that I want to avoid them, but I want to give the ladies the space to grieve that they need without my awkward presence mucking it all up.

"At least she had the mind to prepay her arrangements, so nobody needs to do anything. She didn't want anyone to worry about anything, which is *so* Jeanette. Always looking out for everyone else." She wipes at her teary eyes again, missing her friend deeply. My heart constricts watching her emotions ebb and flow like this because I know what she's going through since I'm going through it too. We all are. "She did everything, funeral, obituary, clothes, service, will, plot, headstone, you name it, it's taken care of. She was nothing if not thorough."

"Wow, it sounds like it would have been overwhelming if she hadn't done that." Chelsie casts me a relieved smile. She's been worrying there is something she should be doing, so hopefully, she can relax now that she knows there isn't. I lightly squeeze her thigh next to me under the table, letting her know I'm here and I'm present.

"Oh yes, she was very clear on her wishes." She reaches over and takes Chelsie's hand into hers, growing serious. "You two will be at the reading of the will on Friday, right?"

Chelsie glances at me. "No... we didn't know we needed to be there...." I just shrug at her. I have no idea what that's about.

"Oh, you definitely will need to be there." She jumps up from her chair and glances around the kitchen, searching for something. "Where the heck did I put my purse? I have all the information in it. There it is." She spots it on the floor next to the counter and pulls out a business card to hand to Chelsie. "Be there at 10:00 AM sharp."

"Yes, Ma'am," I say, taking the card from Chelsie and studying it. I've never heard of these probate attorneys before, but then I really don't know any attorneys. This should be interesting.

I don't own a suit. I haven't since...I can't remember when. Okay, I've never owned a suit, so I have to borrow one from my brother, Theo. Luckily, we're about the same size, so it fits well enough. At least well enough to get by for a few hours. I'm a little broader in the shoulders than him, but he argues the suit jacket must have shrunk during dry cleaning. Sure. Because that happens all the time.

When I arrive at Chelsie's to pick her up on the way to the funeral home, she's standing frozen in the middle of her kitchen while holding two different types of shoes, and she looks like she's about to have a meltdown. She hasn't even acknowledged that I've entered the house.

"Are you okay?" I ask, afraid to move or startle her; she is so spooked. I slowly take a few steps toward her, hands raised in defense.

Her eyes shift in my direction, and I can tell when her eyes focus on me. It's as though she's waking up from a dream or nightmare. I don't know which one yet.

"What?" she asks, confusion now furrowing her brow.

"Are you okay?" I repeat, taking another step closer.

Her eyes travel to the shoes in each hand, and the tears start flowing down her cheeks. My heart wrenches at the sight of her so upset. She's been like this for days, crying at the drop of a hat, spacing out, and constantly losing her train of thought. She is taking Mrs. Bailey's death hard. I close the distance between us and pull her to me, letting her cry herself out. It's all I can do when this happens. Words are useless. All I can do is be here for her.

After a few minutes, she says between hitched breaths, "I just want to wear the right shoes. I want to be respectful, and my shoes aren't entirely...respectful. I don't know."

I frown at this. "What the hell are you talking about? Respectful shoes?" I grab the shoes out of her hands and examine them. I could swear they are nearly identical, but I know it's a trick. They are different somehow, but in some ancient mystical way, guys can't decipher for some reason. I give her the shoe in my right hand. "This one. It's the most respectful of the two." I'll burn in hell later for the lie, we have a funeral to get to and cats to feed on the way.

"Do you think so?" Now she's second-guessing my choice and, honestly, making me do the same.

I study the two sets of shoes again and still see no difference.

"Yup." I nod and put my hands in my pants pockets, just in case they're some sort of tell that I'm lying through my teeth about the respectability of shoes. Definitely not what I thought I'd be dealing with today. "Why don't you finish up so we can feed the cats before the funeral?"

"Shit, I forgot we had to do that. Alright, I'll be right back." She disappears from the kitchen with both pairs of shoes, so I cross my fingers another existential fashion crisis isn't about to erupt upstairs.

I've been feeding Yugo and Edsel every day until

we figure out what to do with them. Neither Chelsie nor I want them to go to a shelter, and we don't want to give them away either. They're in location limbo while we consider all of the options. Edsel was finally warming up to Chelsie before Mrs. Bailey died, so she's warmed up to her right back. It may not even be our decision. There might be a provision for their care already planned out by her. We'll find out on Friday.

Chelsie reappears in the doorway to the kitchen, and even in the depths of her sorrow and grief, she's the most beautiful woman in the world to me. I actually pinch myself even though I know she's mine. I just like giving myself that little reminder every now and then of how lucky I am.

She sighs heavily. "Okay, let's get this over with."

At Mrs. Bailey's house, it doesn't take long for the cats to come out of hiding as soon as the sound of the can opener echoes through the empty house. They emerge faster each day that I've come to do this, giving me hope for their own grieving process. And they're actually eating. They would reluctantly come to the kitchen the first couple of days, only to find out who was there. Then they would wander around the house crying a song in obvious lament for their lost owner. It's been heartbreaking coming here every day to witness their grief.

This is the first time Chelsie's come with me to complete the task and the first time she's been in the house since we were here with Moira. She's frozen in this kitchen now, staring at the table where the deck of cards we used to play with when we would visit sits. She finally breaks out of her haze and picks up the box of cards, rubbing the indent where the hole was punched. As her hand starts to shake, I grab it, forcing her to look at me instead. When our eyes meet, we do what we always do, communicate without speaking. Right now, she's telling me she's beyond sad and still sinking. She's scared to lose anyone else. She misses Mrs. Bailey fiercely. And feels bad for the cats who miss her too. I'm telling her everything will be fine. I've got her. I've always got her. And I love her more than words can say.

I glance at my watch. I hate to interrupt her thoughts wherever they've taken her, but we'll be late if we don't leave now. "Let's go, babe. We don't want to be late. We'll be back soon enough."

She straightens her shoulders, takes my hand, and follows me to the car.

Chapter 41
Something to Remind You

Chelsie

I'm really getting sick of funerals. The overwhelming sense of déjà vu washes over me as I gaze out the car window at the cemetery we're slowly driving through. I was here a few weeks ago with Noah to visit my father's grave. It was about time the two of them 'met,' and Noah even surprised me by asking for some alone time so he could talk to my dad without me overhearing. I don't know what he said or if I even believe that anyone or anything heard him, but I love the idea. He put that loving energy out into the universe, and I love him even more because of it.

And here we are, escorting another loved one to their final resting place. If I never visit a cemetery again, it will be too soon. It's to the point I'm having irrational thoughts about it, thinking maybe I'm cursed and everyone I love will die too soon. Lord knows I can't even keep a houseplant alive. Maybe the karma of all the plants I've killed over the years are catching up to me. What a crazy thought. I need to rein myself in.

Glancing over at Noah as he concentrates on the car in front of us in line, I can study his profile uninterrupted. I love doing this, taking him in when he's unaware. I cherish these moments because I see him for who he truly is. Not that he puts on airs, because he doesn't, but he's more *Noah* when he doesn't know I'm watching. I can read the grief plainly on his face now. His eyes are tired and marked by shadows from lack of sleep, and the lines on his face, though few, are more profound than usual, more pronounced.

He's been so good to me the last few days. He always is, but he seems to have some innate instinct for what I need. He knows when to just hold me, listen to me, or give me words of encouragement and comfort. And he knows when I need much more than that and crave his physical presence around and inside me to remind me I'm alive and loved.

I've never known anything like this before. Hell, I didn't think this kind of love existed, let alone I would ever experience it. But here I am, looking at a man whom I had sworn off seven years ago, and for good reason, who has proven to me repeatedly that people make mistakes and *can* change. This man, who I love with so much intensity it can sometimes bring me to tears for how blessed I am that I'm able to experience this emotion. This man, who knelt at my father's grave and spoke to him from his heart.

All my life, I believed things like this were just in fairy tales, books, or movies. They're not real. True love isn't a thing, or at least not one that happened to me. History had shown that to me over and over. I've never felt worthy. But now, with Noah, I've never felt more worthy.

He catches me staring at him, and he gets self-conscious. "What is it?" The corners of his lips twitch into a small smile, and he reaches over to grab my hand. We've been so tactile lately, constantly within reach of each other for comfort. I hope that part sticks around even when our grief dissipates.

"Just...you," I say, smiling back. "I'm so grateful to Mrs. Bailey for you."

He pulls my hand to his lips, kisses my knuckles, and then smirks. "Think we'll ever be able to call her 'Jeanette?'"

"Nope."

"Didn't think so."

Only a handful of us attends the graveside service. The problem with living a long life is you typically outlive many of your loved ones. Such is the case with Mrs. Bailey. Since Brandon accompanied Normandy, there are a few extra people around, so security guards are at various points of the cemetery. Noah seems unnerved by their presence, but I can mostly ignore them. You tend to get used to things like that fairly quickly.

The other thing keeping people away from the cemetery is the heat. It's the middle of August, and the temperature is over a hundred degrees in the shade. Many things about Las Vegas are not for the faint of heart, with the heat in summer being at the top of that list. It's oppressively hot, making spending any time outdoors uncomfortable and possibly dangerous.

The minister from Mrs. Bailey's church says a few words and tells a few stories that I only half hear. I'm too busy concentrating on holding Noah's hand, probably too tightly, and not falling over from the heat. I'm also trying to calm myself down so I can read the poem I found to pay my respects.

When I'm called up, my voice and my hands shake, but one glance at Noah gives me the strength to go on to read:

"'Do Not Stand at My Grave and
    Weep' by Mary Frye

Do not stand at my grave and weep,
I am not there, I do not sleep.

I am a thousand winds that blow.
I am the diamond glint on snow.
I am the sunlight on ripened grain.
I am the gentle autumn rain.

When you wake in the morning
    hush,
I am the swift, uplifting rush
Of quiet birds in circling flight.
I am the soft starlight at night.

Do not stand at my grave and weep.
I am not there, I do not sleep.
(Do not stand at my grave and cry.
I am not there, I did not die!)"

By the last sentence, tears are flowing freely down my cheeks. And when I'm back next to Noah, I hear a choked sob and a distinctly female voice say, "Oh, fuck."

Turning, I see Normandy with a pained and shocked expression on her face, her eyes wide and mouth agape.

"Norm, what is it?" I whisper, concerned that something has gone wrong due to the extreme heat. It can't be healthy for a pregnant woman.

She grabs Brandon's hand tightly, and her eyes slowly travel to meet mine. "My water just broke."

Nothing else needs to be said because Brandon is on his feet, calling for his head of security, Taylor. There is a bustle of activity as Brandon's orders are thrown about, cars are brought around, routes are arranged, and the hospital is notified of the upcoming visitor. All the while, the few other people attending the funeral watch on with surprised excitement.

Moira starts laughing and is in near hysterics. "Oh, my goodness, Jeanette would love this! A baby! At her funeral!" She's laughing so hard; if it weren't for the sound of her laughter, you'd think she was crying.

She's got a point. Mrs. Baily would have absolutely loved everything about this. Even though she couldn't have her own, the romantic in her would have beamed at the thought.

Normandy lets out a yelp of pain, clutching her belly tightly, and the laughing stops. Brandon is back beside her in a heartbeat.

"Breathe, Normandy. Just breathe like we've practiced." He starts puffing big breaths repeatedly, and Normandy mimics him, her eyes never leaving his. The fear and excitement rolling off the two of them are contagious, and it's hard to contain my own.

After an excruciating minute, the contraction must pass because she can breathe normally again.

"Can you make it to the car?" Brandon's concern and worry slash deep in his face. He's a bit of a control freak, so I know not being able to predict or direct much of this has to be killing him inside.

Normandy scoffs at him. "Yes. I can make it to the car." Her sudden sarcasm tells me he's in for a bumpy ride in the next few hours as the contractions intensify.

"Can I help at all?" Noah's showing almost the same amount of concern as Brandon. Normandy and I share a look, indicating we know women should be running the world.

"Thank you, Noah, but I'll be fine. I just need to walk to the car." She hands me the rose meant for Mrs. Bailey's casket, and then Brandon and Noah do the same before flanking Normandy to walk her to the awaiting limo.

I turn to Moira, still chuckling next to me and wiping her tears away with a tissue. "So, I guess we'll be going now." I glance at the minister, who is unsure what to do. I walk over to the casket and lay everyone's flowers on top of the glossy wood, saying a little internal prayer of gratitude and hope for Mrs. Bailey. I thank the minister and join the others on the new procession to the hospital.

Our grief has been immediately supplanted with happiness and excitement at the new life that is about to enter the world. We've switched from suffering and pain to joy in a tiny heartbeat.

And I can't wait to meet my new niece.

Chapter 42

Light

Noah

The hospital isn't far, making me wonder about city planning and how a hospital could be so close to a cemetery. I can tell Chelsie thinks I'm having deep thoughts by how she's looking at me, which I find extremely funny for some reason. I am very tired.

"What in the world are you thinking about? You just went from super pensive to delight very quickly. Like, scarily fast." She's holding my hand, or I'm holding hers. Either way, our palms are sweaty since we're wired with anticipation for Normandy and Brandon's baby to arrive.

I can only laugh, the rush of each emotion I've felt today draining the energy from me. "Just the rollercoaster of emotions we're going through today. It's a bit much to deal with in one day."

She nods. "It is. This baby was not expected. Well, not today, anyway. You know what I mean." I'm happy I'm not the only one having difficulty with the mood swings of the moment.

Walking into the ER, we're directed to the family waiting area of the hospital's maternity wing. Brandon and Normandy's house manager, Sophie, is already there and is busy texting messages on her phone. How she got here so fast and before us is a mystery I'll need to solve another time.

She jumps up from the bench she's on and hugs us when she sees us. "Joan, Normandy's mother, is on her way to the airport in Utah and will be here in a couple of hours. Brandon sent his plane to go and retrieve her. Hopefully, the baby can wait until Grandma gets here." Her beatific smile is warm. "She's a little early, but that's okay; we can meet her sooner."

"That's a great way to look at it," I say, glad everyone keeps positive. Personally, I'm concerned since the baby's early. But then, I have no clue about anything pregnancy-related besides what I've been told the last few months. And, all the things I've been educated on have had the caveat, *but everybody's different* added to it to further confuse things. "Can I get anyone anything? Soda? Coffee?" I need to find some caffeine because I feel it's going to be a long wait. This will also give me something to do because I am utterly useless in this situation to anybody, except for maybe getting shit for people. It's a role I can handle, though. I take orders and go to search for vending machines.

After a few hours of nothing happening and no word from Brandon, Chelsie and I make our way to the gift shop with a promise from Sophie that she'll text us should any news arise while we're away. While looking at stuffed animals, it dawns on me that I'm being included in all of this without question. It almost doesn't seem real.

I can't say when my relationship with Chelsie was accepted, but there was a definite shift at some point. We became a package deal when invitations were offered for get-togethers, from weddings to barbeques, and now to baby deliveries. I've become a part of this family. And Chelsie's become a part of mine, too. Besides hanging out with River and Mackenzie, we often go on double dates with my brother and his latest attempt at a girlfriend, which almost always fails miserably. He's sure every girl he goes out with is "The One," and that never ends well.

I'm lost in these thoughts when Chelsie tugs on my sleeve for attention, then runs her fingers through my hair. "Where'd you go in that gorgeous head of yours?"

"Here."

"Didn't look like it," she smirks. "You were *gone*."

"Nope, I was here, marveling at the present."

She raises a doubtful brow but nods. "If you say so...I've already paid. We can head back now."

On our way back to the maternity waiting room, we cross paths with Brandon, who appears harried and stressed. He's almost in full-blown panic.

"Brandon? What's wrong?" Chelsie asks, running up to him. "What's going on? Is Normandy okay? The baby?"

He swallows hard as Sophie comes out of the waiting room to check what's happening. "Normandy is fine, but they're going to need to do an emergency C-section."

"What? Why?" Chelsie is feeding off his heightened anxiety and getting caught up in it. "What's wrong?"

"The baby's heart rate keeps dipping dangerously low with each contraction, and they're worried she's not getting enough oxygen. They're prepping Normandy for surgery now, I just have a second, so I wanted to come out and tell you what was going on." He runs out of breath and leans forward with his hands on his knees. He glances up at me, not even for a full second, and the sheer terror in his face strikes fear in my heart.

I pat his shoulder, clueless as to what to say to comfort or encourage him. I am unequipped emotionally for this kind of thing, and my lame attempt at saying anything might make things worse, so I say nothing. What I can do, is lend my strength to Brandon, so I keep my hand on his shoulder, letting him know that I'm present and here for him, should he need me for anything.

Sophie is the only one of us with any words of wisdom. "This is fairly common, Brandon, don't worry. They're doing the right thing. A C-section will solve the oxygen problem." My mind instantly goes to the idea that that's only one problem. What if there are others? I keep my fears to myself since it seems that Brandon takes Sophie at her word and believes it's the only issue. I hope they're right.

"Can I see her?" Chelsie asks, her anxiety climbing.

Brandon grabs her shoulders and shakes his head. "Sorry, Chelsie, I only had this quick minute. I need to run back in there. I'm sorry."

She's not put off at all. "Of course, go. Be with your wife." She pushes him back toward the delivery room, forcing a smile I can tell she only partially feels. "Don't come back until you're a dad."

Once he's out of earshot, Sophie tells us again that it is expected, and there isn't a reason to worry about anything. Knowing that she wasn't just saying something to appease Brandon or us makes me feel better about the situation. It seems to do the same for Chelsie since her shoulders aren't up around her ears with anxiety. We take our seats in the waiting room again and hold hands while time passes at a snail's pace.

Before we hear from Brandon again, Normandy's mother, Joan, makes it to the hospital, and with her, we notice a more significant contingent of security guards is now milling about the halls. Brandon or Taylor must have beefed up the number of guards due to the importance of the occasion. There wasn't any press at the funeral earlier, but that doesn't mean they haven't heard from someone here in the hospital willing to sell a story that the birth is happening. Part of me is sad security needs to be considered, but I'm also glad it's available for them.

While Joan and Sophie talk amongst themselves, I try to keep Chelsie calm and distracted. It's a Herculean task, but I'm up to the challenge.

"So, what are we going to name our kids?" I'm surprised by my own question. Actually, I'm shocked. I don't know where the fuck that just came from, but I can't take it back. *Shit.*

Chelsie turns to face me, her jaw dropped and eyes wide. I think even Joan and Sophie heard us because they get quiet and turn our way. I can feel the heat snaking up my neck and into my potentially frightened face.

"Name our kids?" Chelsie's incredulous. "We're

Ms. Chief

having kids? When did this happen? Was I there for that discussion?"

"I mean someday... not like, right now. Obviously." I want to backpedal so badly and reconsider my words, but they're falling out of my mouth without my assistance. "Down the road like...." *I need to shut the fuck up.*

"I haven't thought about naming kids, let alone having kids, to be honest." She shrugs non-committal. "I figured I'd let Normandy do all that stuff before I decided to do any of it myself. Why?" Her gaze turns suspicious.

I'm unsure if I should be offended that she's never thought about having kids with me. But then, I hadn't thought about it until this minute. Normandy's pregnancy was just a peripheral thing that was happening and didn't affect me at all. Until today. Today Chelsie will officially become an aunt, changing her family dynamic completely.

"You do realize you're about to be an aunt, right?" I smile, deflecting like crazy.

Her legs start to bounce nervously. "I know! I still can't believe it's today, of all days."

Before I can respond, Brandon steps into the waiting room, sleeves rolled up and sweat sheening his forehead and cheeks. "Well, she's here, and she's perfect." The sigh he lets out comes from so deep within his chest that I can feel it. "Ava Harper Carmichael has arrived and is currently bonding with her mom, who is also perfect." His grin couldn't be more enormous, and he gets swarmed with questions and congratulations. Seeing the glint in his eye that is part relief, part pride, and all love is something I now might be interested in finding for myself.

Maybe I've got some soul searching to do. It might be time to consider my future and what I want from life. I know for a fact I want Chelsie to be included in that future no matter what, but beyond that? We'll need to have a few discussions to make sure we align on our ideas about family. If I can be even half as happy as Brandon is right now after the birth of his daughter, I'm looking forward to it.

Chapter 43

Ain't No Grave

Chelsie

I'm an aunt. I'm a freaking aunt to the most beautiful little girl I've ever seen. We only briefly see baby Ava and Normandy in the hospital but leave with a promise to return tomorrow when everyone is in better shape for a visit. Ava is perfect, with ten chubby little fingers, ten chubby toes, blonde hair like Normandy, and the cutest little nose I've ever seen.

Holding her, even for those few moments, got my ovaries screaming for a baby. That's going to need to be a discussion for another time because I am not ready for that quite yet. That talk needs to wait, but it needs to happen, especially after Noah's question today about baby names. I think everyone has babies on the brain, which will pass with time. At least, I hope so.

Noah and I go for the rest of the day without further discussion of offspring. We head to the probate attorney's office the following day to read Mrs. Bailey's will. Moira is already in the waiting room, purse on her lap and a smile. She's wearing a dress. Noah and I are just in jeans. We didn't know what was appropriate for a will reading, so we stayed casual. Perhaps I should have dressed better. Noah doesn't seem concerned.

"How was it yesterday? How is the baby? Is everything okay?" She pats the seat next to her for me to sit.

It didn't dawn on me that she'd want to know the outcome of events yesterday since we left the funeral so quickly. I should have considered the people left behind at the cemetery might be curious about how things went after we all went to the hospital.

"Oh, yes. Everyone's fine," I say. "It got a little scary for a minute, but with an emergency C-section, everyone is healthy and well." I can feel myself beaming with pride, as though I had anything to do with anything. "Little Ava Harper Carmichael is beautiful perfection."

Moira exhales with relief, her chest heaving. "Oh, thank goodness. I was worried about how pale

Normandy was when you all left. I'm glad it went well eventually."

Mr. Forrester, the attorney we have the appointment with, comes into the lobby and greets us, shaking our hands and directing us to a side conference room. He's not much taller than Moira and has a beer belly, but for an older gentleman, he still has all his hair which appears to be dyed brown. His suit is a little wrinkled, and his tanned skin doesn't look like it got that way from the sun, either. I wonder about his relationship with Mrs. Bailey or how she knew him.

"Thank you for coming today," he starts, flipping through papers on the table in front of him. "My condolences to you on losing your friend, Jeanette. She was a good woman, who I only knew briefly, starting back when her husband Wayne passed away, and we needed to transfer some titles and deeds to her name only."

We all just nod, unsure what to say to him. Moira mumbles a "thank you" under her breath, but it carries through the room.

"Right. The reading of the will." He glances up at us with a smirk. "You know this isn't really a thing, right? Normally beneficiaries are notified by mail and given a copy of the will to read for yourself, but Jeanette wanted to be dramatic and specifically asked for us to do this."

Noah starts laughing out loud. "Leave it to Mrs.

Bailey to do something like this." He shakes his head at me. "This is crazy."

"She did have a flair for the dramatic," Moira chuckles.

"This will was filed with the court by my law clerk the day after Jeanette passed. I'll now read it aloud for you three, who are the only humans named beneficiaries."

"Human?" I ask Mr. Forrester.

He holds a hand up. "You'll see why I made that distinction."

It takes several minutes for him to read the preamble and other legal mumbo jumbo naming him as executor of the will, and then he gets to the disposition of assets.

"*I give all my tangible personal property and all policies and proceeds of insurance covering such property to Noah Thompson and Chelsie Blake on the condition that they marry within six months of my death.*'"

"What?" Noah asks, nearly jumping out of his seat, and I can't tell if he's angry or excited.

"Married?" Moira starts laughing again. I'm just stunned. I've never heard of such a thing.

"Can she do that?" I ask. Not entirely mad at the idea, but not sure what to think about it either.

"Actually, she didn't," Mr. Forrester smiles. "It's not in the will, but she did want me to say that to put the idea in your heads." He winks, and my stomach does a flip. It was a joke.

Moira's laughter just about shakes the picture frames off the walls, but Noah and I glance at each other and turn away awkwardly, unsure how to respond.

"What it *does* say is,

"'*With the exception of a gift of $250,000 to Moira Jacobs, I give all my tangible personal property and all policies and proceeds of insurance covering such property to Noah Thompson and Chelsie Blake, in equal shares, to be divided among them by my executor in their absolute discretion. My executor may pay out of my estate the expenses of delivering tangible personal property to beneficiaries.*'"

Is she really giving us all her stuff? That can't be right. She's got to have somebody else to give her things to.

The attorney continues to read.

"'*I give all my residences, subject to any mortgages or encumbrances thereon, and all policies and proceeds of insurance covering such property, to Noah Thompson and Chelsie Blake....*'"

At that point, I completely zone out. Mrs. Bailey left everything, except some money for her friend, to Noah and me. That is insane. Her house and everything in it, her land, and even that oversized garage out back Brandon is leasing housing all those classic cars. I can't believe she would do such a thing.

We weren't family, and we only knew her for a few short months

There's a change in the attorney's tone, and my attention snaps back.

"'...you may ask yourself why I would leave all this to you, and of course, I have answers. Noah. Young man, you are a prince among men. You remind me of my Wayne when he was your age. Galant and chivalrous, passionate, and handy to have around the house. But also kind and good-hearted. Never lose that. And Chelsie. Sweet girl, your heart is so big and so full of life and love for everyone. Let yourself feel and receive that love as much as you give it away. I thank you both for making my last few months without Wayne livable. Without you, I wouldn't have. - Love, Jeanette, "Mrs. Bailey."'"

The tears start again, and this time I notice Moira is crying too. I feel Noah stroke my back, and when I turn to face him, I see unshed tears brimming in his eyes. He's able to hold them back, but he's just as stunned as I am. I never expected anything from Mrs. Bailey. Especially not any of her things, let alone *everything* she owned. It's insane. I thought we were going to get the cats or something like that. *Oh crap, the cats.*

"Does it say anything about her cats?" I can't believe she would leave them out of it. "What should happen with them?"

Mr. Forrester flips through the pages of the will,

then his notes. "I don't see anything specific in the will, and there's nothing in my notes, so they would fall under personal property, which means you and Noah equally own them now."

"Oh. Okay." I look at Noah, who is coming out of his stupor and smiling at me, his eyes crinkling at the corners. "I guess we're co-pet parents now."

"I guess so," he replies, his dark eyes dancing with humor. "It'll be good practice."

I sit back in my chair and arch a brow. "Practice? For what?" I know what he meant, but I can't help prodding him.

"For our own kids, of course." He leans over and kisses me lightly on the lips, not caring there are other people in the room. And as of this moment, I don't care either.

As he starts to pull away from me, I grab his face and pull him into another kiss, this time not as chaste as the last one.

I love this man, and we will be the best pet parents in the world to Edsel and Yugo. We will be the best *regular* parents in the world to our children when they come. I can picture our future together so clearly now, getting married, running Mischief Motors together, raising our own children, surrounded by friends and family. It can't get any better than this. And Mrs. Bailey has seen that we won't have to struggle like most couples our age, and I will be forever grateful to her for that. I wouldn't be this incandescently happy to call Noah mine if not for her. And he is mine. I'm never going to let him go.

Moira starts to giggle, and Mr. Forrester clears his throat, causing Noah and I to break apart but smile at each other languidly.

"Sorry," we say together.

But we're not sorry at all.

Epilogue

Hold

Chelsie

Two Years Later

"Careful, Ava. Jett doesn't like it when you put food in his mouth. Remember when he bit you last time?" We're watching my niece while Brandon and Normandy are in New York for the weekend, and Noah and I's son, Jett, who just turned a year old, is being bossed around by said niece. He's not happy when he gets bossed around, and I don't blame him. Ava can be downright pushy.

"But he should eat sumfing," she pouts, her bottom lip curving and her brows creasing with displeasure. Most things have not gone her way today, and she is not happy about it. She's usually a very generous and sweet little girl, but when Jett doesn't go along with her, like now, she can't cope and tends to melt down. "I don't want him to starve."

"I guarantee you, he will not starve today," I tell her. "You have my word."

She eyes me cautiously as though I would ever lie to her. *I would never.*

"Okay." The pout is still there, but it's lessened just a little bit.

"Why don't you help him build this castle? I'm sure he could use your great flair for decorating."

She reluctantly turns and heads toward Jett, playing in the corner quietly, but her mood lifts at the compliment and suggestion. She does love decorating.

"Where is my wife?" Noah yells from the kitchen as he comes into the house from working in the garage. He has called me 'wife' like some cave dweller since before we were married a year and a half ago, but I love it. He especially calls me that if he's feeling frisky, which is just about all the time. But he particularly enjoys teasing me with it when sex is off the table and only used as a torture device, like now. He knows that the middle of the day babysitting duty does not translate into any kind of sexy time.

"Out here minding the children, husband," I call back, only partially containing my laugh.

The next thing I know, hands are wrapping around my waist from behind, and my neck is being set on fire with kisses up to my ear, where he stops and whispers, "So, when are we going to give Jett a little sister or brother? We could start now...." His warm breath in my ear makes me shudder, and I swear my ovaries explode at his words. He's wanted to get pregnant again since Jett was born, but I've put him off, wanting to enjoy Jett alone for a while. I wanted to give my body a break too.

"What if we've already started?" I ask, grinning to myself.

His hands go straight to my belly, fingers splayed, trying to feel around for a baby as if he could tell this soon.

"Wait, are you pregnant? For real?" His voice rises in pitch, suddenly excited that I might have another child of ours growing inside me.

"Maybe..." I drag it out because it's too much damn fun. "I'm late...?"

"Well, do a test, woman. Do a test and find out."

"It's not like I keep pregnancy tests lying around the house," I laugh, incredulous at his excitement. I wasn't expecting this kind of response. I'm not sure what I was expecting.

"Then I shall go procure a test." And the next thing I know, he's gone to the drugstore and is back within minutes. I've barely had time to register he even did that.

"Honey, I can't take the test until morning."

"Nonsense. If you're pregnant, you're pregnant." He hands me the box and turns me toward the bathroom. "Plus, there are two in there. If this one is negative, you can retake it in the morning to confirm. But if it's positive...."

His smile and excitement are contagious, so I take the box into the bathroom and take the test. Not even a minute passes, and Noah is on the other side of the door asking questions.

"Did you take the test? What does it say?" The excitement is still in his voice, but now it's edged with nervousness.

I open the door to let him in, keeping it ajar to listen for the kids.

"Shhhh, keep your voice down. Ava will hear you and repeat everything you say to her parents. I don't want Normandy and Brandon to know anything until we're positive."

"Fine, I'll keep my voice down. How much longer is the test going to take?" He slides his arms around me again, and I glance up at our reflection in the bathroom mirror. Who would have thought the two of us would be here like this today? Married, with a child and possibly another on the way. And so deep in love with each other, it sickens everybody we meet. Well, not really, but it can get intense between us. It's only in the good ways, though.

He squeezes me briefly, bringing me out of my

reverie. "What? Oh. It should only be a few minutes."

"And, what were you thinking about so intently, wife?" He rests his chin on my head and smiles in the mirror.

I consider what to tell him before speaking. I think about joking with him or teasing him somehow, but I can't. I can tell how much he wants this test to be positive. I want that too.

"Just how happy I am and how much I love you."

"Well, now you're gonna make me blush. Shucks." He plays coy and actually does start to blush. It's adorable. "I love you too, Chelsie. No matter what the test says."

I grab onto his hands and pull his arms tighter around me, using him as a security blanket to wrap myself in. We wait the timer out, holding on to each other, swaying a little, and just enjoying each other's presence as our world might change again in the next few moments.

When the timer goes off, we stare at each other's reflection in the mirror before we each grab for the test. He's damned quick and he gets a hold of it before I can, and he holds it out of my reach so I can't see it.

"Hey!" I try to stand on tiptoe to get it from him, but he's too tall. "What does it say? No fair."

He studies the test in his hand, a smile growing

even wider, and I swear I see his chest puff out a bit. That must mean...

"Congratulations, mom," he cheers, handing me the test. Framing my face with his hands, he leans in and kisses me. At first, it's gentle and sweet, then it turns more passionate, and I start to forget there is a 'rest of the world' besides Noah. When he pulls away, he peers deep into my eyes, so deep I swear he can see my soul, and confesses, "Every day, you make me the happiest man on earth. I don't know how you do it, but you do. And every day, I am so grateful for everything you do, everything you give me, our son, and everyone around you. You are so very special to so many people." He pushes my hair out of my eyes. "Thank you for being my everything, every day."

I can't help the tears that start flowing at his words. I cry all the time anyway. When I'm happy, when I'm sad, and when I'm angry, tears, tears, tears. And now, when I'm ecstatic at being pregnant and blown away by Noah's words, the tears become a deluge. The hormonal roller coaster has begun and begun in earnest.

"I'm only me because you are you," I say in between hitched breaths while caressing his cheek. "Without you, I'd have none of this. This life that I'm living wouldn't exist. I don't think I'd ever be this happy. I'd always feel like something was missing. You are what was missing in my life."

He scoops me into his arms and twirls me around

the bathroom, celebrating our amazing life together that is about to get bigger, which can only mean better.

I'll take better with Noah any day.

- - THE END - -

Ms. Chief Playlist

https://open.spotify.com/playlist/6AoyNlZKe-CO1TYfliSJiiM?si=89062887b1514780

1. Amber Run, *Hide & Seek*
2. Hozier, *Arsonist's Lullaby*
3. The Killers, *When You Were Young*
4. Peter Bjorn, and John, *Young Folks*
5. Black Honey, *I Like the Way You Die*
6. Miles Kane, *Come Closer*
7. Lonely The Brave, *Bright eyes*
8. Nothing But Thieves, *Honey Whiskey*
9. Slothrust, *Double Down*
10. FINNEAS, *New Girl*
11. poutyface, *God Complex (Mojo)*
12. AS IT IS, *ILY, HOW ARE YOU?*
13. Chris Cornell, *Nearly Forgot My Broken Heart*
14. Cage The Elephant, *Trouble*
15. Airways, *Will It Tear Us Apart*
16. Frank Carter & The Rattlesnakes, *Cupid's Arrow*
17. Rag'n'Bone Man, Nothing But Thieves, *Alone*
18. Stereophonics, *Do Ya Feel My Love?*
19. Bishop Briggs, *The Way I Do*
20. Caught A Ghost, *No Sugar in My Coffee*

21. K's Choice, *A Sound That Only You Can Hear*
22. Johnny Mathis, *Misty*
23. Yola, *Stand for Myself*
24. James Bay, Julia Michaels, *Peer Pressure*
25. Bishop Briggs, *River*
26. Palaye Royale, *You'll Be Fine*
27. Liz Longley, *Rescue My Heart*
28. In The Valley Below, *Hymnal*
29. BROODS, *Sleep Baby Sleep*
30. The Killers, *All These Things That I've Done*
31. Holly Humberstone, *Deep End*
32. Anderson East, *All on My Mind*
33. Royal Blood, *Trouble's Coming*
34. Bressie, *Rage and Romance*
35. Reignwolf, *Fools Gold*
36. You Me at Six, *Glasgow*
37. Jill Andrews, *Lost It All*
38. Muse, *Time is Running Out*
39. Damien Rice, *Cold Water*
40. Cryoshell, *Nature Girl*
41. Staind, *Something to Remind You*
42. Sleeping At Last, *Light*
43. Crooked Still, Aoife O'Donovan, *Ain't No Grave*
44. Vera Blue, *Hold*

Contact

My website: http://www.amybookerauthor.com
Facebook: www.facebook.com/amybookerauthor
Instagram: www.instagram.com/
amy_booker_author/
TikTok: www.TikTok.com/@amybookerauthor
Email: amybookerauthor@gmail.com

Add my books to your Goodreads: www.goodreads.
com/author/show/22225202.Amy_Booker

Sign up for my VIP mailing list: You'll be the first to
learn about new releases, sales, available preorders,
and freebies. Note: Be sure to add admin@.
amybookerauthor.com to your contacts before
signing up to ensure the emails go straight into your
inbox.

Near Miss Rock Star Romance Series

Almost

"Time spent telling someone you love them is never wasted."

Audio: Addison
Barnes & Ryan Lee
Dunlap

Sarah Lawrence and Ryan Crawford were best friends who almost had it all, but Sarah pushed him away and he left for LA to follow his musical dreams before they could take that next step. She had good reasons but kept those to herself.

Three years have passed, and Ryan's band, Indigo King, is back in town to record a new album at the studio where Sarah works. They'll both need to put the past behind them to work together again.

They might finally take their relationship to the next level, but the crazy music business and devastating family tragedy may get in the way of their dreams.

Can Almost become Absolutely?

So Close

"Everyone has something painful in their past, don't they?"

Audio: Addison
Barnes & Ryan Lee
Dunlap

Samantha Fisher never thought filming a music documentary of the up-and-coming rock band, Indigo King, would lead to a broken wrist, and a broken heart. But Matt Sturridge, the hot and mysterious drummer, seems to have made driving Samantha crazy his sole mission in life, all while keeping painful secrets from everyone.

Mixed messages? That's not even half of it.

Samantha notices that there's something off about Matt. Since he refuses to talk about it, she is determined to find out what it is, no matter what it costs her.

Sometimes the price of fame is too damned high.

Barely

All who wander may not be lost, but you just jumped off the damned map.

Jude Lockwood loves two things in life: fantasy novels and making music. A self-proclaimed player, Jude doesn't have any room in his rockstar life for feelings or commitment.

Audio: Addison Barnes & Ryan Lee Dunlap

Ren Scott loves two things life: her record store and her baby daughter, Charlotte. Independent and newly single, Ren is struggling to find any time to manage her store while taking care of her daughter, much less date.

When Jude returns home to Los Angeles from a whirlwind tour, his offer to help with Charlotte (a.k.a. "Charlie") turns into a confusing attachment to his best friend and her baby. Soon, all the lines Jude and Ren have drawn between each other are blurring.

With the heart of a little girl in the mix, can they make the leap from best friends to something more? Or is the risk of ruining a decade-long friendship too much?

Near Miss Rock Star Collection

This collection is a bundle of books 1-3 in the Near Miss Rock Star Series.

Indigo King is the hottest new rock band in the U.S., and they're just hitting their stride, on and off the stage.

Audio: Addison Barnes & Ryan Lee Dunlap

Drive Me Wild Vegas Series

Ms. Fortune

There are a lot of ways to impress Normandy Blake. Unfortunately for Brandon Carmichael, being a billionaire isn't one of them.

Audio: June DeBorahae & Ryan Lee Dunlap

Normandy Blake and her half-sister Chelsie just inherited Mischief Motors from their late father, Victor. The company is the most elite private car service in Las Vegas, serving the wealthy and the lucky, and the sisters are desperate to keep it that way. But news of their father's death has mixed reactions from their clients and competitors. And when Victor's connection to the Vegas underworld surfaces, all bets are off.

One of the top tech companies in the world is holding its annual board meeting in Las Vegas, and its CEO, Brandon Carmichael, wants to pay his respects to his late friend Victor while he's in town. Before the meeting, an insider trading scandal has his company's stock plummeting and the SEC breathing down his neck, putting his reputation on the line.

When Normandy and Brandon meet, sparks fly, but not in the fun 'theme park fireworks' way; more like the 'metal in the microwave' kind.

If they can get past the friction, they might be able to help each other. They will need all the help they can get, but be careful who you trust in Vegas.

Ms. Chief

A lot can change in the years after high school. But a lot can stay the same too. For Chelsie Blake, it's both.

Audio: Lilly Drake & Bryant Walker

Mischief Motors is the most elite private car service in Las Vegas, and half-sisters Chelsie Blake and Normandy Carmichael are its co-owners. They don't always see eye-to-eye on how to run the business, and they especially don't agree with Chelsie's attraction to one of their new employees - rugged mechanic Noah Thompson. He also happens to be Chelsie's former high school crush, who embarrassingly shot her down once upon a time, and never really knew she existed.

Let's just say he knows now.

With that painful past, and despite the sparks flying between them, it may take an outside force to bring these two together. A force of nature in the form of a sweet old widow who binds them to each other in surprising ways.

Ms. Lead

Opposites attract, but similarities bind. And to find out those similarities, you need to communicate.

Audio: Lacy Laurel & Shane East

Bianca Torino is the hotheaded Italian Lead Driver for Mischief Motors, the most elite private car service in Las Vegas. Their newest client, reclusive British author Oliver Bellamy, is in town to research Sin City for his next book, and much to her chagrin, Bianca is nominated to be his tour guide.

Oliver is the stereotypical Brit, stoic, brooding, stiff-upper-lip, and all that. But there's a good reason for his reclusiveness. A reason that he keeps to himself.

Until now.

They only have the one month Oliver is in Vegas to figure it all out. And time is nobody's friend.

Ms. Take

Alcohol and bad decisions go together like tacos and Tuesdays, especially in Vegas, where bad choices are buy-one-get-one-free.

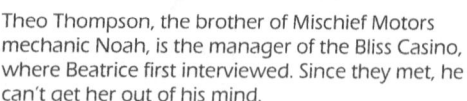

Audio: Samantha Brentmoor & Alastair Haynesbridge

Recent UNLV grad Beatrice Edwards has just landed her first post-college job as the new Public Relations Director of Mischief Motors, the most elite private car service in Las Vegas.

Theo Thompson, the brother of Mischief Motors mechanic Noah, is the manager of the Bliss Casino, where Beatrice first interviewed. Since they met, he can't get her out of his mind.

The new job is cause for celebration. During the festivities, she runs into Theo. And more celebrations ensue. And even more....

Let the bad decisions begin.

Wedded bliss won't come easy, especially when the bride doesn't remember the wedding.

Bea has a violently dysfunctional, yet long-standing family dynamic she can't run away from, even though she should. And Theo can only be understanding for so long.

This is Vegas. What are the odds they'll end up with a Happily Ever After?

Rhapsody Rock Star Romance Series

Coda

Audio: Samantha Brentmoor
& Aaron Shedlock

When the music stops, love begins.

Live fast and die young has always been the rock 'n roll dream. For Murderous Crows front man, Jake Townsend, it just became an actual nightmare. Jake has screwed up before. Hell, his whole life has been a long string of screw-ups mashed together. But this? This is beyond epic, even for him.

Cassidy Young just lost her brother. Her twin. Her best friend. She needs someone to blame, and her late brother's best friend Jake is awfully convenient, and might genuinely be at fault.

Will the fledgling band crash and burn on takeoff when a fatal accident claims their drummer?

Can Cassidy and Jake find their way to forgiveness? Maybe even something more?

Reprise

Overture

Waltz

Sustain

All books are stand-alone, but set in the same universe, so you can pick them up wherever and whenever.

Books are available in audiobook and paperback. Please go to my website for links or to buy direct.

www.ingramcontent.com/pod-product-compliance
Lightning Source LLC
Chambersburg PA
CBHW070908260626
47162CB00007B/2601